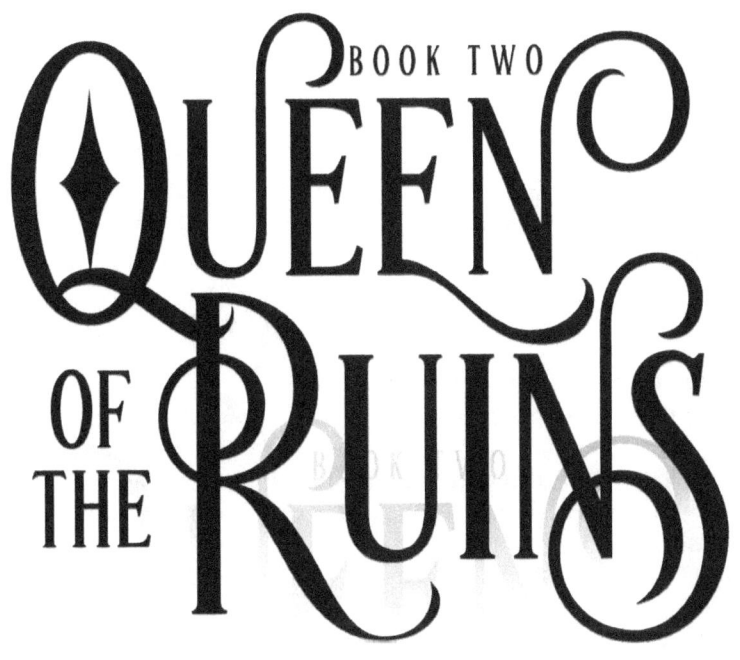

BOOK TWO

QUEEN OF THE RUINS

BY: JODI GALLEGOS

QUEEN OF THE RUINS
Copyright ©2021 Jodi Gallegos
All rights reserved.
Printed in the United States of America
First Edition: April 2021

CLEAN TEEN PUBLISHING
WWW.CLEANTEENPUBLISHING.COM

Summary: While the war between the kingdoms grows, the long-forgotten gods are beginning to take notice. And one of them has been waiting for this moment for a very long time... Queen of the Ruins picks up seamlessly where The High Crown Chronicles left off and draws the reader more deeply into this world of stunning imagery, dynamic characters, and shifting political alliances. A blend of dark, vengeful tone and deeply emotional moments will draw readers through this action-packed novel and leave their hearts thundering until the final page..

ISBN: 978-1-63422-403-1 (paperback)
ISBN: 978-1-63422-402-4 (e-book)
Cover Design by: Marya Heidel
Typography by: Courtney Spencer
Editing by: Cynthia Shepp & Chris Kidler

YOUNG ADULT FICTION / Historical / Medieval
YOUNG ADULT FICTION / Fantasy / Historical
YOUNG ADULT FICTION / Royalty
YOUNG ADULT FICTION / Social Themes / Class Differences

For more information about our content disclosure, please utilize the QR code above with your smart phone or visit us at www.CleanTeenPublishing.com

FOR EVERYONE WHO HAS EVER DUSTED THEMSELVES OFF
AND SOLDIERED ON.

orth Sea
The Gates of Tiernan
The Candor Islands
Fairlee
Tiernan
Allondale
Lithwhit
andyn
Glynnairre
Travion
nified Kingdoms

THE GODS

Omnilus

The original breath in the universes. The great creator.

Creator of the world and the gods. Recognized the gods had too much power which would lead to destruction, so he removed their ability to create life then turned his back on the world he'd created, retreating into the heavens to create a new utopia.

THE ELYPHESIAN GODS

Rūvolo

God of the earth, virility, and aggression.

When man turned against the gods, it was Rūvolo who caused the ground to shake, bringing down the castles of the kings who had betrayed the gods and the remainder of the monuments that had been destroyed by man. Was tricked by Nemii into shaking the earth again, causing the gates of Targatheimr to collapse, trapping the godlings in the underworld forever. Nemii offered to let him be the god of the earth, but Rūvolo grew tired of the fighting among his brethren and retreated into Elyphesus to exist in solitude.

Liræmor

God of the sea, passion and strategy.

Lured seaside maidens into being his lover and fathered more godlings than any other god. Loved the goddess Whenorríga and watched the heavens for her to pass over his waters. He grew angry when she grew to favor Kūbialus. In his anger, he caused great waves to swell, which capsized ships and drowned 300 sailors. Nemii convinced him the only way to win Whenorríga's affection was to prove himself the better warrior. Liræmor aligned with Nemii in the war between gods and men, but when his godlings were lured into Targatheimr, Liræmor threatened to swell the oceans to drown out humans in retribution.

Nemii offered Liræmor to become the god of the earth, but Liræmor retreated to the sea, where he periodically mourns the empty sky above him and tosses the sea in his anger.

Kūbialus
God of force, compulsion, soldiers, and determination.

Loves only himself and war. Kūbialus awards armies for their ferocity in battle and for their thirst for vengeance. Is favored by Whennoríga for his fierceness in war. Kūbialus split the earth so water could flow across the land, carrying soldiers in great ships inland. Whenorríga mistook this as an offering to her, as proof of his love. Kūbialus tempted Whenorríga to ensure her strong winds to help his warriors in battle, but he angered her by also courting the goddess Albati.

Whenorríga
Goddess of the night winds, of the swift-footed, of speed, and protector of sailors.

Whenorríga favored Kūbialus over Liræmor. When Liræmor's anger caused 300 sailors to drown in his seas, the winds that resulted from Whenorríga's fury increased the waves resulting in the death of 3,000 sailors. As a result, Whenorríga was the first god that men turned against.

Nemii
The god of opposition, duplicity, of the sun and the moon, of avarice.

Nemii became envious of the esteem his brother and sister gods were held in. Was responsible for the human uprising. He conspired with both men and gods to establish a dominion over the world but honored his promises to none. He once loved and admired Nithenia above all others and wanted her at his side.

Nithenia
Goddess of bravery, victory, and protector of women and chil-

dren.

Was favored by Omnilus, the Great Creator, which caused great envy among her brother and sister gods. Favors Liræmor among the gods and recognizes his actions to be the result of an impulsive mistake. Takes other shapes and walks the earth, has taken great warriors as lovers and borne many godlings. Stood against the other gods to protect humankind.

Albati

Goddess of love, of ill-fated lovers, of alliances, and of mercy.

Created from the essence of all the gods and from love. Fell in love with a mortal and bore him a godling daughter. Was tricked into aligning with Nemii in exchange for the promise that her lover would be released from the underworld and allowed eternal entry into Elyphesus.

The blood of the false kings will spill upon the earth, nourishing seeds of betrayal. Those who reap power from its cursed abundance and trample upon the legacy of Elyphesia will unleas the fury of the gods. The gates of Targatheimr will burst open and fiery steeds will storm across the earth. A kingdom of darkness will prevail, and it alone shall be blessed by the gods.

~Elyphesian Prophecy

And the heavens boomed and the gods of Elyphesus commanded, "Call forth and we shall answer. Whosoever amongst you that is just, let the gods be your army." Yet no man called, for they were filled with fear and the dark descended.

~From The War of Gods and Men

CHAPTER

ONE

"IT LOOKS SO PRETTY," KATHERINE WHISPERS, TILTING HER face toward the night sky.

From the dark, off to my side, Kennard growls. "It'll be a beautiful death if you don't quit your gawking and pay attention."

Snow drifts from the feathered clouds, landing on us as we lie on our bellies atop a high hill surveying the landscape below. Lilting bits of white fleece dance about as they make their long journey from the slate sky above to the surface of the winter-crisp earth. As a girl, I celebrated every new snowfall, running into the courtyard to stare in wonderment as the miraculous fluff flitted down to kiss my tiny nose and cover Devlishire—and the entirety of the world—in a blanket of serenity.

How fleeting peace—and the memory of it—truly is.

"There." Jamis points to the rise of a hill forty yards from where we lie. He's beside me, pressed into my side to keep me—and himself I'm sure—warm against the frigid night. The snow beneath me has melted, the moisture creeping through my cloak, into my dress, and even into the breeches beneath it. My body is doing its best to warm me and the earth upon which I've been prone for over an hour.

I squint against the falling flakes, my gaze straining in the direction Jamis points. An orange glow lights the valley behind a hill, illuminating the land's subtle rise and casting undulating shadows on the surrounding land.

"Idiots," Josef whispers harshly from my other side. "Dont they know nothin' 'bout war"

1

I smile at the fact that, until three months ago, none of us knew anything about war. A year ago, I was a naïve princess sent to marry the most powerful man in the Unified Kingdoms. But after being betrayed by my father, brother, and their allies, I know far more of combat than most men twice my age.

I study the hill, watching for the shadows of people to move across the glow of the campfire. My ears strain to pick up sounds of camp. Throughout the Unified Kingdoms, battles are being waged daily. A band of knights would make quite a clatter as they shed their armor and weapons, recovered their horses, and settled into rest. Even a group of peasants would make noise, but there is nothing. Only the glow of a fire. A beacon to give away the unsuspecting people who might be gathered around it.

"It's a trap," I whisper. "They know we're in the hills. They're trying to draw us out."

It was only a matter of time before our location was discovered again. For months, we've raided the resources of Roarke and King Lester. We've stolen weapons, food, and livestock almost daily. Acting on information from Legion E spies deep in Devlishire and Carling, we've known when they moved their riches and have intercepted those as well. Once the Alliance of Beasts—as I've come to call them—discovers our location, we move on to our next target. With a band of fewer than twenty members, we're able to move through the Argralands efficiently to keep ahead of the larger troops. But this time, they've caught up to us far faster than expected.

Silence gathers around us as we scan the shadows. Just as I think I was mistaken about troops lying in wait, a bird bursts from a tree, chirping in fear. Instinct kicks in, and we drop our heads. The glow of our faces against the night is likely what they're looking for. Crisp blades of wild grasses poke through the snow and into my face. I reach back. My stiff, numb fingers to pull the cloth of my hood over my head. I peer over the hill again as I draw a dark woolen flap across my nose and mouth, securing it on the opposite side.

Katherine belly scoots alongside Jamis, and Kennard slides into place beside her. The crunch of snow under them seems to echo throughout the night, though I know the sound hasn't traveled beyond our small group.

"They're ahead." Kennard's voice is thick and gravelly, even in a whisper—as thick and war-torn as his body. "There's been no movement from our flanks. We'd have seen them if they'd followed our path."

Jamis nods. Recent experience has taught him to trust in the skills of his most loyal adviser.

I focus again on the glowing hill, unease filling my belly with roiling waves of warning. Pulling my hood from my ear, I close my eyes and listen, straining to hear beyond the obvious in the way Isobel has instructed me. My ears pick up the subtle breeze, the breaths of my allies, the horses hidden in the trees behind us, the crackle of the fire ahead of us, and there, on a subtle shift of air, is a warning. Though I can't make out the words as Isobel can, a message is being carried from one tree to another. Deep in my heart, the goddess Nithenia guides me to hear and understand the message, even though it lacks words as I know them. "They're lying in wait. If we come looking, they'll have the cover of the hills and bushes. We'll have the fire at our backs. They'll have the advantage. There's a small troop, there." I point to the left of the hill.

"And there," Katherine adds with a finger angled to a prominent peak.

Through a series of hand gestures, Kennard communicates he and Katherine will lead the troops waiting in the trees behind us. As they make their way around the base of the hill, Jamis, Josef, and I will move in from the front, drawing out those waiting to ambush us. The plan is counterintuitive, going against everything I, as a queen, ever learned about war. The king isn't sent directly into battle, and he isn't used as bait. And though I was far better trained in swordfight than any other monarch in recent times, my skills were intended for defense. I doubt Esmond, my old trainer and friend, ever dreamed he was preparing me to march directly into an ambush. But I'm a queen in name and memory only now. All I rule is in rubble and those who purported to be my allies won't rest until Jamis and I are dead and our land under their control.

As the others crawl away into the darkness, I roll onto my back, inhaling deeply to calm my body and mind in preparation for the looming conflict. I let my right hand wander to my waist, confirming the presence of the leather belt purse that holds my small dagger—a gift from Esmond, given to me before the Battle of Allondale. Its hilt is small and shaped to fit in a closed fist. The blade is long and narrow—a well-placed jab would puncture a grown man's life force with devastating consequences. My hand follows the familiar path to my hip, patting the sapphire-encrusted hilt of the dagger Jamis gave me on our first and last trip together to Devlishire. Behind that is the solid hilt of my sword, everything I've relied on during previous fights as they should be.

I look to the sky, seeking the vast darkness beyond the falling flakes. *Nithenia, I place my trust in you. Allow my arms to be strong, my blade true, and our victory swift.* Steeling my body for battle, I roll to my right hip and into a low crouch, the weight of the sword on my left hip threatening to pull my back to the ground.

Jamis and Josef are rising to their feet as well. Before standing, I use one finger to draw a pattern of five wavy lines in the snow, the symbol of Nithenia, devised by my sister and me when we were young and beholden to laws banning the worship of the long-forgotten gods. My dark gray cloak falls across my body as I fall into place beside Jamis and Josef to walk into an ambush.

Under the best of circumstances, the darkness of the night enhances the vast emptiness of the rolling hills outside the Unified Kingdoms. But now, as I wait for danger to pounce, the earth itself seems to be holding its breath in anticipation. Silence has fully engulfed the landscape. There are no sounds of forest animals scurrying in the dark, no wolves calling through the night or coyotes yelping their high frantic cries. Only the crunching of snow beneath our boots casts any sound.

Although we know where the enemy troop lies, our gait is slow and cautious, giving the impression we are unaware of the danger that lies before us. When we near the base of the hill, a bush rustles. The movement is subtle, but the leaves on the trees above and the surrounding bushes remain still, indicating the movement was caused by something—more likely *someone*—behind it.

Jamis reaches to push me behind him. Josef angles closer, pinching me off. Despite the number of times I've proven myself in the few short months since the Battle of Allondale, they can't overcome their natural inclination to shield me.

At the ready, mortal. Nithenia's warning fills my head with a keen awareness of everything surrounding me. My right hand grips the hilt of my sword. I lift slightly, pulling it free of the initial resistance of the leather that holds it. I control my breath and center all the energy into my body, allowing it to tumble and roil in preparation for when I call on it.

Crunch, crunch. Our cautious footsteps explode through the otherwise silent night. The bush is only feet away from us now, with the foot of the hill just beyond. My gaze darts along the crest of the surrounding hills, searching for any sign of movement from those lying in wait or our own band of marauders. My mind calculates where Kennard and Katherine should be with their troops by now—at least, I hope they are there. If they were overtaken, we are walking into a trap and our own deaths.

We near the fire, my pupils constricting to shield against the assault of the flame. I focus on the dark beyond, but my eyes betray me.

Snap. The sound ricochets through the valley, followed by an explosion of movement—and then yelling. Men in metal armor burst from behind the bushes. They run at us as more men pour from over and around the hills and from the tree line behind.

With no sign of our troops, Jamis, Josef, and I turn our backs to each other as we draw our swords and step in to meet our attackers. I let out a primal shout as I meet the first blow, easily deflecting it and drawing my blade across the soft, exposed skin of the man's neck.

The night is filled with the grunts and heaving sounds of humans at war and the sharp clatter of clashing blades. Fury driving me, I imagine each opponent is my brother. Images of villagers who yielded to Roarke's rule, only to be struck down in front of their wives and children, fill my head. I swing hard and true, intent on ending his life with each blow.

Our assailants' attention is drawn to the rear line as our troops pour from the shadows and begin taking out the enemy with a stealth they've never experienced. Before they're even aware of the risk, half have been dispatched by our band of knights and forestland warriors. Realizing the risk and having quickly lost the upper hand they were so certain of, the front line enhances their effort. They swing their blades with the strength and desperation of men determined to win. But they are no match for our unit. We've lost more than they can imagine. Fueled by rage, we are an army with nothing left to lose. Each of us is willing to cast our own lives aside to achieve vengeance against the army that stole our lands and those we love in the name of greed.

When the bloody fighting ends, the last alive is a boy no older than fifteen. We always pick a young one, the most frightened if possible. Kennard has driven the boy to his knees and bound his wrists. Katherine, blood-spattered, fierce, and beautiful, holds him in place with an arrow drawn and ready—daring him to flee. His eyes are wide, and his body shuddering against fear and cold as he watches the tip of the arrow that could be unleashed at any moment.

Our troops are busy, scavenging from the bodies in the narrow valley, the scarlet ink of their lives painting the pure white canvas beneath them. Josef cleans his blade with snow as Jamis and I approach the boy. He can barely look away from Katherine. Jamis demands his attention, smacking the wide surface of his sword against the boy's hip. "Who's your king?"

Tears pour from the boy's pale eyes. It's something we're accustomed to. They're young and filled with the purpose that's been demanded: defending their kings and kingdoms. Raised under the rule of the Unified Kingdoms in peacetime, the boys still don't realize the idealized notion of riding out to claim victory in the name of their king is childish and simple. The Unification has crumbled. War-time allegiances will protect these boys or be the reason for their deaths. Their allegiance might have been given poorly if it were even a choice. Most have been conscripted, forced to fight for the king they were raised under or the one who has conquered their homeland. Centuries of theoretical loyalty have left them poorly prepared to make rapid decisions about which side to align with. We try to take that into account.

"I…I's in Prince Roarke's army, sir."

Jamis draws a hand back and strikes him. It doesn't affect me anymore. If I could, I'd strike every person who aligns with my repugnant brother.

The boy lets out a cry, his tears falling faster from his red, swollen eyes. A thick stream of moisture begins to work its way from his nose as well. His shuddering increases as Katherine takes a step closer—her expression daring him to flee. He throws his hands up, wide eyes bouncing from one of us to the other in rapid succession. "Please, sir! They 'scripted me. I'nt 'ave no choice."

Jamis and I circle him slowly. It's a show we've perfected. We assess him, tipping our heads from one side to the other as if considering what to do with him. It only takes us a moment to determine which of us should proceed—an unspoken agreement we've adopted. With this boy, it will be me.

I crouch in front of him, so close our faces nearly touch. Raising my brows and with a voice near a whisper, I ask him the one question I already know the answer to. "Do you know who I am?"

He nods as he tries to lean farther away from me. His skin has blanched, casting the freckles into prominence. His chin quivers.

"Say it."

"Qu-qu-queen Malory," he stutters.

I ensure my voice is low and ominous, a quality that's come about naturally and I've come to like. "Tell my brother I'm coming for him. And if you and I meet on the battlefield again, you won't live to see your next breath."

I stand and stride into the dark without another word. Jamis and Josef fall in behind me, followed by Katherine, Kennard, and the other dozen men in our troop. We let the shadows of the forest envelop us before we even turn to glance at the boy. He can no longer see us, yet he remains on his knees, shivering in the dark. The orange glow of the ambush fire behind the hill casts the only light into the snowy night.

"Make sure he goes," I tell Davion, a fierce Fairlean Josef insisted would be a useful addition to our contingent. Most of the boys we leave behind will flee on their own, usually after waiting a short while to be sure they are, in fact, safe to do so. A few have tried to honor the dead littered around them before moving on. There are a few, though, who immediately run in the opposite direction of our departure. Only twice has Davion had to return and goad the boys to leave, and each was Roarke's soldiers.

We mount our horses, then slip deeper into the woods. The deep regions of the Argralands—forest lands west and south of the Devlishire and Claxton borders—have proven to be as ideal for our needs as Fairlee. The lands are nearly unchartered, uninhabited, and untraveled due to thousands of years of frightening tales and offer plenty of places to hide. We ride for nearly an hour, winding through the trees along a course we now intuitively know until we come to the small pool of fresh water at the mouth of a cave. Several Fairleans remained behind to protect our camp, and they gather around to relieve our horses of their blankets and straps and help carry the cache of weapons and gold pieces we recovered from the bodies.

A fire crackles in the mouth of the cave, heating the inner chambers. Several small animals are cooking over the flames, the aroma filling the camp and making my mouth water in anticipation of my first hearty meal in days.

Davion appears ten minutes later. "He's gone. Headed north." Although he's speaking to Jamis and me, he's looking past us, searching through the people gathered in the main chamber of the cave for Katherine. It was only a week ago I first noticed him seeking her out, though she has yet to notice the increased intensity of his attentions.

"We should clean up," I tell Jamis. After I retrieve clean strips of cloth and fresh clothing, we make our way back into the cold. We follow the familiar path through the dark that leads around the pond to an inlet. The thick overgrowth of trees hang low, the row of brush providing some measure of privacy for my husband and me.

I dip the torn cloth into the frigid water and then hand it to Jamis before drawing my own across my skin. The dirt and grime of the past week in the forest is wiped away from my hands with the scarlet stains of tonight's fight.

Has it been only one week since our last bath?

My skin alights in reaction to the stinging cold of the water against the night. My body embraces the freedom to breathe without the thick covering of smoke, perspiration, and dirt—the result of our new vagrant lifestyle. I could have never imagined the simple act of wiping away filth could bring about such a feeling of decadent self-care.

I pass the rag over my forearms, pushing the braided bangle around to ensure I've cleaned the blood from it as well. With the bracelet clean, I wring out the rag in the water and then wipe my face and neck. I turn my back to Jamis. "Would you?" He fumbles with the pearl buttons along the back of my dress, my skin prickling as each new inch is exposed to the winter air. The cold stings as it assaults my back, but it's the feeling of being alive despite everything that's conspired against me, so I welcome it.

"Isn't it time to give up the gowns?" Jamis's voice is a soft murmur in my ear. Low and taunting. I know where the simple sight of my bare skin takes his mind, and I relish that power. He trails a finger along my spine, his breath coming in hot bursts across my back.

Katherine and I have taken to wearing men's breeches, but we haven't been able to entirely give up our gowns. Though we've given up our underskirts—and the front panels of our dresses have been torn away to allow us more freedom of movement while riding and in battle—we've each kept our two favorite gowns. Our peripatetic new lives are far less nourishing than court life. We've lost much of our softness, giving us the room to pair tunics under our gowns for additional warmth. "I am a queen, and I will wear my finery until it wears away and falls from my body."

"Is that so?" Jamis's fingers slip under the material and lift, causing the gown and tunic to fall from my body as one, pillowing at my feet. The cold air across my body gives rise to a gasp, but I control my reaction and turn slowly to face my husband, arms at my side.

"What is it that you want, *my king*?" I offer a teasing smile as I slowly bridge the small space between us. I'm eager for the heat of his body, but I try to maintain my facade of control. When he pulls me into his arms, I press against him. His kiss is deep and demanding, an evolution from the timid, tender boy I married.

He tastes of war and desperation, bravery and vengeance, and my body responds to its likeness. I reach under his tunic, pushing the material away as I press into his heat, clutching against him, demanding him.

Jamis lifts me, and I wrap around him. He pulls me against him, tighter still as he reaches out for something to stabilize him— the tree that has served us before, though he's more cautious now, not wanting to pull splinters from my backside again.

When our passion is spent—our long, languid sessions of making love in the palace are long behind us—we quickly pull on our clean clothing. As I lift the gown to my waist, Jamis reaches one hand out, his finger traveling along the skin over my heart. "It's almost gone now."

I look down at the design my sister Laila painted over my heart before the Battle of Allondale. The symbol of Nithenia that we created as children is nearly gone. The dark, thick, and black lines are now so faint they may be mistaken for shadow. But though it has faded to the eye, the symbol is burned into my soul. I'm no longer bound by the conventions of the former Unified Kingdoms. There are no kingdoms any longer—their laws forgotten along with all the loyalties that bound us together. And now, my heart belongs to the long-forgotten goddess, the one deity who made sense. A goddess who stood against her brethren to protect the people who put their faith in her alone. A goddess who fought against the strongest of the gods, including Nemii, the god of opposition, met their threats with bravery and cunning—and overcame them in the end.

I shrug as I pull the gown and tunic over my shoulders, turning so Jamis can pull the ties together. "It was only temporary." My fingertips linger on the spot over my heart, where my sister drew the symbol. It was the last time I saw her. Though messengers assure me that she is well and remains in Fairlee, it's been so long since I've seen her.

"We'll be back in Fairlee soon. You'll see her again." Jamis places a soft kiss on my forehead before he turns to gather our discarded clothing. I join him, and we silently scrub the grime and stains from our garments, a task we've grown accustomed to. Jamis tucks the clean items under his arm before reaching for my hand, leading me along the dark path toward the cave.

Everyone looks up as we enter, then turns their attention back to the spit and the animals roasting in the flames. Josef's gaze lingers as he takes in Jamis and me. My skin flushes with heat in response, though I have no reason to be embarrassed at having spent time alone with my husband. Josef's dark eyes harden, and his jaw clenches. In a fraction of a moment, though, his expression relaxes. When he meets my gaze, his face softens, and he offers a slight nod before returning his attention to the meal. He doesn't turn his back to us, though. He never does. I feel as though I'm always in his sights, though I don't find that awareness to be intrusive—or even troubling.

Jamis and I drape our wet clothes over a boulder near the mouth of the cave to let the heat of the fire dry them.

I survey the troops. They're gathered around a secondary fire, one with a stew pot hanging over the flames. Each is sitting on the ground, relaying the excursions and skirmishes they took part in that day. A pile of new swords lies behind them, forgotten amongst the cherished bounty of four skins of wine. Their laughter is infectious and long overdue.

As Jamis moves to join them, Davion scoots closer to Katherine, though there was no need for him to make more room. I eye him and his proximity to my friend. While I'm sure his intentions are good, and Davion is a loyal soldier, I've become cautious of most everyone but the small group of people I know I can trust without a doubt: Jamis, Katherine, Isobel, Kennard, and Josef.

My gaze travels across the group, eyeing each of my closest allies. They are talking and laughing as the wine takes effect, and the roasted game settles in their bellies. Josef is the only one who isn't absorbed in the conversation. He's staring directly at me, as he so often does, and an uneasy fluttering explodes in my chest. The vulnerability I feel when Josef looks at me is unlike anything I feel around anyone else. It's as if he knows some deep truth about me that even I am unaware of. As if I'm laid bare every time our eyes meet.

I swallow and force my attention away from him, joining Jamis at the fire. Sitting close, I hold his arm and lean into him as I accept the wine and take a deep drink. The rich, sweet fluid dances along my tongue, my taste buds reaching up to absorb the delectable drink that has become such a rare treat.

"You should eat something," Jamis murmurs in my ear.

Closing my eyes, I feel the wine warm a path through my body. I reach my hand toward Kennard. "I want another drink."

He looks to Jamis for approval, a habit leftover from our more civilized lives, but he relents and hands me the wine, knowing I am no longer a silly girl who requests permission from her king. I am a warrior queen. If I can kill like the men, I can drink like them as well.

After another deep drink, I pull my legs under me, feet to the ground. It's been two nights since I last slept. Already deeply tired, I am now deeply drunk, too. I push against Jamis's shoulder as I stand. My muscles are heavy, and my limbs are resistant. Our troop will continue to talk until late in the night, but I must sleep. As I stand, I catch Josef watching me, a mixture of amusement and a hint of concern in his expression. I straighten, giving him a pointed look as if to say I am fine and there is no need for his concern. My ankle rolls, but I recover from the stumble quickly. Amusement has overtaken his expression now, and he joins in laughter with Jamis, Katherine, and Kennard. I walk to the back of the cave, lying on an old woolen blanket and pulling another over me.

I'm engulfed in darkness. Sleep envelopes me quickly, only whispers filling my head. It's the voices and words I can't quite make out yet, the ones that have called increasingly since before the Battle of Allondale. It is Nithenia's voice, I have no doubt. Perhaps the other gods as well. Someday, I know I will be able to hear them clearly. I only need patience and faith.

CHAPTER TWO

NIGHT STILL CLINGS TO THE EARTH WHEN I wake. I shake off the horrors that invade my mind in sleep: villages pillaged, soldiers loyal to Jamis dead in the fields, and heads atop spikes upon which my brother's standard flies. And blood—always the blood of those who've perished in my name.

Instinct tells me I've slept a few hours at most. Jamis is beside me, his sleep-heavy arm draped across my waist, body pressed against mine, providing the warmth that is ever-elusive in this new vagabond life we've adopted.

Jamis stirs only slightly as I roll to face him. His breaths are deep, exhaustion finally having claimed him from the constant vigilance required of a king at war. Even in sleep, his brows are furrowed in thought. I pull my hand from under the blanket, then use my thumb to try to wipe away the tension, to relax his expression so I might once again—even for a moment—catch sight of the youthful, optimistic, and open boy I married. The Jamis I was betrothed to loved life. He found a reason to be enthusiastic about every aspect of the world. He was beautiful—his body as well as his soul. But his life turned sour and hard the day he fell in love with me, though neither of us was aware of it then. It was my agreement to marry Jamis that cast the final curse, though I couldn't have changed the path our lives were traveling. My own family betrayed me, forced me to marry him to save my best friend. But Esmond is dead despite my efforts, one more casualty in my enduring life—in my quest to avenge all that's been stolen from me

Everything that once stood beautiful and solid is now in ruins.

The unification between seven kingdoms was more tenuous than I ever imagined, crumbling under the weight of greed. And now the realms are at war, and everyone is at risk. What we don't tear down ourselves is sure to be conquered by distant kings with a thirst to expand their empire.

Murmuring at the mouth of the cave draws my attention. Now that I'm awake, it'll be days before I sleep again. I slip from under Jamis's arm, ensuring the blanket is firmly about his shoulders before making my way to the fire.

The voices are those of Josef, Katherine, and Kennard. They are near the makeshift hearth, Kennard leaning drunkenly against the wall, watching as Josef leans intently over Katherine's shoulder.

I watch from the shadows, my fingertips finding the raised skin on my throat—a remnant from when Lord Cobol attempted to kill me during the Battle of Allondale. My fingers now always find it when I'm lost in thought.

"Ouch!" Katherine casts a scathing glare over her shoulder. Josef stops, lifting his hands away from her.

"I din't mean ta. You've a scar there. The tissue's bound ta be more tender. I can stop."

Katherine shakes her head, drawing her hair over her shoulder so her back is visible. It's then I see the ink pattern taking shape on her back.

"What are you doing?" I step from the shadows and cross the cave, stopping near where Kennard remains leaning against the wall.

"It's a tatt—" Josef begins.

"I know what it is." In the months since we joined the people from the forest, I've seen plenty of their tattoos. They are Fairlean symbols of bravery, though I don't understand the specifics of the different symbols and patterns. I look directly at Katherine. "Why are you getting one?"

The light skin of her cheeks flush, though she makes no move to distance herself from the quill in Josef's hand. She lets out a breath, her shoulders falling. "I'm not getting one. I'm getting *another*."

Kennard taps at my hip. I glance down to see the skin of wine he's holding in my direction.

I accept it, sliding down the wall beside him. The transition to war-time queen has been a difficult one. While I feel an obligation to watch over the ladies of my court, I also realize we are living a far different life now. My court is a theoretical one. Katherine is a war maven now, a battle-tested soldier. And if she wants to be tattooed … "Another one?"

Josef leans back, sitting on his haunches. He places the quill in the wooden bowl of dark liquid he's been scratching into Katherine's back. "I thought she knew."

Katherine shakes her head. She sits up straighter, lowering the front of her gown to allow me to see the symbol over her heart. I gasp at the scrawling pattern across her chest, leaning closer. The artistry is masterful, and I can't imagine how long it must have taken or that it was done in such secrecy. At the center is the head of a bird, an arrow clutched in its beak. The feathers are flames, engulfing and surrounding the bird as it gazes skyward. The tips of the flames reach from her sternum to the front of her shoulder and from her collarbone down to—

I sit back, looking from Katherine to Josef. A dark pit opens in my chest as I stare from one to the other. Prickles of jealousy stab under my ribs as I imagine Josef working so closely and intimately on my friend's bare skin. I shake away my reaction. I'm not envious of Josef and Katherine, only that he sees bravery in her that he's never offered me. I've never been offered a Fairlean tattoo, though I know they have to be granted by someone who sees bravery in a person; one doesn't simply request one.

I am surprised, though, if Josef and Katherine have found comfort in each other. I'd thought she was drawn to Kennard. "I didn't know you were—" I can't even say the words.

"What? No!" Josef is quick to answer. His hands go up as he pushes farther away from Katherine.

Katherine casts him a disgusted scowl as she pulls the gown up to cover her tattoo. "Well, aren't *you* noble."

"Now you've angered the hornet." Kennard laughs as he lifts the wine to his mouth again.

Katherine flushes as she meets his eyes, and I see it. It *is* Kennard she's fond of, that she wishes shared her feelings, though I've never seen any emotion from Kennard beyond anger.

To me, she explains, "I wanted a tattoo when we first went to Fairlee. I saw someone getting one, and I thought it was beautiful. But I couldn't have one then."

"Why?" I can't imagine wanting to mark my skin permanently,

but if my friend wanted it, I'm offended she was denied.

Josef leans on one arm, reaching for a log and throwing it on the fire as he answers. "Because she 'adn't earned it then."

He sits up, reaching for the bowl and drawing the quill through the ebony liquid. "In Fairlee, tattoos 're a gift, a recognition of bravery. Ye can't just get one; it 'as ta be given to ye. When someone thinks ye've proven yer bravery, they'll give ye yer first, of the design *they* choose. 'N the first is always o'er yer heart."

His explanation of the Fairlean ritual makes me feel better, but for only a moment. Josef recognized Katherine's bravery and offered her that beautiful symbol, and now he's giving her another. He's never offered me a tattoo—nobody has. Does Josef find me lacking in bravery? Have I not proven myself every bit as much as Katherine? Jealousy prickles at my skin again, and my mind tumbles. Is it the tattoo, recognition, or attention I want?

"I didn't mean to interrupt." Though I feel like an excluded and petulant child, I manage to make my voice apologetic. "I was just surprised."

Katherine bares her shoulder again. With one more glance in my direction, Josef obliges and resumes scratching the latest symbol of bravery into her back. Kennard is soon breathing heavily. His eyes are still open, giving the appearance he is wide awake, even though I know better. It's a useful trick should anyone happen upon him. They'd be stunned into speech—as almost every member in our small troop was early on.

We talk about our plans as Josef continues to work.

"We need ta attack Brahm next," Josef says. "Rumor 'as it he's feelin' outta sorts. Roarke 'n Lester aren't nearly as concerned fer Claxton as fer their lands. They've given 'im no help. He's been holdin' the southern borders alone. His men'll be tired, wonderin' why they're even aligned wit' da Beasts."

"It's a good idea." Katherine shifts as Josef's quill works farther up on the soft muscle of her shoulder and neck. "We need him to doubt his alliance—to see Roarke and Lester have more loyalty to each other than to him. It's time to hit him, spark some doubt about his position in his alliance."

My brother, the new king of Devlishire, along with the kings of Carling and Claxton, had long plotted my death. The Battle of Allondale was their move to topple Jamis and me and assume our lands. They'd been surprised to find we were not only prepared for them—we nearly bested them. But King Brahm of Claxton is only an afterthought in Roarke and Lester's quest to expand their own rule. They owe him no allegiance, nor will they show him any. They will claim his lands as they plan to do every other king. And when they've devoured all the riches in the Unified Kingdoms, the Alliance of Beasts will turn on each other.

I nod. "There's a Legion E spy embedded in Brahm's court. Last we heard, he's been subtly hinting to Brahm that Roarke and Lester can't be trusted. And the spies amongst Roarke's troops will ensure that their men won't arrive in Claxton if dispatched."

Katherine smiles. "Esmond truly was brilliant, wasn't he?"

I nod, fighting away emotion. My dear friend Esmond had recognized early on that I was in danger. He spent the last months of his life riding about the kingdoms, setting up a network of spies—soldiers, aristocrats, and villagers—who opposed the duplicitous tactics undertaken by the Alliance and vowed to support me. Legion E is so cloaked in secrecy that I still have no idea how vast their reach is.

After I pull a narrow stick from a pile of kindling, I dig it into the base of the fire, covering it in soot. I absentmindedly scratch designs onto the stone floor of the cave with the thick black tip as I listen to their thoughts. The idea is good. We've been targeting Lester and Roarke's resources for months. Hitting Brahm now would make him reconsider his position. I don't doubt Roarke and Lester will leave Brahm to weather his losses. These men only care for themselves and their standing in the Kingdoms. Now that Roarke has claimed the High Crown—with Lester's support—their only interest is in keeping the power they've claimed.

"If we hit him from the south, we'd be in a good position to return to Fairlee. We can drop off our spoils, get some rest, and then head out again." I study Katherine. Her lids hang heavy, and her eyes are swollen. She hasn't slept any more than the rest of us. The three months we've been on the run has been exhausting for everyone. There's never a moment when we can truly relax or even rest. It would be good for us to return to Fairlee. Surrounded by others, we would finally rest. We could eat and prepare our bodies for another long trek. I could see my sister again.

I nod. "We should talk to Jamis. And him." I cast my chin in the direction of Kennard's huge, sleeping frame. We've settled into a system where we are all involved in our decisions. Jamis and I are no longer the High King and Queen, though the titles truly belong to us. We are warriors, members of a tribe, and we recognized early that we all have something valuable to contribute to our long-term survival.

When Josef completes his design, Katherine excuses herself to get some rest. I smile and return to my stick, scratching designs into the ground.

Josef pushes the bowl of ink aside. He sits in front of the fire, closer to me. Over the fire, I swear I feel his heat. It radiates, something I've felt from the moment I met him. I've feared many times that he was fevered, but he simply runs warmer than anyone I've ever encountered—besides his sister, who also runs warm. With the winter cold constantly lurking deep in my bones, I'd love nothing more than to lean into him, but I control the maddening impulse my body urges me to give in to. "Aren't you tired?"

He shakes his head, his brown hair dropping around his face, the waves framing the strongly chiseled lines of his cheeks and brow. "I slept yesterday. Though I'd give m' sword hand for a bedroll to lie on fer an hour."

I laugh. "I thought you were used to life on the move? It's me who hasn't been in a decent bed in months. But you don't hear me complaining."

"'Tis true yer far hardier than I." He leans closer, bumping me with his shoulder to emphasize his jest. "What's that yer drawin'?"

I scratch it out quickly, embarrassed. "Oh, it's nothing. Just nonsense."

"Ye draw it often. When yer thinkin', when yer no' thinkin'. And before we walk into battle, ye manage ta draw it somewhere. It don't seem like nothin'. I think it's very...*somethin'*." His eyes are warm and intense, dark brown pools that invite me to dive in and find comfort, with golden flecks that hint at an energy that will shoot through my body should I touch them.

I redraw the series of lines. "It's a secret symbol. My sister and I made it when we were young. It represents a goddess, but, in the Unified Kingdoms, it was forbidden to worship her. We made the symbols as a secret way to refer to her—and the other forbidden gods."

"Who's yer goddess? The one ye have ta hide?"

"Nithenia. She's the goddess of—"

"Of bravery, victory, 'n the protector o' women."

17

I gasp as he finishes. His expression is smug and teasing, and it does nothing to make me want to distance myself from him. "You know Nithenia?"

"Of course. The Elyphesian Gods 're deeply entrenched in Fairlean beliefs."

I drop the stick to gape at him. "You worship the Elyphesians? I thought you prayed to the forest or something."

"We worship everythin' the gods give us. They gave us the trees 'n the land. Whenorríga gave us the night winds and Liræmor the Great North Sea and all its bounty."

My mind is spinning. I'd never even considered that another modern society would dare worship the Elyphesians when it'd been a hundred years since the last Elyphesian society disappeared.

"Fairlee was once home to the Godlings, ye know."

I nod, excited to recall the stories I'd lost myself in when I was alone in my room—and when I'd been locked away for several weeks in Allondale. "Of course. Forwon stayed in Fairlee to protect the humans from Liræmor when the humans revolted and angered the gods."

Josef nods.

"Can I ask you something?" Though the Elyphesian Gods have always intrigued me, and I felt far more connected to their stories than that of the God of the Heavens and the God of the Earth—the accepted gods of the Unified Kingdoms—one thought always troubled me.

His voice is soft as if I should never have to ask for permission. "Of course."

"Do you think the gods stopped communicating with humans because man defied them, or did they never really communicate because they didn't even exist?" Part of me has always feared my belief was misplaced. That I'm wishing on fairies and dreams, and the gods I think are speaking don't even exist. That everything I feel in my heart to be true is a lie, a fanciful bit of fiction constructed to awe children.

"The gods are there, Malory. But they only believe in those who believe in them."

I feel his words in my heart. I always have. The gods are there. Among men and kings and the people in the world, Nithenia knows me. She recognizes my faith in her. One day, she will answer my prayers. "Thank you."

I smile as I stand, then make my way to the back of the cave where Jamis lies, warm and welcoming. He shifts as I slip my legs under the blanket and slide in beside him. Before I lie down, I look over my shoulder. Josef stares into the fire, the orange glow dancing around him as he breathes slowly. He closes his eyes, leaning his head back and reaching his arms out in front of himself. His lips move, some silent prayer or offering, and then his eyes snap open. He looks in my direction as if he'd been told I was watching.

I gasp and slide against Jamis, my heart pounding in—fear? No, I'm not afraid of Josef. But there's something about him, some ethereal quality—or connection. I don't know what it is, but I'm unbalanced by it. And I'm drawn to the uncertainty of it all.

CHAPTER
THREE

THE CLATTER OF METAL SHATTERS THE DARK SHADOW of my troubled sleep.

The roar of a lion—no, that's Kennard's voice—echoes through the chamber, rattling any lingering moments of peace the orange glow of the sun had yet to chase away. "What th' bloody hell are you doin?"

"Sorry!" Davion stands with his arms full of swords as another clatters to the pile at his feet. Davion is holding one hand out as if to ward off the angry marshal. Though Davion is Fairlean, a people who have always proven to be an equal match for any formally armed military, he's always been intimidated by Kennard. Granted, his enormous size, threatening presence, and battle-scarred body make him an intimidating presence. Still, as I only recently discovered, he's also a Knight of Ballæter, one of the fiercest and most noble houses in all the Kingdoms. An independent township located in the northern edge of Devlishire, near the border to Fairlee and Carling, Ballæter is run by an order of priestly knights who adopt orphan boys and train them to be loyal and lethal servants to the kings, who then pay for their services. But it is rare to know a Knight of Ballæter as they are discreet about their training.

I have a feeling Davion's intimidated manner in Kennard's presence has more to do with the bond that Kennard shares with Katherine, the object of Davion's most devout attentions.

Jamis comes into the cave, bursts of breath visible in the crisp morning air. His brown eyes are puffy. Even the golden flecks that usually cast a glimmer of light in his gaze can't make him appear more alert. I wonder how long he waited to slip from bed after I climbed in beside him last night. He glances in my direction to see if I'm awake. I smile and shrug—this is our life now, noise and interrupted sleep. He looks back at Davion, his brow wrinkling as he takes in the pile of weapons in Davion's arms and around his feet. "What are you even doing?"

"Was jus' tryn'a help. She's takin' a load o' the swords with her, right?" They both lean over to see outside, and that's when I hear the thunder of approaching horses.

She who? I slide from under the blanket, stretching the kinks from my sleep-heavy body as I wind my sword belt around my waist and pull my cloak over my shoulders. I join Jamis as he moves from the cavern. We stand together, staring into the dark that lingers at the trees' base.

With further clattering, Davion gathers the swords, bringing them to lay in the clearing as Kennard grumbles and also rises, joined by the rest of our troop.

Three horses emerge from the trees, their riders wearing thick, gray-and-dark green cloaks meant to keep away the cold and help them blend into the surroundings. Dark hair trails behind the lead rider, and I smile as I see my new friend and ally. *Isobel!*

"How did you know she was coming?" Jamis hooks his thumb toward the tree line that hangs above the mouth of the cave. Josef smiles as he watches his sister's approach. Though they share the same dark hair, Isobel's is highlighted by the presence of woven white and blue shells, which click as she moves about. Now, though, as she rides, the shells cause the colors to flicker about her, highlighting her beautiful bronze skin.

She pulls her horse to a stop and swings one leg over, landing gracefully on her feet in front of Jamis and me. I reach for her hands and squeeze—although we've been through a great deal since we met months ago, we aren't at the level of friendship where I would consider hugging her. "You look well."

"I should. We just relieved some of Brahm's men of this." With a raise of her brows, she drops a bulging bag on the ground between us. The clang of coins jostling against each other is unmistakable. "And this." She holds a hand out to the Fairlean woman who rode in with her. From under her cloak, the lady's arm extends, her hand clutching a sack of coin even more full than the first. Isobel reaches for it, then drops that at our feet as well.

Jamis grins in appreciation of Isobel's haul. "Nicely done. Where did you overtake them?"

Isobel casts a quick, reproachful glare at Jamis. He's either failed to be subtle, or we are just far more attuned to the undercurrents of each other's thoughts these days.

Her answer is casual and assured. "No worries. It was three days ago. We came upon them when we were evenly distanced between Gaufrid, Allondale, Landyn, and Claxton. They had no idea where we came from or which direction we left. And we laid in for a half day to ensure no scouts picked up our trail."

"You were near Allondale?" My heart thuds, my breath becoming trapped. Every time a rider comes in from Fairlee, I fear they bring bad news. I've already lost far too much. I can't bear any more. Especially my sister. That loss would be catastrophic.

At one time, I'd mourned the loss of the kingdom I believed I'd grow up to rule, the family I thought I had, my crown, and the opportunity—as a ruling queen—to determine the course of my own life. But I was a silly girl, and it took true, heartbreaking, gut-wrenching loss for me to realize that. After losing my two best friends, both victims of my brother's greed, I realized what true loss is.

Isobel shakes her head in apology when she sees my expression of hope. "We weren't in Fairlee, and I haven't heard anything about her."

"And my mother?" My mother and sister fled Devlishire the same night, heading in different directions. Though Laila found her way to me in Fairlee, we've had no word of my mother.

I hadn't heard Josef's approach, but he slips between us and lays a kiss on his sister's cheek. Katherine joins us. "We talked last night about raiding Claxton from the south, then heading to Fairlee to regroup."

Jamis is vehement as he shakes his head. His brows pulled together as he leans away. "No. I don't like that idea."

"We have to rest, Your Majesty," Kennard says as he lumbers up alongside our group. Even in the absence of a crown and a functioning kingdom, Kennard can't see Jamis as anything but his king. He gestures to our entire group. "We've been on the road for three months. We've ridden and fought hard. They need a chance to sleep and to eat properly. They need a moment to be home—or near home—so they remember what they're fighting for."

Jamis scans the plaintive, exhausted faces around him. Dirt and grime cling to them. They are gaunt with starvation and physical exertion, hardened by the reality of war and the things they've done simply to survive and ensure the survival of the people we left behind in the safety of the forest and the shattered remains of our kingdom. The thought of spending even a single day back home fills the void of their eyes with renewed hope. "All right, but without attacking Claxton. We stay in the Argralands, then pass to the south of Claxton and Landyn. Then we cut north, straight into Allondale, and into Fairlee as fast as possible. No stops."

Everyone nods eagerly. Only Kennard and I notice the shadow that passed over Jamis's face has yet to clear.

As the others drift away, making plans for the first things they'll do when they get back, I lean against Jamis. "Why don't you want to go back?" I know his feelings about Allondale are mixed. We fought so hard to retain our kingdom and our crowns, but, in the aftermath of the fighting, and with so many scores yet to be settled, it no longer feels like a home—or even a place we can comfortably return.

He turns, and I gaze up into his eyes. For just a moment, I see the boy I married: troubled, unsure of himself, harboring self-doubt about his position and who—if anyone—he could trust. With one finger, he pushes a stray wisp of hair away from my face. "I have a bad feeling, Malory. For days, I've felt dread, as though some impending doom is rolling through the lands in search of us. Last night, I was afraid that was the moment. I'm paralyzed with fear, afraid to make a move, yet afraid not to. I don't want to be wrong and get someone hurt."

I wrap my arms around his waist to pull him closer. "That's why we work as a team. We *all* make the decisions. If it's a bad one, we all share the responsibility."

His brow pinches, and his eyes narrow. He's unconvinced. Jamis is a king. He will take responsibility for keeping his people and his allies safe, no matter what anyone says or how evenly the weight of that responsibility is shared. "Wouldn't it be better if danger is coming for us, that we're surrounded by more of our people and in a place we are more comfortable? We are safest in Fairlee, aren't we?"

He doesn't answer right away, his eyes locked on a piece of my hair he's rolling between his thumb and finger. I give him a quick squeeze. "Jamis?"

His eyes focus again, and he offers a weak smile before kissing my forehead. "You're right. We're safest in Fairlee."

"I'd better go help gather what we can carry with us." I start to move away, but he pulls me back against him.

"Wait, I have something for you."

Giggling, I push back, "I'm sure you do, but this isn't a good time."

He reaches into a pocket in his tunic. When he pulls his hand out, there is something clasped tightly in his palm. "It's a gift, something I want you to have. Something that should only ever belong to you."

I'm intrigued. Though Jamis was generous in bestowing gifts on me during our engagement and marriage, the last gift he gave me, the sword that hangs from my hip, was more for self-protection than an actual gift. Excitement courses through my body, an innate reaction from a previous life that has lain dormant for too long. I pull at his hand. "What is it?"

He gently opens my fingers, so my palm lays flat, then presses his lips to it. His kiss is warm and gentle, the heat shooting from his lips. It travels up my arms and bursts in my chest. Watching my face, he gently deposits the item in my hand and withdraws his own.

I feel the cold of metal and beads. As he pulls away, I notice the flash of white. *Pearls?* My heart lurches, my eyes stinging as my fingers wind through the bracelet. I hold it at eye level, examining it for the first time in over a year. Delicate pearls form a loop with a longer strand of pearls from which a golden medallion hangs: the symbol of the God of the Heavens and the God of the Earth. It's the bracelet I gave Melaine on her fourteenth birthday, the bracelet she gifted me on my wedding day. Tears sting in my eyes. I wipe them away, turning to run into the forest lest anyone see my emotional reaction.

Jamis follows and pulls me to him, hugging me and kissing the top of my head. I shake, wiping madly at the tears, refusing to let them fall. Melaine was my maid and one of my best friends. My brother seduced her, their baby taken from her and claimed by Roarke and his queen, and then her life ended when Roarke slit her throat on his wife's orders. All so my brother could claim the crown of Devlishire—and ultimately the High Crown.

24

Jamis murmurs into my hair as he kisses my head. "I'm sorry, Malory. I didn't mean to upset you. I just thought it was important. I wanted to get it back for you. Something to remember her by."

I wipe my eyes again, the last remnants of moisture battled back into submission. It will do no good to cry—it never does. Grief and fury drive me on, which ensures I give everything I have to give each time I face those who oppose me. Gazing into Jamis's warm eyes, I offer a smile. "I am grateful. I was just caught off guard. I never expected to see them again."

When we knew Allondale would be attacked, we packed all our valuables. Jamis then sent them into hiding. To this day, I don't know where the riches of Allondale are hidden, but if this bracelet has been returned, it means that wherever they are, they are safe—for now.

"How did you get it back?"

"I asked Isobel to find Mereck de Grey, if he was alive, and ask him to have someone retrieve it."

That Jamis would go through so much effort for me, when we're at war and fighting not just for our kingdom but our very lives, is further evidence of what a good man he is at his core. And why he is a far better person than I am. The guilt I've had since being betrothed to Jamis continues to grow in me. Everything that's happened—to him and to his people—is all ultimately my responsibility to some degree.

If it weren't for the greed of my father and brother, and my involvement in the plot to overthrow him, I can only imagine his life would be so much better. The fact Jamis loves me, that he loved me before we'd even met, and I've only come to feel love for him after all we've been through, reinforces the fact I am a far worse person. Even now, Jamis is the person I trust and am most bonded to out of anyone—even my sister. Although I love her, she hasn't been by my side in the last year, hasn't faced and overcome death with me. It's why I trust Jamis above all others. Even now, in quiet moments, I have the fleeting thought, the question that still troubles me: *But do you really love him?*

I reach up, straining on the tips of my toes to place a kiss on his mouth. "You are far more generous than I deserve. I love you." If I keep saying it, it must be true.

I tuck the bracelet into my belt purse, along with Esmond's blade. Memorials to my best friend and the brother of my heart are now side by side and with me always.

We set off after the horses are loaded and camp is broken down, leaving extra items cleverly hidden in the surrounding woods in the hopes that they'll remain should we need ever to return here. Isobel and her troop rides north while we take an eastern trail that will lead us to Claxton's borders.

At a normal pace, the ride could be made in two days, but with our haul of weapons, gold, and armor—and the extra caution we've grown accustomed to—we will surely double that timeline.

The days are long, and the nights longer as we sit in the dark, huddled together to stave off the winter cold. The lucky nights are the ones where we find a cavern of some sort to block the wind.

Josef has taken to telling stories about the Elyphesian gods. During our rest the first day, I made the mistake of telling him about the book I'd cherished so much in my previous palace life. *The War of Gods and Men* was a gorgeous book, from the leather cover to the hand lettering and vivid paintings of the gods at war. I laid awake many nights reading and rereading each of the tales in the book.

Josef passed a hand as if wiping away the relevance of the stories I adore. "Ah, those 'r all the stories that ev'yone hears. They're the borin' ones passed on by borin' men with no inclination ta tell the real stories—the interestin' ones. Fairleans been tellin' stories 'bout the gods fer hundreds of years without books, an' yet we never seem run out'a new ones ta tell."

"Then tell me one story I've never heard," I challenge him.

"All right. When Nithenia was a wee girl, jus' comin' into knowin' 'bout her power and her position within the gods, she walked the earth fer seventy years—"

"I already know that," I interrupt, certain I know the story he's preparing for. Everyone has heard how Nithenia defeated an army of men—and defied Kūbialus in the process—to become known as the protector of women. I can't imagine he believes I wouldn't have come across some unique story. I've read every book in the Devlishire library about the ancient gods.

"But do ye know 'bout the porcupines?"

I'm careful to answer. I don't want to admit to something I maybe don't know, but I hate to admit Josef may have more knowledge about the gods I profess to believe in than I do.

My voice is quiet as I answer, realizing I've never wondered about the story behind the facts. Nithenia is known to have used porcupine quills as quivers in her arrows, but I never thought to question why. I just accepted it as a fact. Perhaps Josef does know more about my gods than I do. And I know already that I'll listen to every tale he wants to relay, and he will tell me everything I crave to know.

CHAPTER

FOUR

WE ALL SIT, TRANSFIXED, AS JOSEF RELAYS THE tale of Nithenia, the goddess who was forced to walk amongst humanity. Taking the form of a young girl, she was welcomed into a kind family. But when the Venbrúids raided the town, the children fled into the Argralands.

As the pirates searched for the children, Nithenia fashioned a bow and arrow from Danailor rods, the quills of porcupines—and a single diamond.

"And as the Venbrúid raiders neared the children, Nithenia drew back the arrow, prayed to the only god she'd ever depend on—herself—'nd released the arrow."

I'm breathless as Josef finishes his story. I add the only other bit of the tale I know, my voice nearly a whisper. "But the arrows—the diamonds—they turn to stone when they touch the blood of her enemies."

Josef smiles, his eyes intense as he nods. We both linger in an awe-swept state of wonder, the magic of the story filling the spaces between the trees, between us all. "That's right. They turn to stone so no person can claim the riches of her arrows or a memento of war."

"Aye, ta find one o' them arrows, though, eh?" Davion's voice breaks the spell. I breathe reluctantly, thrust back into reality.

I survey the group. Jamis meets my gaze, his eyes narrowed, jaw set. I offer a smile, heat spreading across my face. I break eye contact with him, putting on an air of ease. Why do I feel ashamed? I did nothing but listen to a story. He stands in a quick motion, then heads for his horse. "We should move on. Telling tales gets us no closer to Fairlee."

With an apologetic glance at Josef, I follow Jamis, mounting my horse and falling in alongside him. "Did you ever read tales of the Elyphesian gods when you were young?"

"You know it's forbidden in the Unified Kingdoms." His voice is hushed from years of abiding by the Unification laws, of whispering anything that went against them. It's as if Jamis still doesn't realize the Unification is over. The kingdoms are at war. We are no longer High King and Queen. Only the rulers of a nation in rubble.

"Of course." The guilt I carry at having been the cause for everything that's come about in Jamis's life prevents me from pushing it any further. The amount of anguish he carries because of the people we have lost and the fight that still lies ahead of us weighs heavily on his face every day. I won't cause him any more stress if I can help it.

Our group rides in silence for hours. Only the crack of twigs giving way under our horses' hooves, and their soft nickering as they carry us through the forest, make any noise. We're all silent, scanning the surrounding hills and tree line for any sign of threat. Tempers are tight amongst us all, and it becomes easier not to speak than to risk an argument. We need a break. We need to return to Fairlee to find some sense of ease—even if just for a few days.

The days are long, and we are forced to forage for berries when we grow hungry. The small game has gone to ground as the snow is falling again, and we haven't seen any big game since we entered the Argralands. We make camp each night, two people sitting guard in the trees or on a hilltop, each taking a shift. Jamis and I sit guard together on the third night. We are side by side at the top of an old stone wall, abandoned by unknown generations and crumbled under the weight of neglect.

"I didn't mean to snap at you. You should be able to read about anything you choose."

I reach for his hand and pull it beneath my cloak, clutching it in my lap. The warmth of him, his nearness, is always a comfort. I lean my head against his shoulder. "I shouldn't say things that trouble you."

A quiet laugh escapes him, his shoulder bouncing in time with it. "When have you ever really held back? Even when you were cautious with your words, you only veiled their *meaning*, never the *words.*"

"I was rather bold, wasn't I? It's a wonder you ever agreed to marry me."

When I came to Jamis, I was a seventeen-year-old girl, the heir to the throne of Devlishire. But my father's greed—surpassed only by that of my brother, Roarke—left me as a pawn in a plot to overthrow Jamis, then the king of Allondale and High King of the Unified Kingdoms. Angry at my father's betrayal, I vowed to protect Jamis, though I had to be cautious. It was difficult to navigate a new court and new land while determining how to warn my new husband. Sadly, the one skill I learned was to tell the truth in a way that implied what the listener wanted to hear while masking my true message. It's a skill I used against Jamis far too often and have become too comfortable with, to the point I often don't even know my own truth.

Such as if I really even love him. I force the errant thought from my head. Of course I love Jamis. He's my husband, the one person I'm bonded to beyond all others. We have risked our lives for each other. We've sworn ourselves to each other. He has proven time and again how much he loves me. *But that doesn't mean you feel the same way.*

"I love you," I tell him—and my fickle mind.

Jamis squeezes my hand, leaning into me. "You're my everything, Malory. All I have left. The one thing I can't bear to lose."

My heart explodes. He loves me so much. Losing *me* is his greatest fear, yet my mind is still more focused on getting vengeance against my brother than on saving Jamis. *I am a wretched person.*

We break camp early in the morning, while darkness still blankets the land. We'll ride into the thickening forest land to Claxton's southern tip, emerging where a sparser tree line gives in to grassy fields before we cross the river into Landyn. Our horses will have to maintain a run through the fields to clear them before the sun rises, lest scouts see us in Claxton.

When we arrive at the border, we pause in the tree line's safety, scanning the moorland ahead for any sign of scouts. An absolute silence hangs heavily in the air, the type that accompanies a snowy night when the entirety of the earth seems to rest under a blanket of white.

Gray blades of grass and dark stones rise above the ground's surface, casting shadows that make the land appear to dip and roll. My breath puffs in front of me. Sparkles of frost hang in the air, illuminated by the cast of light from the falling snow. A chill runs along my back, my shoulders quivering in response. Is that a warning sign or a response to the cold? I've become more attuned to my internal warning system since the Battle of Allondale, but the cold is interfering with my ability to discern the true origin of my ill feelings.

Kennard slips from the trees to my right. Katherine, followed by Davion, approaches from the left.

"I don't see anything," Kennard whispers.

"Me either. It's completely quiet. No sign of troops or that they've been here recently."

Jamis nods once, though his face is pinched in concern as he scans the surrounding area again. "It feels wrong. It's too dangerous."

My heart thunders at his hesitancy, his sense of danger. I survey the distance we'll have to travel. At a full run, we'll be exposed for minutes before we make it to the river. Even in the warmest weather, the horses will be slow to cross, but it'll take even more time with the amount of ice accumulating. And then several minutes more to cross the fields of Landyn back to the tree line's safety.

"Then we go further south," I decide, Jamis's unease leeching into my senses.

No time. The whisper echoes through my mind as it always does. *Draw!*

I pull my sword from my belt.

Accustomed to taking cues from each other, my group draws their weapons as well. Swords are drawn, bows held at full draw as we scan the fields ahead and forest surrounding us. Straining my ears, I reach out with all the awareness I can muster, trying to sense the threat before it's upon us.

To your back, girl. I spin to face the dark spaces lurking between the trees. Our men spin as well. And then I hear the crunching of snow under the feet of a troop. As their heavy breaths cut through the dark, our breaths come ragged against the cold as we steel ourselves for the confrontation.

Jamis pivots, grasping for the reins of my mare. She shies, pulling away, and he nearly stumbles as he yanks her. "Mount up, now. Run!"

"There's no time!" The dark spaces between the trees are moving now, the heaving mass of bodies running toward us beginning to take shape.

Kennard's voice is a low growl as he warns the group about the impending onslaught. "At the ready."

"Oo-oo-pah," Davion says in a low voice. It's the call of Fairleans, a rallying cry of sorts.

"Oo-oo-pah." Josef's answer is a whisper.

Jamis's face blanches as he looks from me to the tree line, dropping the reins and drawing his sword.

"Nithenia, guide my blade." The words have barely left my lips before primal yells erupt from our attackers, and they burst from the trees at a full run.

Knights in dirty white surcoats, an amethyst eagle with gold talons stitched to their chests—the colors and emblem of Claxton—lunge at our line, their weapons drawn. My heart surges, my limbs flushing with the heat of the one instinct that drives us through every battle: the thirst for survival.

Guttural grunts echo through the empty night as we trade blows with all the force we can muster. I block and strike, watching for any opening with which I can draw my blade across flesh or drive the point through while being mindful not to give anyone such an opportunity to do the same.

Men seem to pour from the trees. We are truly outnumbered, though we've been this way before. But we fight on, meeting the frontal attack while being pushed back toward the river. Slowly, we are losing ground.

Startled, our horses have retreated to the line of the ice-covered river.

King Brahm's men are pushing in, edging us farther apart as they work to separate our line.

"Run, Mal." Jamis is breathless as he issues the command.

Josef, still within steps of me, glances over his shoulder. With a surge of ferocity, he cleanly drops the two soldiers closest to him and then crosses the distance between us.

I angle off, ready to take each other's backs, but instead of positioning behind me, he shoves me, his hand connecting forcefully with my hip. "Go!"

I don't have a chance to refuse. We're quickly surrounded again, and I lose sight of Jamis and Katherine through the sea of white and purple.

"No! Let go of me." Katherine's voice shatters through the low wall of grunts that clings to the ground level, echoing into the sky.

"Katherine!" Davion's voice erupts from behind me, and I catch sight of him. He's running *toward* the horses. Coward!

Kennard, his head visible over the troops surrounding him, is fighting his way toward Katherine, but her curses are nearing the tree line. They are carrying her away. I enhance my efforts as well. If I'm to be defeated, they'll have to earn the honor of killing me. I'll never accept defeat.

From the corner of my eye, a familiar form stumbles and falls to the ground. *Josef.* Brahm's men swarm toward him, eager for the opportunity to easily dispatch one of us.

"No!" Jamis runs into the fray, yelling for Josef to stand—begging him—as he fights back the small band. As the assailants turn on Jamis, Josef rises to his knees. Blood stains his temple, and it has left a path to his jaw. He staggers as he attempts to stand.

An explosion shakes the ground. My knees buckle, and I fight to maintain my footing.

Have I been struck from behind?

Light flashes, cutting sharply through the dark and searing into my eyes. I squeeze my lids together, tucking my chin away from the explosion. It's only a moment until the yellow glow—and the confusion—subsides. I blink rapidly, trying to make out the chaotic scene around me, but dark circles hang in front of the scene. Someone moves from behind me, emerging to my right.

"Close yer eyes," Davion commands right before the light explodes through the night again.

Whatever Davion did gives us valuable seconds. We scramble to dispatch several of the knights surrounding us—which leaves us with even numbers.

Realizing they no longer have the upper hand, the Claxton army turns, retreating into the trees.

Kennard leads Katherine back into the clearing, her face—once the pristine beauty of a lady of the court—now snarled in a fury. "I'll *cut* that bastard's *throat.*"

Scanning, I take a quick inventory of my innermost circle: Katherine, Davion, and Kennard. To my left, Jamis is on his knees in the snow, struggling to stand as Josef assists him. My heart plummets. "Jamis!"

I run to him. He has one foot under himself, and he's pressing up to standing as I approach. Josef grips his elbow, providing leverage and speaking in a low voice, his brow knitted. Jamis pulls his dark gray cloak around him as if bracing against the cold, but not before I see that he's holding his left arm tight against his abdomen.

I push past Josef and reach for Jamis' arm, but he turns away, evading my attentions. "What happened?"

"I just hurt my shoulder. It'll be fine." He smiles and reaches his right hand to hold my chin up, looking into my eyes. "A few days rest in Fairlee, and I'll be ready to go again."

Doubt flutters through me. I take a breath to argue, but he silences me with a kiss. "My warrior queen. You always amaze me." We take just a moment to survey the scene around us. "Get the horses, why don't you? I'll get everyone ready."

I nod before heading to the river. The horses are walking lazily. With the chaos of battle over, they've turned their attention to grazing on the blades of grass that peek from the snow. Gathering the horses by the reins, I return to my group. Most of our troops are mounted up, awaiting their orders. Davion lingers near the tree line, scanning the ground as he makes slow circles. He bends and pulls at some leaves, rolling them between his palms as he surveys the other grasses and leaves. I've seen him forage before, but never after a fight.

Jamis, Kennard, and Josef stand in a tight circle, talking in hushed voices. As I approach, they break up, Josef accepting two horses' reins. "Ye can take Katherine's ta her. She's picking through the bodies." He gestures to her with his chin. I lead her horse toward her, careful to avoid the bodies. Though I have no respect for those who carry out my enemies' orders, I won't disrespect the dead by allowing my horse to trample them.

"A few gold coins, but their swords are old. I'm surprised they're even carrying them."

"Brahm likes to keep the king's coffers filled with riches for his own spending. Why arm your knights when you can buy pretty jewels?"

As we mount up, I hear popping noise followed by a low moan. When I turn, everyone is concealed by their horses. I ride nearer. Jamis is still gripping his arm to his side, his face is pale, and I realize that it must hurt him far more than he wants me to know.

A familiar scent catches my nose, the subtle stench of burnt flesh. I turn my horse, riding back through the bodies. My brother's armies are ordered to set at least one captive afire, but Jamis and I will tolerate no such desecration. As I move, the odor dwindles. *Perhaps it was only a memory?* But no, I've come across the horror of my brother's victims too many times not to recognize the smell of freshly burnt human flesh.

Another moan grabs my attention, and I pivot to find all except Kennard on their horses. Clicking my tongue, I give my horse a tap. She moves, returning to our group. There, the aroma lingers again, fresh and tart in the crisp winter air. But I have no time to dwell on it.

"We'll cut due north, ride past Lake Gaufrid straight into Allondale, and into Fairlee from there." Kennard swings a leg over his horse, giving a quick kick. The stallion steps off at a brisk pace, slowing only when we reach the river.

The horses are reluctant to cross the water. We have to drive our heels into their side with each step, but their pace increases once we cross.

I sidle in beside Kennard once we're a good distance from the river. "Why are we cutting through Landyn? We planned to skirt its southern border before heading north into Fairlee."

"No reason to risk another attack, is there?"

"Isn't that what we're doing by riding through the kingdoms?"

"It's the fastest way, m'lady." A lifetime of training and service to royalty have fully engrained Kennard with formal manners that haven't been easy to let go of. He still acts as though he were a servant to a king.

Dark tendrils of doubt and deceit are prickling at my brain. I look ahead to where Jamis rides beside Josef. His back is bent slightly, his usual regal posture crumpled under the pain in his shoulder—is it his shoulder? "And why are we suddenly more concerned with speed than caution?"

Kennard snarls—another impulse left from our early days together in Allondale—the days when he doubted my intentions with his king—for good reason. "Because we are too tired and too weak to face another fight. If you'd like to take on the world yourself, then, by all means, do so. But we are returning to Fairlee."

Feeling as though I've been well and soundly disciplined, I stop questioning him. I drop back to ride alongside Davion, where I keep my eye on Jamis.

As the pale orange glow of the sun begins to taunt the indigo night with the promise of a new day, I consider Davion for the first time since the fight. I'd been so sure he was running away from the fight. I'd been angry at that moment. The thought that someone who feels strongly for Katherine would be so quick to leave her filled me with fury. If I'd had a spare moment, I would have ended his life right then. But he hadn't run. He'd come back with—what?

My voice is low, and I focus on the surrounding hills and tree lines as I talk. "What was the explosion? What did you do?"

He smiles. "T'was Fairlee Fire. A mix of sulfur, stygialas blossoms, and danailor resin boiled together. Tis poured into shells, sealed, and stored underground for ten years. Once the shell is broken, and th'air hits it..." He shrugs, using his hands to indicate the explosion I'd witnessed.

"Amazing," I whisper.

He nods. Even though he knew about the explosive, he still recognizes the amazing impact it had in battle.

"How come you haven't used it before?" Thinking back on all the fights we've been in over the past several months, I recall the times we were desperately close to losing.

Shrugging, he glances over his shoulder to where Katherine rides behind us. "The stakes were high this time."

I nod, a little smile playing about my lips as I realize what the stakes were for Davion, what he couldn't bear losing. Glancing back to her so he's aware I know what he's talking about, I nod. "They were. Thank you."

We ride on, the day growing long before the sun has even risen above the tree line. The promise of sunshine is overtaken by a thick gray gloom that passes overhead from the north. The cold air increases as we pass the shores of Lake Gaufrid. A bitter breeze pushes the water along, so it laps higher up the shore than normal. The breeze swoops from the air, across the water, and assails my face with an icy mist.

I pull the hood of my cloak over my head, clasping the bit of cloth that covers my mouth and nose. The cold has settled deep into my body, and I can't shake it any longer.

My legs ache from the amount of time I've already spent in the saddle since awakening. Though I'm not one to complain or beg for considerations, my bladder soon begins to demand a respite from the constant jostling of my mare's tired gait.

I speed up to ride alongside Kennard again. "We've been riding all day. We should rest. Maybe get out of the saddles for a few minutes to stretch our legs."

He glances back at the others, then ahead toward Jamis and Josef. "You rest. We'll ride ahead. You can catch up."

"What?" We've never split up to allow for rest. His refusal to stop fuels the apprehension that's plagued me. "What is going on?"

His gaze cuts to Jamis before returning to meet mine.

I kick at my mare, and she trots ahead. Kennard calls after me, his voice urgent. "M'lady!"

I ignore him. Maneuvering my horse along Jamis's left side, I realize his posture has fallen farther forward, his right hand propped on his horse's withers, reins loose in his hand. His left arm remains clutched across his front. He and Josef both turn as they hear me coming. Jamis tries to straighten. They gaze from me to each other, their eyes wide, the colored discs swimming in pools of guilt. Jamis's skin is pale, graying, and damp with sweat though the air remains chilly.

"What are you hiding from me?"

He opens his mouth to deny deceit, but I reach out, yanking his cloak away. The leather gauntlet on his left hand glistens with moisture. His surcoat, the deep blue of Allondale, darkened with the filth of months of travel and battle, is stained dark where he holds his arm.

Realization slams into me, a jolt of panic that floods throughout my body. He wasn't clutching his arm to his side because his arm is wounded. No… he's clutching his *arm* to a wound.

I grasp the reins from his hand, drawing my horse and his into an immediate stop.

Both Josef and Kennard yell my name as if to stop me. "Show me," I demand of Jamis.

Pain flutters across his face, the physical combined with that of having to admit he's injured. His breaths are ragged as he leans right and pulls his arm from his wound.

The cry escapes my mouth before I even realize what I've seen. I lean closer, touching his surcoat as if my touch will make this any less real than it is, any less catastrophic of a realization.

Jagged, torn fabric frames a wound that puckers and gapes as Jamis moves, trying to hold himself up. Scorched bits of fabric and flesh blacken the center of the wound, where they'd tried to cauterize it. *The smell of burnt flesh*, I realize. Bits of leaves have been packed into the wound.

Each movement causes more thick red blood to trickle from the torn flesh. When I pull my fingers away, the tips are painted with the crimson essence of Jamis's life. My breath carries with it one word, a beseeching call or a curse—I'm not sure which. "Gods."

Josef leans over the withers of Jamis's horse, trying to hold my gaze, to bring me from the panic that threatens to engulf me. "Malory! We have to ride on. We have to get him to Fairlee."

I nod, numbed by the sudden urgency of the situation. Kennard and Josef have known since the fields how bad Jamis was injured. Suddenly, I feel we can't move fast enough.

When we reach the southern border of Allondale, a troop of knights meets us. Sir Walter, the Grand Master of Allondale, is with them.

"The route is clear into Fairlee, Your Highness." A question passes through his eyes as Jamis simply nods and rides past. My expression tells Sir Walter all he needs to know, the silent answer to his unasked question.

"Can you tolerate a quicker pace, Your Majesty?" Kennard is growing concerned. He rides to Jamis's right side, pushing my horse away. He and Josef glance at each other, concern etched in the sets of their brows and clenching in their jaws.

Finally, Jamis nods, though he makes no move to speed his horse. With a look between each other, Josef and Kennard move their horses closer. Josef takes the reins while Kennard reaches for Jamis's arm, steadying him as the horses take off at a run.

I heel my horse, willing her to keep up, not bothering to look at who is following, though, from the thundering of hooves against the ground, I would guess everyone has joined in the desperate race to get Jamis into the safety of Fairlee.

We ride hard for two hours until we reach the village, passing the open and crumbled wall surrounding the castle we called home until months ago when we were attacked and driven from our sanctuary into the northern forest land.

Our horses trample through the puddles and rutted roads. Jamis leans dangerously, being tossed from one side to another. As we near the tree line, Josef pulls Jamis's horse to a stop. Kennard pushes himself back farther on his horse, then pulls Jamis to join him. Jamis is draped across the animal, his arms and legs hanging limp as Kennard kicks it into a run.

As I heel my horse, my gaze catches a gray, misshapen reminder of the risks of our new lives. At the base of an ancient tree, its towering limbs reaching out, sheltering any who seek shelter, lies a pile of gray stones. The thick seal of mud fills the spaces between the stones, keeping out weather and insects. Beneath those stones, at the base of the tree, lies Esmond.

Forcing my eyes from the burial site of my dearest friend, I focus on my husband lying limp across a horse, bleeding as they race through the thickening maze of trees and shrubbery.

Kennard's horse darts around bushes and trees, finding its path through the now-familiar woods.

I trail farther and farther behind, desperately heeling my poor mare, trying to impart on her the importance of keeping up with the larger, stronger stallion. But we continue to fall farther behind until I can no longer see Kennard in the darkening sky.

Each lurch of my horse that carries me farther into the dark forest feels as if it's pulling me farther from Jamis. Just as I'm about to be fully engulfed in despair, I smell the smoke. It's the rich aroma of wood burning with some kind of game-filled meals being cooked over them. An amber glow shows through the trees, a beacon leading me into the primary camp deep inside Fairlee.

I pull my horse up short, scanning the crowd gathered around Kennard's horse. They are carefully easing Jamis from its back. Several men carry his limp body. His eyes are open, focused on the trees above, but seeing nothing. Kennard dismounts in one motion, and I see the trail of blood across the horse's back, along Kennard's arm, and the front of his tunic. Jamis is carried into the healer's tent. Kennard stops at the doorway, aware that he can offer no help to his king beyond that entryway.

I push past Kennard to run to Jamis's side. Squeezing between the healers tending him, I tear away his surcoat and leather to expose his bare, bloodied skin. "Jamis! Open your eyes and look at me."

"Malory, get back or leave!" Across Jamis, I notice my sister for the first time. Laila, covered in my husband's blood. *What is she—* and then I recall Laila is training as a healer. We left her behind for her safety, and my little sister—the girl who was always determined to find her place in the world, her calling—has been learning the art of healing. My eyes sting, so happy to finally see her and so desperate for her to give me some measure of hope. "Help him," is all I can manage before fear clamps at my throat, blocking any other words from spilling out. As I slump, I'm suddenly lifted and pulled from the tent.

"Let them work," Kennard says, holding me tightly against his chest as we both stare into the tent as Laila and the other healers call for tools and potions. Katherine arrives on her horse, approaching me as one would a wounded animal, a hand held out, reaching for me, yet not quite daring to touch me lest I turn on her. I don't blame her. I tend to strike out when I'm wounded.

I reach for her hand, pulling her to stand beside Kennard and me, but I can't let go of him. He's the largest, most stable—thus *safest*—presence right now. He's my lifeline, and I know he's as afraid of losing Jamis right now as I am. Jamis is our reason and our means for everything.

Josef sits quietly on a stump behind us, watching his longtime friend battle on the edge of life and death, closer to death than any time we've been through yet. "He should have left me," Josef says. "He's injured because he saved me."

I can't deny his words. Nor can I comfort him when I agree. Jamis might not be injured had he let Josef fend for himself—or let him die. *But Jamis would never leave him,* I remind myself. *Josef is his dearest friend, and Jamis wouldn't have left any of us behind.*

We watch for hours as they tend to Jamis, watching for any signs he's awake and ready to recover. I wait for him to turn and give me the smile that has reassured me so often. But he lies there, unaware, as an elderly woman sticks her fingers deep into his wound, then introduces a bit of iron, pulled directly from the flames of the fire, into his flesh. Though Jamis doesn't move, Kennard begins to sway. Josef leaps up, easing him to the stump. Kennard shakes his head and growls. "I'm fine, the queen..." But as he struggles to stand, he sways again.

"I'll tend ta the queen. You rest." Josef pushes him back to the stump, where Kennard lowers his head into his hands.

Josef embraces me as Kennard had, his arms around my shoulder and waist as we watch the efforts to revive my husband. Finally, when I can stand no more, I ease onto a large log that someone dragged over, Josef beside me, our hands clenched together and eyes fixed on Jamis.

It is hours before the healers begin to clean up Jamis, wiping the blood from his abdomen and face. They spread a colored paste on his wound before covering it. When he's been buried under piles of blankets and furs, the healers finally step from the tent, leaving one old lady—Florie Cavell, the lead healer—sitting beside Jamis.

Laila wipes her hands as she exits the tent. Exhaustion pulls at her face, and she moves with heavy limbs. When Josef releases me, I go to her. We collapse into each other. "Is he okay?"

She pulls away, leading me by the hand to Jamis's side. "We did our best. Florie cleaned his wound, stopped the bleeding, and sewed him up."

I look to Florie, hoping my face conveys what I can't say—that I'm thankful for her efforts. The old lady pulls a thick padded wrap over her ears and averts her eyes, discouraging any words. From my months in Fairlee, I know that nobody speaks to Florie, that she rarely speaks herself, and that everyone drops their voices to whispers or less when she is around, though I don't know why.

Laila drops her voice, leaning to speak directly into my ear. "It's a bad wound, Malory. He's lost a lot of blood. We've done all we can. Now, we wait."

I near him, but as desperate as I am, I'm terrified to touch him.

"It's okay," Laila whispers. She reaches for my hand. Lifting Jamis's blankets, she places my hand on his chest. He's warm, and that single fact fills me with a glimmer of hope. Dropping to my knees beside him, I begin whispering in his ear. I tell him how much I love and need him. I know now, despite the doubt and questions, that it's true. I love Jamis, and I can't bear the thought of losing him.

"Sit here." Laila taps me on the shoulder.

I stand, taking the stool she slips beside Jamis's bed. As I sit, I catch sight of outside the tent. Josef remains, though everyone else has gone in search of food or warmth. His expression is intense, a mix of fear and sadness. I know he's concerned for his friend, but I'm too selfish to invite him in. I sit beside Jamis, spending the remainder of the night brushing my hands through his hair and whispering words that I hope are both healing and encouraging.

Finally, I give in to the physical and emotional exhaustion. Laying my head on the bed, I whisper my love into Jamis's ear until sleep finally claims me.

CHAPTER

FIVE

"ALBATI, GODDESS OF LOVE AND ILL-FATED LOVERS, GODDESS of alliances, hear my prayer." I whisper the call over and over, for certainly if Nithenia can hear my calls, Albati can as well.

The great goddess loved Mandiah Pellah, a mortal, and bore him a daughter in secret. But when the gods turned against each other, Albati stood with Nemii, who promised to grant Mandiah eternal life in Elyphesus. But the duplicitous god killed Albati's lover and lured their daughter into the underworld with the other godlings.

The fact Albati turned her back on humanity doesn't deter me. If any goddess understands my love for Jamis—my *need* for him— it's the goddess of ill-fated lovers. For what two lovers have been more ill-fated than Jamis and me?

I call her name again, begging for her intervention.

Jamis hasn't woken in two days. The wound in his belly continues to seep. Blood mixes with yellow and orange-tinted drainage, staining his dressings. Freshly washed bandages hang near the fire to dry. Florie and Laila—who carefully studies and repeats everything the old healer does—frequently change out the dressings while periodically dabbing some salve or another across his wound. One always remains in the tent, sitting near the crackling fire as they mix roots and oils to create fresh ointments.

I marvel at how quickly my little sister has adapted to life in the forest-tented community. As a princess, she was raised with the belief that rudimentary healers consorted with demons, and their gifts were the result of evil spirits and demons who would

42

demand payment for their opposition to the natural order of life. But Laila has managed to transition smoothly into this new life. As much as I would prefer to see her returned to a life of satin gowns and jeweled slippers, I am comforted to see how strong and adaptable she truly is.

The slow rhythm of Jamis's chest as it rises and falls hypnotizes me. I grip his hand as I watch him for any movement behind his lids or—Elyphesian gods willing—the moment he'll open them.

With no change, I return to my prayers. "He is my love and my ally, and we need you to intercede on our behalf. Please, Albati, you are kind and beneficent. We *need* you."

A quickening comes over me, brief but intense. The hair on my arms rises in awareness, and a chill runs along my spine. An indiscernible whisper fills my ears, causing tingles to travel from the tips of my ears and across my scalp before shooting through the length of my body.

I look to the top of the tent, and Florie, seated in front of and focused on the fire, thick muff over her ears, glances up as well.

Albati has heard me. Of that, I have no doubt. But did Florie hear?

The whispering breezes through my mind again. Florie turns to me, one brow raised in question as her eyes meet mine. She turns away, focusing on the fire and the roots she is mashing with renewed vigor.

Hope floods through me, warming the cold pit that has burrowed into my core. Albati is resistant, but she has heard my pleas. I lay my forehead on my arm as I hold Jamis's hand and resume my whispers again, an unending stream of prayers to the great goddess who is spurred by love. I'm careful to include an occasional appeal to Nithenia, asking her to intervene on my behalf with her sister.

A warm hand on my shoulder brings me back into the present. I leave my head down for just a moment. It's only been two days since Jamis was injured, but it feels like so much longer since I've felt the calming, supportive touch of another person. Being a queen is an isolating position. I frequently miss the warm embraces from my childhood. But being a queen at war is even more isolating. Nearly every moment is devoted to survival. The connection to what we are fighting for is often forgotten or remembered in too-brief moments, stolen during brief respites from the surviving labors. I take one more moment to lock away the touch in my mind, to feed it into my soul, and then I lift my head.

"Ye need ta get some rest 'nd somethin' ta eat." It's Josef behind me. His leg brushes against my back as he shifts, pulling my shoulder with a gentle pressure intended to turn me away from my husband.

"I'll stay with him until he wakes." I shrug my shoulder from under his grasp, angling toward Jamis.

"Yer no good ta him if yer not takin' care of yerself, Mal."

"I can't leave him alone."

"I'll sit with 'im." He taps my shoulder gently, then my back, his hand pulling to ease me from the stool.

I'm exhausted, my body cramped from sitting on the small, hard stool. With my attention turned to myself for once in days, I register the weight of my limbs and the empty churning of my belly. Nodding in acquiescence, I stand. My joints are stiff, resistant to this sudden change in position. My knees give for just a second. Swaying, I clutch Josef's arm to stabilize me. His face pinches in concern, and I know he will personally escort me from the tent if I don't interfere now. I smile, tap him on the arm, and step past him. "Don't leave him."

Josef's response is delayed, and I fear he'll follow me, but he shakes his head and sits. "You've m'word."

I emerge from the darkened interior of the tent like a babe into a new world. Daylight stings at my eyes, though the sky remains dappled and dark with the threat of yet another winter storm.

Smoke from the fires dances among the tents, rolling along the earth beneath the tree branches, which were pushed to the ground by the accumulating weather's weight. The warm scent of burning wood and game lures me to the edges of the clearing where the vendor stalls have a selection of stews, roasted meats, and potatoes. The orange glow from the mouths of stone ovens act as a beacon, promising the savory comfort of fresh bread cooking in their depths.

"Ye've built up quite an appetite, I'm sure, m'lady," a Fairlean lady says in greeting. Her salt-and-pepper hair is in a long braid, wrapped about her neck as a scarf. "Been at war fer months. We've worried fer ye."

"Thank you," I say as I accept a wooden bowl with thick, steaming stew and a piece of bread. I retreat to the log benches that surround the primary fire pit to claim a seat.

There are small groups of people mingling together—Fairleans and Allondaleans, who once never dreamed of entering each other's worlds until they were brought together when Allondale was invaded. They are huddled in conversation while others are busy chopping wood, whittling spears, and sharpening knives. Among those busily preparing for the next battle, young children run about playing ball, kicking the ash-filled leather balls through the crowds of adults. Once evident by the pigmented bands of color painted on their faces and bodies, the forest children blend in with the others. Many of the village children have adopted the decorative style of the Fairleans, and I'm unable to identify which are from the forest and which came from the village.

I watch the children, remembering the first time I'd ventured into the village with Jamis. As a girl and the heir to Devlishire, I'd never been allowed to go into the village. Aside from my unsanctioned trips outside the castle walls with Esmond to play along the river, I'd never been outside the castle grounds or surrounded by villagers. My only trips outside Devlishire were formal ones in which I was transported by carriage from my palace to the next and back again. The warmth and connection I felt as I stood among the people of Allondale and watched joyful children playing was greater than I'd ever felt in my own country—the one I was betrayed by.

I blow on the stew before taking a bite. The flavor is rich and bold, the roasted meat, carrots, and potatoes tender as I bite into them. My mouth explodes in appreciation, my stomach growling with impatience as it waits for the delicacy to be delivered.

"May I sit, Your Majesty?"

I don't have to glance up to know who it is, but I raise my head and smile anyway. "Of course, Kennard. Would you like some stew?"

"Already ate," he says as he sits beside me—cautious as always not to touch me. Despite our current lack of a true kingdom, Kennard is a true Knight of Ballæter, loyal to his king and true to his formal training. The war hasn't been difficult for Kennard. Instead, it's the lack of formality Jamis and I have fallen into as warriors among warriors.

"How's King Jamis?"

The words catch in my throat on their way out. "Still asleep."

Kennard keeps his eyes on the fire, but he nods as if he'd known but was simply trying to find a way to begin a conversation. A long silence settles over us, weighted by our tumultuous past.

Though we discovered that we do, in fact, share the same loyalties, there was so much initial acrimony between us, so many things that happened and have remained unsaid, we've yet to achieve true comfort in each other's presence. Jamis is the bond that holds us together. Should we lose him—I can't even consider that.

My voice is low, and I broach the one thing I've never brought up with Kennard, the one lie I *know* he told me. A lie that only recently came to light, but one I still harbor ill feelings about.

"You told me that Jamis executed Esmond."

His shoulders slump, his head falling forward. He closes his eyes for only seconds before straightening again, facing the fire as he nods. "I *implied* Esmond was dead. And I'm sorry."

The old hurts rise, consorting with new ones, clenching my heart in their grasp. When I feel the salty constriction of emotion gathering in my throat, threatening to pour into my nose and spill from my eyes, I force it all back. "Why?"

He shakes his head as though even he doesn't know—or doesn't want to say—and then he meets my accusing eyes. His voice is low, and I notice a sheen of moisture in his eyes, an emotion I've never before seen from Kennard. "I thought it would be easier. To believe him dead. To move on. And I thought you might be more loyal to the king if you believed Esmond was forever gone."

"How could you possibly think it would be easier for me if Esmond were dead?"

His gaze returns to the fire. He blinks rapidly, his emotions retreating, replaced by the stoic manner for which he's known. "Because that's how I had to think to go on. When I lost the person I loved."

Kennard was in love? My mind reels. Never have I imagined that the strongest hand to the throne of Allondale, the warrior knight from the House of Ballæter, had ever been in love. Who was she, and when had he ever had the opportunity to fall in love? Kennard was an orphan, adopted into the order of priestly knights at a young age—the knights of Ballæter adopted all its orphans by the age of ten—and then my father purchased his services. He was gifted to Allondale upon Jamis's birth. Kennard's life and duty haven't allowed him to spend time with maidens, and knights of Ballæter are expected to be celibate—not that I'd expect anyone to adhere to that kind of lifestyle. "Who was she?"

He stands abruptly. "It doesn't matter. I shouldn't have said anything. I want you to know I'm sorry. I really was trying to ease your pain—and the king's."

Like that, the strained space between us returns.

He clears his throat, hooks his thumbs into his sword belt, and shifts from foot to foot. "Isobel returned with a message. I'm to tell you that your mother is in Gaufrid. She's with King Carolus."

Relief for my mother floods through me. I've heard nothing since Laila arrived to tell us of the night they fled Allondale in different directions. "Thank the gods. Has she sent a message?"

"Nothing, Your Majesty. There's also been nothing more from King Carolus."

Carolus, King of Gaufrid, had been committed to peace. He is the sovereign of the only neutral kingdom within the king's council. But when Allondale was to be attacked, Esmond somehow convinced Carolus to ride on our behalf. His men helped us to turn the course and saved mine and Jamis's lives. But once the Battle of Allondale subsided, King Carolus and his men returned to Gaufrid and have refused to give any further aid.

But if my mother—the king's childhood love—is in Gaufrid, she may convince him to come to our aide again.

"In two days, Isobel, Katherine, and I will ride to Gaufrid to appeal to the king," Kennard says. "We've got to get more men. We're spread too thin. If we don't move against the Beasts soon, they'll bolster their troops. We won't be able to oppose them then. We'll lose, and Roarke will destroy everyone who stood with us."

I'm torn. Vengeance has driven every step I've taken against my brother. I want nothing more than to be there as all he's yearned for falls from his grasp. I also desperately want to see my mother. I know I should be at the forefront of an appeal for help, but I can't leave Jamis. "I should ride with you, but—"

"The king needs you," he agrees.

"Take Josef. And Davion as well." I can't bear to think of any going without the others. They've been a formidable troop while on the road together. I only wish I could ride with them to see my mother and challenge King Carolus. He made promises, led us to believe he would align with us should war erupt in the Unified Kingdoms, but then he delayed. Even after he provided aid, he retreated. He's no ally at all, but I believe his love for my mother is where his strength lies. After decades of being kept apart, she is with him, and he will defend her to the very end. Even if he never comes to our aid, he will have done what I deem his most important duty—protecting her.

With my meal complete and a chance to stretch my limbs, I return to sit sentry until my king awakens. As I near the tent, I see subtle movement inside, the light of the fire illuminating the gesticulations of Josef as he talks to...*Jamis?* I rush into the tent, knocking into a small table beside the bed as I do. Josef stands aside as he sees me enter.

Jamis is sitting up, blankets propped behind him, He offers me a weak smile, but his brows are pinched in pain as he reaches a hand for me. His voice is a dry croak as he says my name.

I take his hand, placing a kiss on his brow before accepting the stool beside his cot. His brow and hand are warm beneath a moist sheen of sweat. I try not to show my concern. "I'm so sorry. I shouldn't have stepped out."

He shakes his head. "Nonsense, Josef said you've been by my side for days."

I glance over at Josef where he stands by the small fire, his eyes fixed on the flames. His ear is angled toward us, and I have no doubt he's listening. Suddenly, I feel in the air that the conversation I interrupted was far more in depth than either will ever admit. "And Josef has been waiting just outside for you to wake up."

Jamis casts a hard glare at his old friend. "Yeah, so he said." His expression softens. He reaches for me, placing his palm gently against my face. Although when his brow tightens again, I know the movement is causing him substantial pain. I reach for his hand, pulling it away from my face, though my impulse is to close my eyes and let him comfort me. To let him be my calming influence and my strength.

I hold his hand in both of mine. "Florie and Laila worked so hard to save you. When this is all over, we'll have to—"

"Malory," he interrupts. His eyes are pools of unspoken worry. He shakes his head once. It's a subtle movement, one I want to have never seen.

I squeeze his hand with a pointed look, unwilling to assume the doubt he's trying to convey. "We *will* do something wonderful for them when you're better, and this damned war is over. To show them our appreciation." I stumble over my words, so much guilt and worry cluttering my mind. "I don't know what I would have done if they hadn't saved you, Jamis. I would be broken without you."

Although his lids are beginning to fall, his look is tender, exhaustion weighing heavily on him already. "You aren't one to ever be broken, My Queen." His smile is weak. Before he drifts into sleep, he reaches for me, the tips of his fingers pressing into the soft flesh under my chin. He draws me toward him and places a soft kiss on my mouth before he releases me, leaning back against the blankets and giving in to the sleep that's come to claim him.

I spin on the stool, then shoot across the tent in one large stride, striking Josef in the arm and hissing, my voice low so as not to disturb Jamis. "What did you tell him? He was angry with you. Why?"

Josef reaches for my arms. His height, size, and nearness suddenly feel threatening. His presence is too much, and I pull away. "Mal, I din't say anythin' to upset 'im. He'd been dreamin' or somethin'. He's speakin' nonsense. I tried to make sense—"

"*What* did he say?"

Josef studies me calmly, but he's delaying, considering what he'll say. "He said 'e dreamed it all. The battle, 'is wound, right 'ere, right now. Says 'e dreamt it all."

The dull drop in my stomach churns the stew I ate earlier as I recall Jamis telling me about the bad feelings he'd been having. A feeling of impending doom was how he phrased it. He was afraid to take that route through Claxton, yet I'd insisted. We'd all insisted it was the best option. And now Jamis is injured—what he feared now come to fruition. But did he tell me everything? Had he dreamed beyond the attack in the wood?

Guilt comes over me, accompanied by an awareness that I did this to him. I may not have been the hand that thrust the blade, but, once again, everything I've done since I first spoke his name and conspired against him has led to this moment. I have led us to the point at which Jamis must walk the rocky crag between life and death.

I study him as he sleeps, Josef beside me. My voice is a whisper as I broach the last question. "What else? Why is he angry with you?"

Josef's gaze snaps my way. He shakes his head, then stomps from the tent without a backward glance. Have I pushed him too far? Is there something he isn't telling me, or is the thought of losing his lifelong friend too much to bear? Perhaps the amount of loss I've suffered has made me calloused to the feelings of others. The number of people I love to my core has vastly decreased in the past year because they either proved my love was unwarranted or because they were ripped from me. Esmond and Melaine were both torn from my life—from life itself. My father and brother betrayed me by plotting my death. The only people left whom I love deeply are Laila, my mother, and now...Jamis.

I do love him. I know that now. It isn't simply a fondness or a mutual dependence. I *have* come to love him, and I am a horrible person because it took the threat of losing him to admit that to myself. Our love may not be the all-consuming passion of fanciful tales, but it is born of trust and comfort, and it grows over time. *And I do love him.* I resume my watch, easing onto the stool beside Jamis. I whisper, asking—*demanding*—that he get better. And then I turn my pleas back to the gods.

CHAPTER

SIX

JAMIS MANAGES TO SLEEP THROUGH THE NIGHT, AND he's greatly improved in the morning. His wound has even stopped seeping. By midday, he's eating solid foods, though in small amounts.

Florie leaves his bandages and care to Laila, who swells with pride at being trusted to manage his care independently.

"You've taken to this," I say to Laila as we sit to let Jamis eat.

She grasps my hands, the enthusiastic princess returning beneath her soot-smeared, beaming face. "I never imagined it would be so rewarding. And I never grow squeamish at the blood or the wounds."

I squeeze her hands. I'd expect nothing less.

"I even helped birth a baby," she says. "It was spectacular."

I shudder. Though I've seen the horrors of war—men eviscerated and desperately clinging to their entrails and life as both slowly seep through their fingers—the thought of childbirth seems brutal.

Laila laughs, glancing between Jamis and me. "Someday, it won't seem like such a horrible idea. The two of you will have brave, beautiful children who will rule all the kingdoms. *Fairly.*"

Jamis sets his bowl aside, a shadow having taken over his expression.

Laila scoops up the bowl. "Would you like something different? Some bread, perhaps?"

"No, thank you. I've had plenty." He offers her a grateful smile, then asks for Kennard, Josef, Isobel, and Katherine. "I'd like an update; I've been negligent for far too long."

51

I stroke his arm. "You've been wounded. You're hardly neglecting the war. It'll rage on without us, I'm sure."

He throws an irritated scowl my way. "We have a responsibility, Malory. I can't let the Beasts ravage the kingdoms at will. I'll lead the armies from my cot if I must, but I won't be cut completely out. I'm wounded, not an invalid."

With his trusted advisers—myself included—gathered in the tent, Jamis is apprised of the Beasts' latest actions and how the kingdoms we're allied with are faring.

Kennard is the first to speak while the others hold back. They all have bad news—for bad news has become our custom—but only Kennard is brave enough to be the first. "King Herrold is dead. He and his sons reclaimed control of Landyn, but the king was murdered in the night. A spy stole into the castle and slit his throat. His heirs have fled Landyn with Queen Ann. Their mother has remained to hold Landyn for them."

Jamis's eyes are wide, surprise dropping his jaw before he responds. "Margaret Saint-Léger is Queen Regent?"

Kennard nods. We all join him, nodding to emphasize the veracity of what he's said. We'd been just as surprised as Jamis by the turn of events in Landyn.

Jamis takes a deep breath. "She has always been a force to be reckoned with, hasn't she?"

"King Merrill is ailing as well. Most of his troops and the villagers fled north to Fairlee. They may have made it into Ballæter. But the Beast's troops have set up a line between the castle and the river. They damned the arm that led to the castle. They've had no water for three weeks, and servants we've been able to question report the stores weren't built up, that King Merrill didn't believe they'd be attacked.

"Fool." Jamis shifts in the bed, a wince pinching his face, but he quickly assumes a calm demeanor, realizing how close he is being watched. "And Carolus?"

Isobel speaks up, a breeze moving through the tent as she does, only light enough to prickle at our skin and make its presence known. I've become accustomed to it, as though the trees that speak to her are joining her, making their voices known as she speaks. Or perhaps they are carrying her words beyond, to the ears of others who can hear them as she does. "We've confirmed that Queen Enna is safe in Gaufrid. King Carolus has sealed off the entry points surrounding the castle. His troops are lined along the exterior walls and those at the inner bailey. Gaufrid is nearly impenetrable when it isn't locked down. But King Carolus hasn't responded to any messages and has made no effort to support our troops or our cause."

"We need him. He's a fool if he thinks he can wait this out. Does he think the rest of the Unified Kingdoms will fall, and Gaufrid will be left unscathed?" Jamis clenches his jaw, his mouth pursed in frustration.

Behind Kennard, Josef speaks up. "We're leavin' t'morrow. We'll ride ta Gaufrid 'nd convince Carolus to align with us 'nd fight the Beasts. He's a smart man. He'll see there's no other way."

Jamis's gaze meets mine. The air in the room shifts, and I feel its weight as a somber realization settles in. No one—Josef, Kennard, Isobel, or Katherine—will ever convince Carolus to help us. They don't know him—he hasn't watched them grow, hasn't been on the periphery of their lives, watching from a distance and wondering how his life could have been different. He isn't in love with their mothers. They'll never sway him.

"You have to go," Jamis says. His voice is soft—as much a cushioned statement of a fact I also realize as an inevitability he's been hoping to avoid.

I shake my head, even though I understand there's no other way. I don't want to leave Jamis until he's fully healed, but everything we're fighting for might depend on having the troops of Gaufrid behind us. Our numbers are dwindling, and we've spread our resources thin to attack the Beasts on multiple fronts. We need men and alliances of our own—stronger than the political allies Jamis and I secured before we were attacked. We need wartime allies—kings who are unafraid to fight against the Beasts' greed and injustice. But war is tiring and lonely.

I look at Jamis, a silent plea pulling at my brows. *Don't send me.*

He reaches out, his palm open, calling for me to accept it, but to do so means I will be walking out of here and back into war—alone. This brief respite, these few days of not fighting, were enough to ease the constant fear and stress of war from my body. It was a tension I hadn't noticed when I was always on the alert—always fighting—and I'm resistant to putting that armor back on. I'm reluctant to heaving the weight of leading an army back across my body, my soul. I raise my hand and slide it into his warm palm, watching as his fingers wrap around mine. His thumb is soft as it traces over the subtle scars that now line my hands. He nods, sadness filling his eyes. I know he wouldn't ask this of me if he didn't think it was the only way if he didn't believe me capable of convincing King Carolus to help us. I nod back, our understanding—as well as the entirety of our relationship—wrought of the undercurrents of war and our dependence on each other.

"We ride out tomorrow," Kennard says.

Jamis's eyes remain fixed on me. His voice is low but commanding—still a king's even if he's unable to ride with his troops. "Ride out at night. Head directly toward Gaufrid, but be cautious. It's a two-day ride under the best conditions. It should take you three, maybe four, to travel through the hills depending on how many troops you come across. Don't tempt fate." He gestures toward me. "Convince him."

I'm lost in my thoughts as the others discuss strategies for dividing the Alliance of Beasts. We've always known that King Brahm was just a number, someone who was easily enticed into the plot between Devlishire and Carling. He'd foolishly believed himself an equal participant in the plot to usurp Jamis and claim the High Crown for Devlishire. While King Lester would have the advantage of his daughter being married to the heir of Devlishire, King Brahm was promised lands and riches when the other kingdoms fell under their rule.

But with our constant bombardment of his troops and riches, Brahm has come to realize he's been thrown to the wolves at his door—or rather, the castaway lone wolf of the Devlishire clan—while Carling and Devlishire have a solid alliance and are working actively to shield each other from attacks.

A young girl, perhaps seven, runs to the opening of the tent. She comes to a lurching stop so fast I fear she'll topple right over.

Kennard's voice, gruff as ever, booms through the tent. "What is it, Ayleth?"

Her golden hair is a mass of wild curls, dark soot has been smeared across her forehead, and a narrow band of dark red and black are painted in a line that reaches from one ear, across the bridge over her nose, to the other ear. Her tunic has hand-drawn symbols in various colors, and her dark olive cloak and hood are covered in small bits of mismatched fur. The thick leather boots seem far too large for her narrow legs as if they might slip right off if it weren't for the dyed scraps of fabric wound tightly around their tops. But more than being surprised to see this young girl, I'm stunned that Kennard—who I've come to figure only genuinely likes Jamis and Katherine, while, at best, tolerating the rest of us—knows this girl by her name. I'm not even certain he knows my name, only my title.

The girl lifts a sealed parchment from under her cloak. Her voice is proud, and she holds Kennard's exasperated look without shrinking away. "A message for the king, sir."

"Well, bring it here then." He holds a hand out toward her. She comes in, deposits it in his palm, and then stands with her little fists clasped at the waist. Her brows raise, expectation on her face as she holds Kennard's gaze. He shifts, his lips pinching together as he rolls his eyes and reaches into his jacket pocket.

I strain in my seat to see, watching Kennard's massive hand hovers over the tiny girl's open palm and drop—*a cube of sugar?*

"Thank you, Kennard, sir." Ayleth squeals in joy and runs from the tent, clutching her precious reward to her chest. Kennard's upper lip strains against a smile, the skin at his eyes crinkling as he watches her retreat. He turns to find five pairs of wide eyes—and open mouths. His usual gritty persona snaps right back into place as he pulls his shoulders back and scowls. "That runt is a pain in my arse.

While everyone else turns their attention to the folded message Kennard has handed to Jamis, I can't help but offer a one-sided smile at Kennard and his farcical ambivalence to the adorable little girl.

Jamis turns the parchment over in his hands. The seal—black wax with an *E* impressed into it, a sword lying beneath the letter, and a single paw print beside it—lacks any kingdoms' color or emblem. I realize the color indicates this is correspondence from a dark operative, someone deeply embedded someplace, but where?

Jamis holds the seal up for everyone to see.

Katherine gasps, locking eyes with Kennard. Their bond, which they strengthened on the battlefield and during training sessions, is one I'm nearly envious of. She glances at Isobel as well before she whispers the words I'd hoped for. "Legion E."

Jamis snaps the seal, then opens the parchment. The message is brief, and he hands it over. My fingers shake as I read the message.

Dwindling resources in Devlishire. King and queen are relocating to Carling in three days. Will be heavily guarded, Advance troops to ensure a safe route. Highest chance of defeating all the Beasts is when they are in the same cave.
~E

My mind is numb as I read the words and realize the implications. I glance from the dark ink, the words hastily scribbled on a spare piece of parchment, to Jamis and the others. "Legion E is still at play." I'd suspected—*hoped*—but it has been weeks since we've had any real communication.

This message confirms that Legion E, a secret legion of lone soldiers, villagers, servants, and even titled dignitaries, working unseen throughout the Unified Kingdoms, is still in existence. The secret sect, some of whom came together to fight for us during the Battle of Allondale, work as dark operatives, passing information from within the other kingdoms. Most importantly, Legion E was assembled by Esmond before his death. Though he was young, Esmond was a skilled and respected knight in my father's army. He'd established Legion E to help protect me. But this—a seal with an emblem—tells me that Legion E is a legitimate uprising in the works.

I fold the broken pieces of the seal back together, running my finger over it. Immediately, I know the meaning behind each symbol, even though Esmond could have never intended one. The E, of course, for my friend's name, the man who established the network, who sought out and convinced so many men to risk themselves to advance the cause of goodness in the kingdoms—or at least the lesser of two evils. The single paw print, a lone wolf, symbolic of me, the solitary member of the den of wolves, the kingdom I was raised in. The standard of Devlishire is a black cloth with a scarlet wolf, the color and spirit of our kingdom. And once I was cast out, betrayed by my father, I became a solitary wolf, a beast with no pack.

But the sword under the E, which is a tribute to my friend and the swords laid at his feet as he died, is the proper tribute for a dying hero.

Rage lights a fire in my core, my mouth dries, and my hands shake as fury creeps in. *Roarke.* I vowed to kill him, to avenge Esmond and Melaine, and in retribution for everything he's done to try to destroy Jamis and me. For all the innocent people who died or were left bereft by his greed, I've vowed to kill him. Images flash through my mind: beautiful Melaine crying her love as he slit her throat; Mary Talbot with a blade protruding from her chest on her wedding day; the blond curls of little Peter Quimbly, his mud-covered body in the fields behind Quimbly manor, and his mother's look of horror as I handed his corpse to her. And Esmond.

Eyes burning, I look up at Jamis.

"No, Malory. Not yet."

"He's going to be in Carling." I stammer the thoughts out as they roll through my mind. "We'll attack his cavalcade. We can hide in the—"

"Malory! No." Jamis's voice is harsh, and it induces a coughing fit. He grimaces as he holds his wound.

Kennard and Josef have moved in around me, as though they'll have to hold me in place to keep me from rushing from the tent to slay my brother this very minute.

It takes just a moment for the fury to clear and rational thought to take its place once again.

Jamis reaches for my hand. "I haven't forgotten about him. We *will* bring him to his knees."

I open my mouth to speak, but Jamis—knowing my true heart—says it first. "We will *kill* him for everything he's done. And you, my love, will draw the blade that cuts him from this world. But, *for now*, it's too great a risk."

Josef speaks as well, his voice calm, almost pleading with me to agree. "He'll be heavily guarded. They'll *expect* an attack on the King's Road. 'S not the time, Mal."

I nod, looking at Jamis. I don't want him to worry, not when he expects me to ride to Gaufrid and convince King Carolus to help us.

When we're alone again, and Jamis's eyes are fighting to stay open even though exhaustion is quickly claiming him, he pulls me to him. The cot is narrow, but I lay beside him, careful not to press against his wound. He wraps his arms around my shoulder and pulls me tight against him, nuzzling into my hair. I feel the gentle pressure as he places a kiss on my temple, but he doesn't release the kiss until exhaustion finally claims him and sleep slackens his body.

There, alone in the inky night, I allow everything I've kept deep in the dark confines of my secret self to bubble up unchecked. And with my husband's breaths to comfort me, I wade into my fear, heartbreak, anger, and the deep loneliness that seems to hover over me, despite the people surrounding me. Doubt creeps in, suggesting that perhaps Roarke isn't responsible for everything that's come about.

Doesn't it all come down to me after all?

Though I soothed myself with the thought that my father and Roarke had orchestrated this vile plot to grab the High Crown, I participated and then opposed it. If it weren't for me, perhaps only Allondale would have fallen. It would have been a swift and quickly forgotten battle. Surviving only in the annals of some dusty tome on the shelves of libraries throughout the Unified Kingdoms.

Are you ready to surrender, mortal? I thought you were more resilient than that.

I sit up, swinging my legs from the cot, and rising into a fighting stance. My hand reaches, but my damn sword is across the way, propped beside the fire.

It wouldn't help you, anyway.

It isn't a voice, but a series of breezes that pass through the tent, carrying the message. I strain my ears, but it isn't the voice of Nithenia, nor what I assumed to be Albati's earlier response.

No, the wind erupts in the sounds of laughter. *I am not Nithenia, nor Albati, though I've listened to you with as much interest as they.*

"Who are you?" My whispered demand is low so as not to wake Jamis, but I'm certain my volume is irrelevant.

Undecipherable whispers erupt throughout the tent, each faint voice drowning out the others until the original one speaks again. *I'm the one who's waiting for you, Malory.*

A low rumble sounds in the distance, then a thunderous burst explodes, shaking the ground. Despite the noise, Jamis sleeps soundly. No dogs are barking, no people stumble from their tents, awoken from their slumber. The tick of something landing on the roof of the tent draws my attention. It's followed by another and then more as the skies open up and pour rain.

I hear the scuff of footsteps and turn as Florie enters, carrying a fur over her head. She drops the fur beside the fire and turns, pulling her muffs from her ears. Her dull green eyes scan the tent before falling on me, her brows drawn tight, gaze piercing, a flicker of fear dancing across her irises. "Who was it?"

My suspicions were confirmed. "You can hear them, too."

CHAPTER

SEVEN

"It's a burden I bear," Florie says, turning away from me. She gives a cursory check of Jamis's wound before reaching for her discarded fur.

"A *burden*? You can hear the gods. It's a gift."

She turns on me, her eyes burning with an irritation I've never seen in her. The heat of her anger causes me to step back. "Yes, I can hear them. I *always* hear them. I defeated my devils—I was only a girl when Nemii sent them for me—and yet I'm still bombarded by the constant talking, arguing, and laughing of the gods. I hear the screams of the godlings from Targatheimr and the cries of the gods in response. The *gift* you're so enamored of never stops."

"That's why you cover your ears."

Sadness nearly mutes her voice. "I nearly went mad as a young girl. It isn't the same as listening to people talk. My head is filled with indiscernible..." She struggles for the word.

"Whispers," I offer.

"So you hear them as well."

"Only a few. This was the first time I heard that one."

She pulls the fur over her head and steps into the storm. "Best hope you never hear it again. Your devils will come for you as well."

"What devils?"

She ignores me—or can't hear me for the covering over her ears—and retreats into the rainy darkness.

I'm the one who's waiting for you. The words, as well as the voice, haunt me the rest of the night. Who is waiting for me? It was the voice of a god, but which? My instincts are certain, but fear clouds the message.

Nemii, the god of opposition, the trickster of the Elyphesian deities. He was responsible for turning humanity against the gods, and the gods against each other. He occupies his opposition by sending seven devils—borne from the guilt, hubris, or fears that haunt their minds—to distract them as Nemii weaves his plot. Even the gods succumb to their devils. Albati did, too, as did Liræmor and his brother Rūvolo.

Why would Nemii send seven devils to Florie? And why would the god of opposition have to wait on me? *No, it must be another god who spoke.*

Sleep is elusive because of what happened in that tent or the journey ahead of me—I don't know which. Once the rain subsides, I give up on rest and venture out of the tent to the fire.

Laila is seated on a bench, sipping from a mug. She hands it over when I sit beside her. The tea is bitter, but I welcome its warmth as it seeps into the coldness of my body. Laila leans into me, laying her head on my shoulder. It's the action of a bygone time, and I realize that despite being so deeply entrenched in war and Laila's newfound skills as a healer, she's still only a fourteen-year-old girl. A girl whose family and country have fallen apart, who has been driven from her home, and who watched her father and brother turn into monsters—and her sister a vengeful hellion.

"You're leaving tonight," she says.

"Yes."

She sits up straight, reaching for her tea. "Do you remember when we first went to Allondale?"

I nod. It's a day that haunts me, the day my family and I rode into Jamis's kingdom under the pretense that we were only there to welcome a new sovereign and new High King. In reality, we were there to prove him inept to hold the crown and—unbeknownst to me—marry me to him. My father also planned to kill me while blaming Jamis—thereby giving my father a reason to invade Devlishire. He intended to reclaim the High Crown for Devlishire, and he was willing to sacrifice his firstborn to make that happen.

She smiles, and a blush creeps across her light bronze skin. "I was mad Jamis only paid attention to you. Jealous."

"It didn't last long."

"I just want you to know I'm glad he picked you. Not that I'm glad for all you've been through. I would take that on if I could. I just mean I could never have weathered all you've been through—nor even anticipated what was happening. I would have been a victim of father. You were meant to be here, Malory. You are smart and fierce in ways they never anticipated. You truly were born to be queen, and I'm so proud of you."

My words are low, a whisper I can only risk my sister hearing. "What if I fail?"

She angles toward me. "I don't think you will. You don't see yourself as we do, Malory. You are more powerful and resilient than you realize."

"I don't feel powerful." But that isn't true, is it? Because I do feel strong and invincible, but only when fueled by vengeance. That isn't how I want to live, though. Some part of me still yearns to live in peace—to be a ruler who is wise and outmaneuvers her opponents in political strategy. War has left a dark chasm in my soul, one which can only be filled with blood and vengeance, and that isn't the queen I imagined myself to be.

"Look around this camp. Everyone here believes in you. There's even a myth about the rise of one great ruler—ordained by the Elyphesian gods. Some people are convinced it's you."

"Nonsense." *I'm waiting for you.* The voice again—along with those that already speak to me. Is it nonsense? Will the gods return to the earth—and would they choose to endorse Jamis and me against Roarke and Lester?

Jamis awakens a short while later. "I could hardly sleep," he says, though the fact he barely moved all night indicates that isn't the case at all. "I've been thinking about Gaufrid. It's dangerous."

I nearly crumble in relief. He's right. It's far too dangerous a trek for me to make without him. We should wait until we can all travel together until we have a full army to ride into the kingdoms with—not small pockets of troops acting on our behalf but separated by great distances.

"You can't travel by horse. You'll have to walk."

"Walk? That'll extend our trip by *days*. Just to *get* there." I find little comfort that Jamis still believes me capable of going out on my own.

"It'll be safer. Horses are noisy. They can't be silenced. You must get to Gaufrid and talk to Carolus. You can't risk the sounds of heavy hoofs or neighing giving you away."

I sit beside him and hold his hand, trying to reason with him.

"It'll increase the time it takes me to get back to you."

"You are my queen. Each moment without you will be an excruciating wait. But I need you to be queen more than I need you at my side. We have to endure. We have to defeat Roarke and Lester, or they *will* defeat us. I want to be by your side to get our vengeance and avenge the people we've lost. Nothing would make me happier than to stand by the queen who toppled nations to reclaim the High Crown."

The High Crown means little to me anymore—a tarnished symbol of greed and lies—but I do have a vow to enforce. I will seek retribution for Melaine and Esmond. I will get vengeance for everything that's been taken from me, everything that's been plotted against me. For driving me into the shadows of the forest and into a vagabond life at the mercy of the night, for his attempts to bring about my death, for bringing Jamis so close to his own, I will kill Roarke. And I must do everything it takes to bring me to that moment.

I nod. "I'll tell the others."

"I wasn't prepared for that." Katherine's eyes are wide as she considers the journey. Everyone else simply nods before pulling supplies from their saddlebags and rearranging them into a single pack.

"You'll be fine," Kennard says. He gives her a pointed look. "You're not that girl anymore."

Katherine straightens her shoulders, nodding at the praise. "Right, then." She joins the others as they go through their packs, pulling out incidentals they'd planned to carry when the horses were the ones who would be bearing the weight.

I'm quickly done with my pack, taking only a waterskin, some food, and a clean gown with the front skirt panel torn away. With my sword and daggers in my belt and vengeance in my heart, there's nothing else I need.

The sky is darkening, and we gather in Jamis's tent to review our plan. I sit beside Jamis, my finger drifting over the scar on my neck. He instructs Kennard, Josef, and Davion to keep us safe—as if Isobel, Katherine, and I were somehow helpless maidens. He gestures at Davion. "And do you have more of the…"

"Fairlee Fire." He nods, holding up five fingers. I don't know if I feel more or less comfortable knowing Davion carries so much explosive power in a bag that'll only be feet from me at any given time. One poorly placed step and our path will be rocked from under us.

The others drift out to give Jamis and me time to say our good-byes. Tears sting at my eyes, threatening to spill, though I force them away. "I've never gone into battle without you by my side. I don't even know how to do this."

He grips my hand. "You spent your life preparing for this. Esmond prepared you. You were ready to be a warrior before I came into your life, and you can do it in my absence."

"That's what troubles me—your absence."

His smile is a kindness that masks the shadow of sadness pooling in his eyes. "If you need me, close your eyes and call with your heart. I'll hear you, and I'll be with you. As will your gods—trust in them."

He pulls himself up on one elbow, trying to mask the wince of pain the movement causes. He reaches for my cheek, pulling me into a kiss. His mouth is soft as it lingers on mine, Jamis's fingers wrapping into my hair, pulling me harder against him for only a fraction of a heartbeat before he lies back against the blankets piled behind him. His eyes are red and intense. "You are the sum of all that matters in this world—I regret nothing for it all brought me to you. Now, go get what is rightfully ours."

It's all I can do to walk away from him, to face this next challenge while knowing he's here in Fairlee waiting. "Ask Josef to come in before you leave," he calls.

A crowd has gathered around us as we pick up our packs. "He wants to talk to you," I tell Josef. A moment's hesitation takes over him before he trudges into the tent, head low. I wonder about the cause of the recent strain between the two old friends, though neither will discuss it.

Laila presses a small clay pot into my hand. "In case anyone is wounded or sick. A teaspoon in boiled water three times each day should help."

I slip it into my pack, then lift it over my shoulder. The bag's weight isn't too much now, but I'm certain that it will feel far more cumbersome after days of walking.

Josef joins us near the fire. I survey him for some clue as to what they talked about, but his expression remains blank. He focuses on our gear and accepting the good wishes our people bestow on us as we head away from them and into the woods.

We walk through the night, our bodies pliable and strong from the days spent feeding and resting. Our path will take us north of Carling, then we'll move south across the King's Road into Gaufrid. The risk of crossing paths with knights from Carling or Devlishire is far less in this direction than if we'd gone immediately south and through Allondale. The biggest risk of passing Carling will be when Roarke and Phoebe are in Carling. Their procession will be leaving Devlishire today. The knowledge increases my pace and strengthens my endurance.

Josef meets my pace, walking beside me as the sun's orange glow brightens the sky through the trees. "I know what yer thinkin', and we ar'nt goin' ta attack yer brother on the road. There's six o'us 'nd hundreds o'them with nowhere ta hide."

"I know that," I'm furious he would think me so stupid. *But I am so stupid, am I not?* That's exactly what my inner drive was propelling me toward—always toward Roarke.

"We should slow down, be more cautious now that the sun's up." Isobel pauses, listening to the breeze. "They're scouting the forest. Preparing for the High King."

"He's *not* the High King. He is a subverter, a false ruler." My venom-thick voice nearly echoes throughout the forest.

Isobel is serene as she responds, everything in her demeanor intended to soothe the rage building in me. "I know that. It's what they are calling him. I only relay the message."

I turn back to my path, though I allow Kennard to set the pace—as excruciatingly slow and cautious as it is. We stop midday to eat and then again in the early evening. Davion and Katherine drift north of us to hunt as we make our way. They catch up to us with two rabbits between them. We take some time to roast them over a fire and rest our feet. After we've eaten, we resume our walk again. Our days of rest are soon forgotten as the heaviness of exertion seeps back into our limbs.

For six days and nights, we trek through the shadows of Fairlee, sleeping in short bursts when we find a rocky crag or cave to conceal us. Our pace slows, and our progress grows more cautious as we pass south along the west of Carling. Each step could be the one that causes just enough noise to give us away.

It's midday on our eighth day when the trees grow sparser and the russet-colored dirt of the King's Road is finally visible in the distance. "We 'ave to wait until dark," Josef says, scanning the horizon in all directions.

"Well into dark," Kennard agrees.

We settle in at the base of trees where we can rest and keep our eyes on the road and our surroundings in every direction. An occasional cart travels past, hauling produce from the fields to the villages and likely to Castle Carling. I imagine how simple it would be to overtake one of the farmers, drive the cart into Carling, and kill my brother. I let my mind imagine all the possibilities as I continue to watch for threats. Only our breaths, subtle movements, and the songs of birds singing above fill the air around us. The quiet soon becomes nearly overwhelming until a snap echoes from behind us. We whirl toward the sound, Katherine with her bow at full draw, Kennard, Josef, and Davion each with a blade in their hands, ready to throw.

A small cry echoes, and then I see who has snuck up to us.

Kennard jumps to his feet and snatches the interloper up, shoving her to her belly on the ground as he drops beside her. "Ayleth, what the devils are you doing here?"

The poor little girl is shivering in fear. "I wanted to help."

Stunned, I gape at Josef and Isobel. "She's been tracking us for eight days?"

They both shrug, and Isobel offers, "She's Fairlean."

Kennard growls, "Well, she can't come with us. Get back to where you came from, girl. It's too dangerous."

"Sending her back to the camp on her own isn't dangerous? She'll stay with us. But Ayleth, you do as your told." I can't bear the complexity of having a child to look after, but there's no way to spare anyone to get her back safely.

"She's not my responsibility. Someone else can look after her." Kennard crawls back to the tree, resuming his watch.

I look between Josef and Isobel, hoping one will assume her charge since she's their people. But they are considering each other, each silently warning the other not to take her on. "Fine, she'll stay with me. Ayleth, come here."

The girl pushes through the grass and leaves on the ground, moistened with the recent snowfall. Her olive-green cloak darker where the dampness has begun to seep into the wool. The maroon and black line over her face remains intact, her ice-blue eyes are intense as she vows, "I won't be no trouble, m'lady."

I turn away from her, doubtful but not wanting to tell her that.

We wait, long after the dark reclaims the earth, staring intently at the space between the shadows for any sign of movement. The King's Road is patrolled even in times of peace. With the lands ravaged by war, and Roarke traveling, the patrols are certain to be more frequent.

An owl hoots high above us. The sound of the river flowing in the distance, signals the relative stillness in the night. We slip from the tree line, our pace cautious. We duck behind trees and bushes while we can until we reach the open space that we will have to cross to get across the road and into the trees on the other side. We will be exposed for several minutes, and I calculate my slower pace as I now have Ayleth to get across as well.

We look at each other. I wrap my hand around the girl's, then nod my agreement. We burst from the foliage and run as fast as we can, everyone else far outpacing me as I tug on Ayleth's hand, near-ly pulling her from her feet in my effort to hurry her. My heart is thundering. The noise we're making seems to reverberate through the night, leaving no doubt to anyone nearby that we aren't sup-posed to be here. The dirt is hard-packed and sends a jolt through my feet and into my body with each step. The uneven surface, rut-ted from wagon wheels and horse hooves, conspire with the dark, threatening to roll my ankle. My toe catches the rise on the other side of the road, and I tumble into the grass. The air is knocked from my chest, and I struggle against a growing panic as I feel Ayleth tumble on top of me.

"Mal!" Josef's voice is an urgent whisper through the darkness. In seconds, he's beside me, pulling me up as he reaches for Ayleth, throwing her onto his back as he hauls me up the grassy hill and into the safety of the trees.

He drops my hand, and I lean onto my thighs to catch my breath.

"Twelve hells," Kennard curses. "You're lucky there was nobody there. And you—." He points a finger in angry accusation at Ayleth, who hides her face against Josef's back.

Isobel interrupts. "We'll be to Gaufrid by midafternoon if we keep going."

I nod. Midafternoon seems so far off, but the thought of see-ing my mother would keep me going for longer than that. But more important than my desire to see my mother is the opportu-nity to find out why Carolus turned his back on us after coming to our aid so briefly.

There is another matter to discuss with my mother, though. One that's been lingering since I last saw Roarke and, be it a vicious lie or one more secret that helped construct my life, I will find my answer.

CHAPTER
EIGHT

THE WALLS OF GAUFRID LOOM HIGH AGAINST THE horizon late when we are finally able to see it in the afternoon.

"I've never seen anythin' of the sort," Davion stops walking to take in the sight.

Though I've never considered it before, Gaufrid is an amazing kingdom to behold. I visited it as a girl, but I also studied it and every other kingdom with my teacher, Master Llewellyn. My old teacher was an intolerable bore, insisting that we review each realm's bloodlines, architecture, and archaic historical facts, when all I wanted was to lose myself in magical tales of the gods. But now, I'm far more appreciative of Master Llewellyn's lessons as they prepared me better to travel this world.

The village itself is a wondrous series of cobbled roads in concentric arcs, each intersecting passage offset, so no single route leads directly to the castle. There are no less than a hundred dead ends that one could find themselves in as they attempt to reach the castle.

Where the village draws to an end, a narrow expanse of land lies bordered by a curtain wall that reaches far into the sky and in an arc around the stronghold. Castle Gaufrid was built on an island in the middle of the magnificent River of the Kings—originally named River Déiha, or River of the Gods, until claimed by the kings during the Unification. The narrow inlet and massive wall protect the castle from land-based invasions. Only the portcullis allows passage from the village into the grounds, and now it lies closed while all along the wall, armed knights look out at all angles for threats to the kingdom.

I take in the valley and village below. The hill we're on is at the edge of the forest. Once we begin downhill, we'll emerge into a clearing where we are sure to be spotted by the guards. There's a risk they will shoot on sight, rendering the question of *whether* we can navigate through the labyrinthine village moot.

Squaring my shoulders, I grab Ayleth's hand. "Keep your weapons sheathed and hands visible. Maintain a slow pace. We can't be seen as a threat, or they'll kill us before we reach the bottom of the hill."

"I'll take the lead," Kennard says, stepping past me.

"No." I grab his forearm. I'm the queen of a fallen realm here to beg for aid and the daughter of the deposed queen who is in hiding behind those walls. And lest we forget, I am also the sister of the heinous ruler who has brought about bloodshed in seven empires. I won't be seen as hiding behind anyone. "I'll lead."

From the moment we step from the cover of the trees, I feel the soldiers' acute attention and the threat of the weapons they've certainly aimed at us. With my head high and shoulders back, I maintain a confident, though unthreatening pace. When we speak, it's in low tones and only to calm each other or point out potential threats.

"To the right," Katherine says from behind me. I cast a glance, immediately spotting the men she's referring to. Three are dressed and moving as though tending the field, only their clothing is fresh, and the moderately sized pile of alfalfa was long ago dried out. I imagine they've been moving that same pile around for weeks.

We draw more attention as we enter the village. The sound of our footsteps echoing through the narrow, cobbled streets draws curiosity. Wary faces peek through darkened windows and doorways. Although some doors slide open to allow hidden occupants the opportunity to peep out at us, others slide closed against the threat we might bring with us, preventing us from tainting their homes and their lives.

At the first intersection, I pause, unsure which path will lead us to the gates of the castle. I'd prefer not to become lost in the village. It would make far less of an impression if I were to wander aimlessly for days before reaching the gates of Castle Gaufrid. How can I convince Carolus that I can defeat armies if I can't find my way through his village?

Closing my eyes, I send a silent prayer to Nithenia, asking for her guidance. The whispers envelop me, and though I can't hear the words, a surety settles over me, and I turn to the left. Each subsequent turn is guided by intuition—or by my goddess—though my mind would argue that each turn was wrong if left to my rationalization. Sometimes it seems we're walking away from the gates in one direction and then in another. Rarely does our path seems the one most likely to lead directly to the gates.

"I d'nt like this," Josef whispers.

We're nearing the wall. There can't be more than two roads between us and it. The sun is low on the horizon, and the castle's shadow falls across the village. No less than a dozen arrows are trained on us as we make our way ever nearer to the castle—and those are the ones we can see. I do not doubt that each of the arrow slits in the rising towers behind the wall has a man behind it watching us as well.

Stepping from the narrow alley, a full platoon of knights greets us from their station in front of the portcullis. They wear the green tunics of Gaufrid, the stitching in gold. On each side of the massive gate flies the standard of King Carolus—gold cloth with a winged ram of emerald color. The guards draw their swords the moment they see us. "Halt!"

My group reacts, the rustle of motion reaching my ears as they—accustomed to acting on impulse—move to draw their weapons.

"No." I hold up a hand to remind them to remain calm. They slide their weapons back into place and hold up their hands, palms to the knights, proof they are unarmed. "I am Queen Malory of Allondale. I'm here to see my mother."

The guards swiftly surround us. I look about, expecting more to pour through the gates. Gaufrid is well fortified, having only one entry that doesn't require crossing water. There are plenty of knights at the front gate and along the top of the wall to hold this point.

An additional group of knights descends from the top of the wall using a staircase so narrow that they are forced to angle slightly sideways and take careful steps while leaning close to the wall. Stones jut from the façade. One wrong move, and they could be jostled against the wall and caught off balance, plunging to the hard ground below. There is no railing and nothing to cling to, which also means that any invading troops would find it impossible to fight their way up the steps as there isn't enough room to swing a sword—no matter which hand you favor.

I raise my hands to the level of my hips, palms outstretched, and repeat myself. "I am Queen Malory of Allondale. The true high queen of the Unified Kingdoms. My mother, Enna of Devlishire, is a guest of King Carolus, and I request the king's permission to pass through his gates and see her."

At my side, I see the subtle twitch of Kennard's fingers, eager to draw a blade. I cast him a glance that definitively tells him that he is under orders to remain calm.

Josef and Isobel hold the guards' harsh glare with a look that says they won't draw first but won't be easy targets should they be drawn against. Poor Ayleth is at my side, certainly unaccustomed to being at the attention of armed knights. I maneuver in front of her, though she remains calm, her body relaxed as I try to shield her with one arm.

The guards murmur amongst themselves, and I grow tired of waiting for them to decide. "I'll wait. Send someone to notify King Carolus at once. You *won't* keep me at the gates all day. I'm the High Queen, and my *request* is only a courtesy."

The commander of the guards lets himself be known as he nods to another of the soldiers. The man breaks away and runs to the wall, following the narrow steps until he reaches the top and crosses the escarpment out of our view.

The wait is eternal, growing shadows ticking off each minute as the sun descends below the ridges of the distant Argralands. I shiver as the cool air seeps in unchallenged by the retreating sun, but I don't dare draw my cloak about me lest the guards mistake me for reaching for a weapon.

A group of men in detailed tunics and jeweled medallions gather on the battlement directly over us. They confer for several moments before they disperse, and then the messenger knight descends the stairs, looking more relaxed than when he'd left. He speaks in a hushed voice to his commander, whose shoulders drop slightly as he turns to assess us with fresh eyes. No doubt, he'd hoped to slay someone today to prove his worth to the king, only to discover he's drawn against a queen.

The commander bows, and his troops quickly follow suit though some still maintain a bewildered expression. They're unaccustomed to a queen walking to their gates—much less arriving unannounced. "Apologies, Your Majesty. King Carolus welcomes you to Gaufrid." He stands and sweeps his hand toward the stairs. "I'm afraid this is the only access to the castle. The portcullis has been lowered until the war is over. King Carolus won't risk an invasion, especially with Queen Enna in residence. We could perhaps arrange for—"

"The stairs are fine, thank you." I sweep past him, too near my mother to be kept from her any longer. But as I approach the steps, I realize just how narrow and dangerous the climb truly is. A heavy weight falls in my stomach as I survey the climb.

"I'll go first," Josef steps past me. "Take my hand."

Though my pride insists I not be seen having any weakness, fear at the thought of being so high up and on such a precarious footing wins over.

I nod, and Josef slips his warm hand around mine. He steps close, looking directly into my eyes, his gaze infused with calm. "We'll be fine. Take Ayleth's hand."

Numbly, I grasp for the girl's tiny hand. She doesn't cling to me as I do to her, though, she seems more accepting, as though she's only doing this to comfort me. And I'm grateful for it.

Josef takes the first step, pulling me along. My foot resists setting in place on the first step, and my knees refuse to lock, But I push on, climbing while every fiber of my being shrieks to return to the safety of the ground. My legs wobble as though they'll give up and throw me from the wall should I insist on going any higher.

We continue climbing higher and higher into the night. The pewter stones blending in with the inky sky as the dirt below is absorbed into the blackening night. Being unable to see the ground enhances my fear, and my trembling increases. I cling to Josef's hand—my only lifeline as I take another step and sway a bit. The stairs are impossible to anticipate, each with varying and awkward height and a narrow ledge that only the ball of my foot fits on. My shoulder catches on a stone jutting from the wall, and I sway forward. Josef pulls me toward him, using his shoulder to pin me against the wall as his eyes—wide with fear—beg me to be more careful. "We're almost there." He squeezes my hand in reassurance.

I look back at Ayleth, realizing I'm gripping her hand so tightly that I'd have taken the poor girl with me had I plunged off the edge.

Ayleth remains completely untroubled by our height and unsure footing. With her smaller stature, perhaps the staircase doesn't seem as narrow. I try to deflect my terror. "She's doing fine."

Josef nods once, unconvinced at my attempt to deflect. His steps are slow and cautious as he pulls me along. Each step higher into the night sky increases the terror growing within me, but I'm determined to reach the top of this wall and my mother beyond it. I haven't survived a plot against me and months of war defending my crown and my kingdom to perish in a fall.

Josef crests the steep top step and reaches, pulling me up with a tight grip on one hand and another around my waist. I release Ayleth as I climb to the top and cling to him for several seconds, willing my legs to stop shaking now that I've reached the battlements. My heart is thundering in fear. My body feels alive, energy coursing through me. Josef's voice is a whisper, gentle and urging, so close it tickles my ear. "Malory?"

Dropping my arms from him, I turn away. My heart explodes in my chest from fear, exertion, and—

"Your Majesty." I release my grip on Josef, spinning to find a man in an emerald surcoat, the stitching and decorative elements in gold. His breeches are silk, his black boots so thoroughly buffed that the light of the torches dances in their sheen. The finery of the coat and gold that hangs from his neck indicates he's a member of the court, although I don't recognize him. He offers a deep and respectful bow while the pinch of his brows and nose signal his surprise at having to greet a queen with such a tattered appearance.

For the first time, I imagine how I must look to others. Impulsively, I run my fingers through my hair, drawing my loose braid over my shoulder as I try to tame the stray hairs and appear somewhat presentable.

"I am Lord Ignalius, Majordomo for the House and Kingdom of Gaufrid. We are pleased to welcome Your Majesty. And if I may ask, who are your…traveling companions?" His gaze lingers on Josef before traveling over the rest of my motley group of warriors.

"These are my guards and my most trusted advisors. I assume they will be welcomed and made comfortable?"

His disgust at their appearance is less veiled than when he takes me in, his upper lip pulling tight at one angle on one side, but he complies as he has no choice. "It will be the king's pleasure. This way, please, I'll lead you to your chambers."

"I'd like to see my mother."

"Of course, Your Majesty, but perhaps…you'd like to make yourself more presentable before presenting in court?" He doesn't say anything else, only leads us into the castle.

People in the hallways stop to watch as we walk past. By their finery, it's obvious they are members of Carolus's court. Each surveys us with the same pinched faces Lord Ignalius met us with, making no effort to disguise their disgust at our appearance—and perhaps our smell. They draw away as we pass lest our filth leap across the width of the hallways and infect them.

I cast a subtle glance about my group for the first time, taking note of how others might see us. While we only notice we are alive and full of vigor, I now see us through the eyes of gentler creatures: royals and titled people, even the servants. We must look like we've crawled from the dark forests, which, in fact, we have. But I remind myself of how much we've overcome, of how I should have been long dead by now had my father's plan come to fruition. But I'm not dead. I'm a queen and a warrior. I pull my shoulders back, meeting each person with direct stares that dares them to look upon me as anything less than what I am: a warrior and queen.

I offer a saccharin smile to a young maiden with a dour face and too-plump bosom bursting from the top of her silken gown. "Lovely dress. Probably a bugger to wash blood from. Oh, for the leisurely life of waiting about while someone else saves the realm. Right, Katherine?"

"Not everyone's cut out for war," Katherine answers as we sweep past the now appalled maiden.

Lord Ignalius pauses at a door and knocks. The thick oak door swings open, and a harried-looking maid steps aside. I imagine she's been quickly preparing the room for me since the first knight delivered the message I was outside the gates. She bows deep, her red face glistening with beads of exertion. The fire has only recently been set as it hasn't yet had time to warm the chamber. The bed is wide enough only for me—or perhaps Ayleth and me. Thick emerald-colored blankets are piled upon it, and a canopy drapes from the golden hooves of the winged rams that are perched atop each post. "Samrah will be available to help with anything Your Majesty should need," the man offers from the doorway.

"If it isn't too much trouble, I'd like my ladies with me. Perhaps two more cots can be brought in?" We're used to sleeping as a group, but I know it won't be appropriate to have the men in the same chamber if I'm presenting as a queen. But I won't let us be broken up into any more groups than necessary.

"Of course, Your Majesty."

I decide to push the issue. "And my men will be nearby?"

Lord Ignalius refers to the maid, who shakes her head to tell him she doesn't know where the others are to be housed—or if any considerations have even been made for them. But I'm not about to leave Davion, Josef, and Kennard to be put up in another wing.

"I will need them to respond immediately should I feel my safety is threatened. We are at war, after all."

"Your Majesty, I can assure you that your men will come to no harm within these walls."

I don't respond, but let him know with my eyes and stiff posture he can't deny me this request no matter how he wishes to.

"I'll see to it, Queen Malory." He gestures for Kennard, Davion, and Josef to follow him.

Josef lingers, reluctant to leave us. I give him a nod, telling him he should go. Samrah watches me intently, so I can't say anything. I can't have anyone know these people are anything more than my staff. Should anyone ever suspect I care about these people, they would be used against me—just like Melaine and Esmond. I can't bear to have anyone else I care about die in my quest for vengeance. But I also can't give up on my quest for it.

Lord Ignalius pulls the door closed as they finally exit.

Samrah pulls a chair near the fire. "Ye can rest 'ere, Yer Majesty. I ordered some water fer ye to clean up and some fresh clothes. His Majesty has requested you to accompany him and Lady Enna for supper when yer ready."

"My companions will be joining me, as well. Please ensure the gentlemen are attended to." I ease onto the chair Samrah offered as Katherine and Isobel pull others into place beside me so they can bask in the warmth of the fire, too.

Samrah slips through a door in the rear of the room.

The crackling fire is so warm and welcoming I could almost climb right into it to chase away the chill that's seeped into my bones from so many months in the elements. It's astounding how simply being behind the cold, stone walls of a castle—which used to feel positively frigid as a young princess—now seems to offer protection against the true depth of cold that permeates the world.

Only Ayleth remains in the center of the room, watching as Katherine, Isobel, and I hold our palms over the undulating flames. I beckon her over. "Come warm up. You must be freezing."

Her steps are hesitant as she approaches the fire, assessing us before holding her own hands to the fire.

"Isn't that better?" Katherine asks.

"Better," Ayleth agrees, though it's almost as though she's studying us and responding as she thinks we expect her to than with what she honestly thinks. She is a strange girl. Though I'm intrigued by her unique nature, I sometimes wonder where Kennard came across her and who her parents are.

Samrah returns with several other maids. They haul in bowls of warm water, infused with the scent of lilies and roses. We scrub the grime from our skin and drag brushes through our tangled tresses, taking turns to help Ayleth as the mechanics of bathing and cleaning seem lost on her. Isobel tames Ayleth's wild curls, tucking them into a complicated pattern of braids that any lady would envy.

The gowns we're given are silk—deep garnet and dark spruce for Katherine and Isobel, and a little gown the color of juniper berries for Ayleth.

"The king'd be honored if ye'd wear this," Samrah says. Two other maids bring in a gown of deep emerald—the color of Gaufrid—with a full skirt. Elaborate stitching decorates the bodice, which glitters with crystals. It's obviously a gown crafted specifically for Gaufridian royalty, and I assume it's left from his wife's wardrobe. Queen Mathilde died in childbirth nearly twenty years ago, taking their unborn son with her. King Carolus has grieved the loss of his wife and my mother before. He never pursued another marriage and refused to consider any betrothal presented to him. Some claimed he was so heartbroken over his wife and child's loss that he vowed never to love again as he couldn't bear the inevitable loss that love brings with it.

Shuddering at the thought of wearing a dead woman's gown, I concede. I need to convince Carolus to align with Jamis and me once and for all. There can be no more neutrality in the Unified Kingdoms. He will be *with* me, or he will last see me when I bring his own rule down around him. "It's lovely. Thank you."

The gown *is* exquisite. My shoulders are bare, and the long, fitted sleeves cling to my muscled arms before billowing out at my wrists, leaving flowing material to hang free, blending in with the flowing material of the skirt. The bangle I usually keep snug about my forearm and hidden beneath my sleeves won't fit under this gown's sleeves, but the flowing material will conceal it at my wrist. The bodice's details are so intricate it has the stiff control of a corset, causing me to struggle to draw each breath.

Without the heavy decor of jewels I was accustomed to in Devlishire and Allondale, though, my bare neck and shoulders feel far too exposed. I finger the scar at my neck, more aware of it without the thick layers of clothing and my cloak to hide it.

A sharp rap on the door echoes through the room. Samrah opens it, stepping aside for a young page. The boy is no more than seven. His curly auburn hair is cropped close to his head, making his plump cheeks more apparent. He stands just within the doorway and bows. "Your Majesty, King Carolus. requests you join him in the grand hall for a feast in your honor."

I pull my royal pretenses around me like a shield and nod, following him into the hall. Katherine, Isobel, and Ayleth follow at my heels. At the intersecting hall, Kennard, Davion, and Josef wait. They've also been provided fresh—and court appropriate—clothing. Though they all look spectacular, I nearly laugh at the sight they make in proper court garb. Each resembles a nobleborn man, only their hands, impulsively reaching for the comfort of their now-missing swords—and then to confirm the placement of each of their numerous other hidden knives—gives away their true, battle-tested nature.

"Your Majesty…" Kennard bows, basking in the comforting sight of his queen in a gown and no longer dressed as a vagrant. He stands, pulling at the surcoat that seems to make him feel confined.

When I smile, he falls into step behind the boy, followed by Davion and the girls.

Josef seems to take no notice that his clothes are different from those he's worn on any other day. He's just as comfortable in court finery as in the leather and wool I've always known him to wear. But with his skin clean of the usual cover of war and survival, the pale patchwork of battle scars across his hands and neck are now more obvious. He bows his head, reaching for my hand. "Your Majesty."

"My Lord," I joke with a smile. I let him go through the act of placing a kiss on my hand. It is soft and brief, and the world shakes beneath my feet as his lips linger against my skin. I pull my hand away, the breath driven from my chest.

I hurriedly maneuver past him, following the others. I think I hear his low voice from the poorly illuminated hall behind me, saying, "You look magnificent."

The labyrinthine halls of Gaufrid make the walk seem eternal. Not only is my mother here, but also the man who can offer help in my war against the Beasts. So much is dependent on this meeting. The steady thump of my heart echoes our footsteps as we're led through Castle Gaufrid to the Grand Hall. I force my mind to my purpose, and my husband, who lies in wait for me—dependent on me to secure additional armies to reclaim our kingdom and our titles.

CHAPTER

NINE

A LARGE TABLE SITS IN THE MIDDLE OF the hall. It is twice the width of the formal banquet tables in Allondale and double their length. Massive chandeliers hang low from the vaulted ceilings, each with tiers of candles burning against the darkness, their faint amber glow illuminating only the guests at the table, leaving the remainder of the hall in the shadows.

While there are a fair number of people gathered around the table, the hall could hold ten times more—and none would brush the arm of another. I've seen it do so under better circumstances. The dark, empty corners of the hall are thick with ghosts of bygone fetes.

"Queen Malory of Allondale," a servant announces. Even in Gaufrid, I am now only referred to as Queen Malory, not *High* Queen. Is this a simple comment to the uncertainty on the title's future, or has Carolus already consented to the idea of Roarke ruling the realms?

King Carolus stands, and everyone at the table follows suit, but I see only one other person.

"Mother!" Although I want to sprint directly into her arms and collapse, I maintain a regal gait.

"Your Majesty." She reaches for my hands but curtsies. She stands straight and wraps me into an unencumbered hug. I melt against her, pulling her tight to me and losing myself in the comfort of having my mother at my side again. In the year since I was sent from Devlishire, I often searched my memory for the tender moments with my mother. After father died and Roarke assume the throne of Devlishire, I feared for her, especially after she fled in the middle of the night. My greatest fear was that she would be killed, and I'd never see her, but now it's as if I'd never felt her arms around me.

"I've missed you so much," she says—not in the whispered confession of our time together under my father or Roarke's rule. This time, she declares it for anyone to hear. She feels no need to worry how anyone would perceive her love of me or how that impacts her loyalty to them. "And Laila?"

"She's safe," I confirm and watch as her shoulders relax a bit more. Two of her children, at least, are safe.

I hold her at arm's length and gaze at her again, grateful to be able to see her if only for a short time. I fight away the tears at the experience of this one joy among so many heartaches. I can't allow my mother to see me weak, can't make her concerned for me at the risk of herself. And I can't have Carolus or any of his court members think me weak, thus unworthy to align with. Reluctantly, I pull away from my mother and greet King Carolus.

I dip into a shallow curtsy—a symbol of respect though I'm not required to bow to him. His eyes are heavily hooded, and the color is lost in the shadows of the dark hall. Silver threads have colored his wavy hair since I last saw him. His expression is one of joy, but I sense the dark shadow of trouble looming behind his eyes. "King Carolus, thank you for welcoming my companions and me into your house. Your kindness is greatly appreciated."

He steps forward, and the kind smile he's always greeted me with reappears. "We were so happy to hear you were safely at our gates. I'm afraid we've heard conflicting reports since the Battle of Allondale."

The guests at the table return to their seats, casting curious glances toward me, and the group assembled behind me. Carolus finally takes note as well. "Forgive my manners, please have a seat. I'm afraid I'm unable to introduce you—" He stops, obviously unwilling to offend anyone, though he might rightfully assume they are all untitled and unaccustomed to being seated with nobility. Fine clothes and rose water can't mask their true selves, but none are ones to be intimidated. I introduce each with pride as they take the empty seats at the end of the table nearest Carolus and my mother.

"Lady Katherine Prescott of Allondale. Josef of Fairlee and his

sister, Isobel. Davion Demarsk. The young Ayleth. And Sir Deme-
trius Ralevian Kennard of the House of Ballæter." Kennard's eyes
snap to mine as I announce his true name, whispered to me one
night by Jamis as we watched on a hilltop. I shrug one shoulder
in response, pleased with myself for keeping such a secret and for
having revealed it so perfectly. I do like to keep him on his toes—as
he does me.

"It's a pleasure to have you all join us. We can't wait to hear
about your travels and what you've experienced during the war."

As the servants carry platter after platter into the hall, depos-
iting them on the tables and pulling the covers off with great flair,
a few of the guests keep their attention firmly on us. We take our
seats, lured by the aroma of freshly roasted meats, root vegetables,
and baked goods. Davion peers in all directions, his mouth opening as he takes in the sight of so many options. Though he maintains control for the sake of table manners, I can see his fingers
twitching at the thought of piling items onto his plate.

I look to Ayleth, certain that the girl from the forest has never seen such an abundance nor such variety, but she appears as
unaffected as always. She accepts a small bit of meat and roasted
potatoes.

"Here, try this." I spear a fork into a spongy pastry, lifting it
onto her plate. I add a dollop of honey and fresh berries then nod,
encouraging her to sample it. She takes a tiny bite, her expression
a mix of curiosity and consideration. She chews and then swallows,
appearing underwhelmed as she sums up her thoughts on the delicacy. "It's quite interesting."

Carolus and my mother laugh, and the other guests join in. "It
is indeed quite interesting young one," the king says. His manner
with her is as kind as it ever was with me when I was younger. He
beams as Ayleth digs a spoon into a bowl filled with cubes of sugar
and deposits the pile onto her plate.

"You arrived on foot," mother's eyes are troubled as she says
this.

I nod, swallowing the small bite of meat I'd just slipped into
my mouth. "Jamis thought it'd be safer than to bring horses. We
made our way here without being detected, so it seems he was
right."

"I just never imagined you'd—," she struggles to find the words
to express her thoughts.

"Of course she did, Enna. Malory is resilient. It runs in her blood to adapt and overcome." Carolus reaches to squeeze her hand before giving me his attention fondly. "We hear stories glorifying your presence on the battlefield."

One of the men in attendance leans, looking down the table as he addresses me. "Oh, yes. Each of my daughters eagerly waits for the latest tale of your adventures."

My adventures? Do these people not realize we are at risk of being overrun and killed? That there are men in the kingdoms whose orders are to do just that? That my brother is offering a reward to the person who brings my head to him? Across from me, a storm brews behind Kennard's eyes, and he clutches his fork in a tight fist. Katherine moves with subtle grace as she places a calming hand on his forearm.

I lock my neutral, political demeanor in place and offer the man a small smile. In my lap, concealed by the table, my fingertips find the bangle. I spin it, letting it exert a calming influence on me. "How reassuring to know that so many celebrate our accomplishments."

"You may very well be the one who can end the war among the kingdoms and establish peace again." The man is far too eager. I assume he's the sort to declare a stance dependent on the person to whom he's speaking.

I look to Carolus, fighting the anger that threatens to taint my response. With all my willpower, I try to ebb the rising tide of emotions—fury as well as mourning. I must remain competent and controlled, I can't risk emotion. "A task that would be easier to bring about if my allies kept their word and came to our aide."

All eyes turn to Carolus and slack momentarily claims his shoulders before he regains control. He offers a simple nod, his mouth curling in consideration before he lifts a silver goblet to his mouth and takes a sip. "That is a discussion for the two of us, I'm afraid, Your Majesty."

"Then perhaps we should have that conversation." I don't want to appear desperate, but nor will I be pushed aside. I'll never allow anyone else to think I *can* be pushed aside.

My mother interrupts, looking between us, attempting to avert an impasse. "There are many conversations to be had."

"Tonight seems like a good time," I say. I have questions for her, too.

Katherine's wide eyes bounce between our faces. Though she's become accustomed to war, Katherine is also accustomed to life in court. As attentive as she is, though, she can't translate the undercurrent of messages happening between King Carolus, my mother, and me well enough to realize they're about both *war* and court.

Josef leans back in his chair, watching and absorbing. Beside me, Ayleth's attention has been drawn to the high ceilings. Davion and Isobel seem happy to be filling their bellies so long as they have the opportunity to do so. Isobel has discovered the cubes of sugar that Ayleth is intently picking from and is paying little notice to anything else.

The rest of the meal is heavy with apprehension. My group knows the importance of securing the aide of Gaufrid and the fight we will weather without additional forces. I assume Carolus's court knows why he has failed to provide the support he offered, and they agree with his decision. But the past is thick with secrets, some of which I've only recently come to know. I need my mother to answer those before I leave.

When the last platter of food has been carried away, Carolus stands and excuses his guests—and mine. "Queen Malory, Lady Enna and I have matters to attend to. If you'll excuse us."

Both Josef and Kennard narrow their eyes, reluctant to leave me alone. I nod that it's okay, but Josef hesitates before he pushes his chair back. "I'll be waitin' outside the door if ye need me."

An echo ricochets through the empty room as the thick doors are pulled closed behind the last guest, leaving us at the massive table. Though I'm seated directly beside my mother while Carolus is next to her, the distance between us suddenly seems impossible.

"I was relieved to hear you'd safely found your way to Gaufrid," I say to my mother. Glancing at Carolus, I offer appreciation for the one thing that binds us. "And I'm grateful you've shielded her. Her safety is imperative."

He nods, casting a gentle look at my mother, which she returns.

I start the conversation, unwilling to wait any longer. Good or bad, all our secrets must be laid bare. When I walk out of this hall, it will mean an agreement has been reached. "Shall we begin with old business?"

Mother's brows draw together, and she presses her lips tight.

"You're lovers," I say without further preamble. I've known my mother and Carolus were in love as teenagers, though the High

King at the time arranged for their betrothals to others. They've long maintained a friendship. Now, I realize they've carried a torch for each other all these years. But something Roarke said the last time I saw him—as I was being forced to kneel before him— made me realize how sheltered I have been. He called me a bastard and our mother a whore. "Now and previously."

Carolus holds my gaze, giving away nothing. I have to admire the way he protects my mother's honor even now.

A quiver takes over mother's voice as she answers my accusation. "I did everything to honor my duty to Devlishire. I married the king, and I produced heirs. I stayed in Devlishire for my children and the country. But my love for Carolus has never waned— nor his for me."

"Your mother was always true to Grayson in her deeds, if not in her heart."

"That tells me *nothing*," I challenge. For the first time, the fear I had for my mother and my joy at being reunited with her pales against the anger I'm carrying. "Am I the heir of Devlishire?"

She begins to nod, but I interrupt. "A *true* heir?"

They exchange a glance. It's my mother's resigned expression that tells me what her words are reluctant to. I push the chair back with my legs and lean over the table. Fury makes my head pound, heat flaming through my body. The threat of tears burns my eyes, but I drive them away. "How could you? You let them threaten my life. You let me risk my own under the belief I had been denied something that was mine. And all along it was Roarke's. I could have easily walked away and let him claim his rightful prize."

"But it isn't his either," she says, her own eyes shimmering with the weight of her deceit. "Nor is it Laila's."

I sink back to my chair. Though Roarke had declared me a bastard, I'd never imagined the same could be said for all the heirs of Devlishire.

Carolus clings to my mother's hand, but his eyes are downcast, guilt fixing them to the table in front of him.

"You're my father." It's no longer a question nor a suspicion. Everything I thought was true about my life has been a lie. A wave of nausea overtakes me, but a glimmer of rationality surrounds me. I've long wondered how my father could conspire in a plan that was intended to bring about my death. Was he so heartless and focused on acquiring the High Crown that he could send his child to death, or did he always know that I wasn't truly his child? "Did my father know?"

"No. He had no idea. Your father died believing you were his child."

Darkness moves across my heart again, a thick curtain of resignation dropping across the hopeful reaches of my mind. I have two fathers, one who plotted my death while the other lived in hiding and now refuses to come to my aide.

Mother comes to sit closer, pulling a chair so she can grip my hand. I can't meet her eyes. My mind is reeling with the storm of lies swirling about me. "Malory, I was afraid, and I did what I thought I had to do. I had to produce heirs for Devlishire, so I did. But there were risks you can't even imagine."

"Greater risks than my father plotting my death?" I jerk my hand from hers. "You knew about that plot, yet you let me walk right into it. You trussed me up with a fancy gold belt and a whispered warning before sending me to my death."

"I didn't know they planned for you to die. I'd never have allowed that had I known."

"And what do you know, Mother? What caused you to be so fearful of him that you'd whore yourself out to give him heirs?"

Carolus drops his fists on the table. "Malory!"

"Don't get involved," I growl, baring my teeth.

The door opens behind us, but Carolus and I hold each other's hard glares.

Josef's voice is cautious, but I hear the edge of a threat waiting to be unfurled if needed. "Are ye a'right, Mal?"

"I'm fine."

The door closes, a soft click sounding as it locks in place. I lean back in my chair, desperate to regain control, to force the flames of emotion from my body. I draw in a deep breath, then exhale the tension in my muscles with it. I turn my attention to my mother, my hands folded across my lap so she knows any other touch from her is unwelcome. "Tell me. Tell me how this came about. Why you did this."

My mother pulls her majestic persona back over her, replacing the regretful mother in front of me with a resigned queen. "I'm the heir of a fallen nation and descendant of two others. I was sent to Tiernan as a girl. Carolus was also there, and we fell in love. But Carolus's family wouldn't allow him to marry me. Glynnairre had fallen, and I have no claims to any other kingdom. King Edward—the High King at the time—arranged for me to marry King Alexander of Devlishire—the only king whose family would consider me. Two weeks after we married, he…fell."

She stumbles over the words. Even Mother doubts it was truly a fall that killed her first husband. According to Jamis, the rumor was Alexander had been pushed by his younger brother, Prince Grayson—my father.

She continues. "I agreed to marry Grayson after a period of mourning. But when we failed to produce an heir after two years, I became desperate. Because of the lingering threat, I did the only thing I could to give him heirs. I went to Carolus."

"You couldn't have known he'd be barren. Wouldn't it have been better to let him think you were the barren one and set you aside? He'd have remarried, and you'd be free."

"But I'm not free," she whispers. Carolus nods, encouraging her to go. Whatever truth lies ahead, they have carried it between them. "I agreed to marry Grayson within days of Alexander's death. I wasn't thinking properly. I was shocked and numb. I'd just come to Devlishire, and the thought of being sent away was terrible. Where would I go? I had no nation. My family had perished in Glynnairre, and our descendants would never welcome a distant cousin to their lands when they were already locked in conflict about the true succession of their crown. One more unmarried descendant in the mix could sway the power to one side or the other. Carolus had married Mathilde by then. So, I agreed to remain the Queen of Devlishire. But just after Grayson announced our engagement, I discovered that I'd conceived with Alexander. I went into confinement at Rosalia House under the pretense of completing my mourning. The baby was taken from me immediately after his birth. The last I saw of him was when he was placed in a wet nurse's arms and led from my chambers."

Hells! I sway in my chair, thinking I might stand, but unable to. Energy courses through my body, but I don't know how to expend it. Never had I imagined my mother would tell me more than that she was Carolus's lover. "I have a brother?"

"I don't know. I have no idea where he is—or if he's even alive. Grayson had him taken away. He wouldn't risk any superceding claim to the throne of Devlishire. He always told me that only he knew where the child was and that my son's life depended on my actions. He told me he would have the child killed if he ever thought I was failing him. He wanted me to be his wife and queen. For a time, that was his only obsession. I had to give him heirs of his own, or he would have killed the baby. I'm afraid I never thought ahead to the danger I'd be putting my other children in. I was young, desperate, and stupid."

Carolus leans forward to catch her eye. "You were in an unfor-givable position." He turns his attention to me. "You've seen what Grayson was capable of at the end of his life. It's hard to imagine, but he'd mellowed significantly by that time. In his youth, he was volatile and paranoid, imagining threats around every corner. His army was far more skilled than any other in the Unified Kingdoms because he sent them into war far more often than any other king. He kept your mother in terror for years. It was only when you were born, and then your brother and sister, that he softened toward her. He believed she'd finally proven her loyalty to him. He became a different person, but he never let her forget that her first-born was in the world somewhere, and his life was dependent on her loyalty."

I study my mother, sunken against her chair, the weight of her past hanging heavily around her. The sheen of the mother of my memories no longer exists. Though I love her, she is just another woman who was forced to make horrible decisions, much like my-self. She is another woman who was denied what she wanted, who tried her best to maneuver under King Grayson's threats, to do her best with the least resultant damage. And she's also just another woman who may have failed under his control.

"Where is he? Where's— " I don't even know my brother's name.

"Erik," she offers. "I don't know. I've had people search, but nobody seems to know. I begged King Kyste for help but soon af-ter Carolus and I left, he ordered the gates of Tiernan closed. Few people have traveled in or out of those gates in twenty years."

Though I've heard stories about the King of Tiernan all my life, I never thought about him as more than someone that father cor-responded with. The reclusive King Kyste of Tiernan is powerful. Tiernan's wealth is rivaled only by that of Travión. And its network of spies is deeply entrenched within the Unified Kingdoms and throughout the world.

There's nothing I can do about an unknown older brother. He's long lost, and his existence does nothing to impact my goals. I've wasted far too much time on something that doesn't affect my current situation. I turn to Carolus—my true father. "Why have you ignored our pleas for help?"

He sits back with a nod. Knowing this discussion was coming doesn't make him any more eager to have it. "I'm forbidden."

"Forbidden? By whom?" Carolus is the king of Gaufrid. Though his country has always maintained neutrality within the Unified Kingdoms, it was by choice, not because it was obligated to do so.

"I made a deal to keep your mother safe. I had to choose—either help you and Jamis or help her."

"But your men rode in and helped us. In Allondale. They came to our aide."

He acknowledges this, though his brows are pinched. He looks to my mother, hesitant to admit that he chose her, knowing she would never have agreed to that had she known. "The deal was after that. Your mother had fled Devlishire. Someone came and offered to deliver her safely to me. In exchange, I had to swear not to offer you any help."

From her lack of reaction, I surmise Mother has heard this story before. "Who made you the offer?"

"I'm forbidden to say."

Forbidden? Well, that is easy to settle. I turn to my mother. "Who brought you here?"

She shakes her head. "I don't know. I rode from Devlishire in the direction of Gaufrid. Somewhere near the hills of Hadley, I sensed I was being followed—or watched. It was very strange. I woke up here with Carolus tending me."

It makes no sense, and I'm furious Carolus and my mother are making this so difficult.

"Who followed you? Did they carry a standard?"

"I-I truly don't know. I didn't see anyone. I thought I heard … whispers, maybe. But that was it."

Whispers? Were the gods at play in bringing my mother to Carolus? Or is he hiding an alliance with Roarke? I stand again, tired of the endless game of deception that winds throughout the kingdoms. Everywhere I turn, there's another barrier, another excuse. "If you align with me, we'll take on whoever is threatening you—as well as my enemies—together. I will stand by you, but I need your help."

"I'm afraid the risk is too great, Malory." His face is drawn and somber. "I won't risk losing her again."

"Not even for your daughter?" I immediately hate using the knowledge against him, knowing I drew on it deliberately in an attempt to sway him.

He considers my words for a few moments before he continues. "I'm forbidden from sending my troops to your aide. But I have no control over the actions of the men who've abandoned my kingdom to fight for the true High King and Queen. I think there may be around…oh, two hundred men considering just that."

I hold his gaze with a steady consideration, then counter. "I think you might find that four hundred men have abandoned their posts. Perhaps even five hundred."

The edge of his lip twitches, hinting at an underlying smile. Pushing to his feet, he offers my mother a hand. As she stands to join him, he nods. "I think I heard four hundred. But we'll touch base in the morning when I've gotten a more detailed report from my Grand Master. Goodnight, Your Majesty."

I receive conciliatory smiles, everyone too drained from the revelations of the evening to offer more.

"Carolus," I call as they cross the room. They both stop and turn expectantly. "I am going to kill Roarke. It makes no difference if he's my brother or your son. I will kill him. And Lester too."

"I know." His voice is even and resigned. There's no doubt or regret in his voice. Even Mother seems to accept that this is what may come to be. Either my brother or me will be dead by the hand of the other.

After they exit through a doorway beside the fire, I pull open the oak door leading into the hall.

Josef paces in the corridor, rushing toward me when he hears me come out. "Well?"

It's all too much. In the dark hall, my carefully crafted emotional armor crumbles. My arms and legs begin to tremble, and my knees give way. I crumple to the floor in the middle of the hall. Numbness and fury collide in my body. Everything I've thought about myself and my family had been carefully crafted lies, constructed in the wake of murder, deceit, and greed.

"What in all hells did 'e say? What's 'e done, Mal?" Josef lifts me. With one arm around my waist and another on my arm, he leads me down the hall until we find a dark corner with a settee. The padding is thick, and I sink into it as Josef sits beside me.

I lean forward, elbows on my knees, and bury my face in my palms. I can't cry, but neither can I stop the trembling.

Josef lets me sit for several minutes before I feel the warmth of his palm on my low back. His voice is low but urgent as he tries to urge me back into the present. "Tell me what happened. Is he goin' ta help us?"

I turn to face him, a shuddering breath escaping. How do I even verbalize what happened in that hall? I force the easy answer from the depths of my aching chest. "No."

His shoulders slump, and he nods slowly as he considers what this means for our cause.

I push aside my shock and steel myself to tell him everything. "He can't officially help us. But we'll get troops, four hundred."

Confusion knits his brow. "But you said…"

In that darkened corner, squeezed together on the small settee, I tell Josef everything. I tell him about my mother, about Carolus, and the man I thought was my father—the man I once loved and revered but grew to detest after he betrayed me. Even though he honestly believed I was his daughter, the man orchestrated a plan that would have led to my death in his effort to claim the High Crown. And when I'm done, the numbness seems to have spread from me to claim Josef as well.

He sits without moving for several moments, a stunned look upon his face. Finally, he reaches for my hands, holding them gently between his own. His thumbs trace the alabaster pattern of scars that line my hands as he struggles for something to say. "I'm sorry, Mal. I had no idea ev'rything ye went through before ye came to Allondale. I had no idea 'bout any 'o this."

His words are kind, but confusing. "How would you?"

He opens his mouth to respond, but words seem to fail him. Instead, he shrugs in apology. "But he's goin' ta give ye men. That's good. Even if he won't commit his full army, he's given ye nearly half."

I nod, focusing on the little good that's come from this journey. I now have four hundred extra men. "And he'll keep my mother safe. He's seen to that."

"Who did he make a deal with?"

"I have no idea." I can't imagine anyone powerful enough to influence Carolus to make that decision. "But he looked afraid at the thought of opposing whoever it is."

"Is it Roarke?"

"No. When I told him that I'm going to kill Roarke, he didn't seem affected at all."

"Who could hold more power than Roarke or Lester?"

I look directly into his eyes, determination lit anew, warming all the cold depths of my heart. "We won't know until they're dead."

I'm afraid that he'll deny me immediately, but Josef meets my gaze, a smile pulling at the corner of his lip. He knows I won't be swayed, and he's willing to go along with whatever I'm planning. I have no doubt.

Josef walks me to my room. Before he reaches for the handle, he admonishes, "Don't let your plans keep you awake all night. Who knows when you'll sleep in a bed again?"

That he knows my thought process so well makes me smile. Impulsively I step closer, throwing my arms around his neck. He briefly stiffens before relaxing. Leaning into my hug, he wraps one arm around my waist, pulling me closer. Though my natural inclination is to melt into the warmth of contact with another person, I find the strength to pull away. Not, however, before I whisper into his ear, "Thank you for understanding. And for standing by my side. Always."

He stands straight, looming over me in the darkened hallway, though neither of us steps away. Josef looks into my eyes and moves slightly, pushing the door open. He steps back so I can pass through. "Goodnight, Mal."

In the room, Isobel, Katherine, and Ayleth lie sleeping near the fire, their breaths deep and slow.

I step into the chamber, then close my eyes as the door is pulled closed behind me.

CHAPTER
TEN

SLEEP ELUDES ME ONCE AGAIN LIKE IS SO often the case these days. I lie awake most of the night, rolling the bangle around my arm, my fingers trailing the braided bumps and grooves. My mind is a swirling storm of plans, reflections about everything I've learned about my family.

Grayson of Devlishire wasn't my true father. While at one time, I would have rejoiced at that knowledge, I find no comfort that Carolus *is* my father. Was my childhood so pointless that any man could have served as a father? Was there any value in having him in my life?

Was he simply one of my devils? Placed by Nemii to interfere in my path?

"Don't be ridiculous!" I chastise myself in a whispered voice.

Of everything that's keeping me from sleeping, my new comfort with Josef is the easiest to reconcile. I'm appalled to have shared so many private things with him. Last night I laid bare every awful secret in my family to someone I trust in battle, but whom I have never truly bonded with on a personal level.

I turned to him simply because I'm lonely and afraid. Jamis is generally always at my side to calm me and offer support. In his absence, I simply reached for something familiar. It just so happened that Josef was there when I needed to be comforted. I don't genuinely feel anything romantic toward him. He's handsome, rugged, charming, and intriguing—that truth can't be denied. But I don't have *feelings* for him. He's simply someone I trust and with whom I have a familiarity.

Shutting my mind down, I don't allow any other ruminations about Josef. I haven't betrayed Jamis. Forever bound to him, I will never give him a reason to doubt my loyalty. Had Davion been at my side—or, god's forbid, Kennard—I would have found some comfort in their presence as well. Having Josef at my side was simply circumstantial, and I won't give it another thought.

For the remainder of the night, my thoughts turn to planning. With four hundred additional men, I could easily move against Carling. The Legion E spies confirmed that Roarke's move to Carling is so he and Lester can consolidate their men. Between heavy losses from the war and the men who've deserted the king's posts, both armies are dwindling. Roarke's remaining knights are now divided between the wars, simultaneously protecting Devlishire and him as he travels. Carling is far less secure than Gaufrid—or even Allondale—and has far too many small and forgotten entryways.

I crawl from my bed while the sun still hides below the horizon. A maid sits in the hall, drowsing in a chair. She startles awake as I exit the room. "I'd like my clothes. The ones I arrived in."

She hurries down the corridor. When she returns several minutes later, she clutches my gown with its partial skirting, my boots, and my pants. Samrah follows behind, looking as though she was just woken. Her hair pokes at several angles from a hastily piled updo. Her arms are draped in my leather belts—all of them.

Once I've dressed, I find my way to an enclosed courtyard near the back of the palace. Panels of wood and glass cover the exterior wall that leads into the gardens during warmer weather. Through the windows, I look over the barren landscape that leads to the river at the south end of Gaufrid. It was just over a week ago that I rode through the lands beyond, still unaware that Jamis had been injured before we fled the borders of Claxton.

"I'm afraid it's only a stark shadow of itself right now," Carolus says as he comes to stand at my side, looking out the window at the sparse, withered garden.

"Aren't we all?" Last night's emotions have faded, but I can't muster the fondness I used to carry for this man. He's still my true father, but he's lied to me for my entire life. Everything he's said and every kindness he's ever shown me has been offered under false pretenses. But I also can't hate him because, despite everything, he saved my mother. Whatever agreement he made to accomplish that goal, I have to appreciate it.

After he snaps his fingers, a maid hurries to exit through a doorway. She returns a few seconds later, carrying a tea tray. "Would you join me? We have some details to work out."

We take a seat at a round table. The stone floor causes the chair to be uneven. As I sit, I'm pitched to the side as though I'll be tossed from it. My stomach lurches at the sudden movement. Carolus grasps the back of the chair, steadying it as I scoot to the table. He places a soft hand on my shoulder, ensuring I'm stabilized before he takes the seat across from me and waits for the maid. The older woman is efficient as she pours our tea. Questioningly, she glances to Carolus, who nods once and waves his hand, excusing her so we can speak alone. "I was sorry to hear of Esmond's death. He was a brave young man, and he cared deeply for you."

My nose itches and my throat tightens, burning with emotion. As I've become accustomed to doing, I push the sadness away. "He came to you before the Battle of Allondale. You agreed to help, and then you broke your word to him."

He nods, setting his tea on the table and leaning back in his chair, his arms draped across his lap. "I sent my men into Allondale to help turn the fighting back in your favor. Did it not work?"

"Yes, but the war isn't over."

"And I explained I was given a choice. Enna was my choice."

I take a sip. The tea is strong and bitter, but I need the moment to control my thoughts and suppress the emotion that's so tentatively managed these days. "And you won't tell me who made that deal with you? Who you fear?"

"I can't. But they are worthy of the fear." He holds my gaze, his gray eyes—my eyes, I realize—solemn in their conviction.

"Maybe I'll find them, too. After I kill my brother."

"Not every fight can be won on sheer determination, Malory. Some are too much to endure, and some losses too devastating to comprehend."

Is he explaining his reasons for avoiding war, or is he warning me against pursuing this other person? "I'm prepared to spend the rest of my days fighting against every evil deed that's been visited upon the people of the Unified Kingdom—and further if need be. I won't be frightened away. I vow that on Nithenia's name."

"Ah, yes. I have heard you're known to invoke the names of the long-forgotten gods. Interesting."

I sit straighter, lifting my chin in defiance of the Unified Kingdoms' customs and the rulers of the past. I am the queen, and I vowed early on I would call upon whichever gods I chose once I held that title. "Interesting?"

"Yes, interesting that you now call upon the gods who turned against each other to help you during a time in which so many of your own have turned against each other."

"The Elyphesian gods turned against humanity only after people turned away from them. Why would they remain on earth when people were destroying temples and denying their eminence? The godlings were cast into Targatheimr, and the kings demanded the people accept the God of the Heavens and the God of the Earth as their deities."

"And where did the lessons of the God of the Heavens and the God of the Earth originate?" He isn't challenging me, nor does he seem to be judging my beliefs, only leading me to consider.

Suddenly I feel uneducated and ill-informed about the religion I was raised with. My fingers find the bangle, running it over its surface and twisting the pliable rope as my mind reaches for what I might remember of the religious history of my girlhood. "I don't know. We were taught the Doctrine of the Gods. We read the scriptures daily. But there was no history, only lessons and expectations."

"Perhaps the doctrine was written by the kings of so long ago. Curious that they would follow the lessons of gods they didn't know the origin of. Or perhaps they *did* know and simply chose to overlook them," he says and lifts his teacup to his mouth again, blowing before he takes another sip. "Perhaps they weren't *new* gods after all, only the remnants of the old."

His eyes cut to an entryway then find mine again. His voice is low as he continues. "Now, about those men who've deserted my army. I believe you'll find that four hundred and seventy-three men have joined your ranks. As I understand, they are waiting for you in Fairlee, a day's ride west of Carling, near the road to Ballæter. I'm compelled to demand that you return my men."

Silence settles between us, though the air is thick with information. I clear my throat and sip my tea. "I'm afraid I can't grant your request; everyone who fights on behalf of the High Crown has volunteered to do so. I command them only in matters of war. They are free to choose whom they align with and for how long."

"Then I see we are unable to agree, and I must excuse myself. I'll see that your mother comes to bid you well." He stands and smooths his surcoat.

As he passes me, he places a hand on my shoulder. In a low voice, he adds, "I am truly sorry for the role I played in betraying you. It was never my intent to do anything other than love and protect your mother."

And with that, he is gone. My chest tightens. There was a time not so long ago that I would have rejoiced to discover that Carolus was my father. He was kind and jovial, everything Grayson was not. But I've had far too many lies in my life, and each one gets harder to accept. Also, I love my mother and have always admired her. Accepting Carolus as my father means admitting that my mother is far less honorable than I ever thought her to be. And as angry as I am that she's deceived me, and that her own choices have helped bring about the life I now live, I don't want to hold that against her. I love her no matter what, and everything I thought I'd be as a queen I modeled after her. To know that my mother was a liar and an adulteress is a harsh truth that I can't yet fully accept.

Roarke's angry words whisper an accusation in my mind before I can shut them out. *Like mother, like daughter?*

Mother is hesitant as she enters, as though she's a child about to be scolded. Each slow step seems to delay the inevitable. She slides into the seat that Carolus abandoned. Her normally bronze skin is pale, and I wonder if it's from the stress she's been under lately or from being in hiding for so awfully long now, first to avoid Roarke and now to avoid the war. "Do you hate me?"

I want to confirm I do, in fact, hate her. But the high wall her betrayal built across my heart crumbles at her question. "No. I could never hate you."

She stands to embrace me. I rise, stepping into her arms. Her thin frame is brittle against my own, made hard and muscular from war and wandering. After we sit together at the table, I quickly update her about Laila and everything that's happened. Mother shakes her head in wonder. "She's a healer, and you're a warrior. Never did I imagine my daughters would grow to be such forces to be reckoned with."

"You know I have to kill Roarke," I reassert. "For what he's done to me. For Esmond and Melaine. And because he'll kill me if I don't."

She nods, a single tear falling over her lashes and weaving a path over her high cheekbone and into the hollow of her cheek. "It's unbearable to watch my children be torn apart by the same thing that drove Alexander and your father apart. The High Crown was intended to be the thing that held the kingdoms together, but it's become that which has divided them most often. Greed, betrayal, and death seem to have replaced all the good the crown was supposed to signify. Had I known it would all lead to this—"

She doesn't give voice to her last thought, but I can imagine she's regretting every decision she's made since she left Glynnairre. Each of those steps led her to where we are now and helped cobble the path to this moment. Much as my ideas as to how Devlishire could bring about the end of the reign of Prince Jamis of Allondale led me to this moment.

"We can't erase the past, Mother. We can only set about to repair the damage we've done, and I'll undo my damage if I have to do so with my dying breath."

She nods to show her understanding before taking a deep breath. Her gaze travels across the weather-stained gown to the torn-away panels, the dark breeches tucked into the heavy black boots of some long-forgotten, fallen soldier on the fields of—was it the village of Tarpoli? Alanium?

"You look so—"

"Dirty?" I interrupt. "Being forced to hide in the forests and fight for your life will do that to a girl."

"I meant, valiant. Like a warrior. Not just the sword at your hip and the practical attire, but your eyes, your disposition. You're a far more developed soldier than your father ever imagined you'd become. We've all heard stories about you, and I doubt any are exaggerated."

"It's likely they are. There's little glory in war, Mother. It's done in necessity, we continue—and we win—or we risk death. Each hour of every day is a risk we face."

"You're leaving, I take it? You've got a new army to command."

I nod and take one last bite of a biscuit, letting the buttery texture melt on my tongue before I sip from the fine teacup to wash it away. It's one last act of civility before I return to the nomadic life I've adopted. "I'll be back when I can. But you know that we may never see each other again?"

She comes to embrace me as I sit, absorbed in the anesthetic emotion of my new life. I can't dwell on the fact that I'm leaving her again. Any emotion besides anger is too dangerous now. I pat her arm and stand.

Before I leave the room, I turn back to her. She's staring out the glass into the stark winter garden, her shoulders trembling as she quietly sobs.

"Mother?"

She turns, wiping her tears away with a delicate lace kerchief. "Yes?"

"Don't ever refer to Grayson as my father again. Nor Carolus. As far as I'm concerned, I have no father."

CHAPTER
ELEVEN

WE LEAVE GAUFRID WITHOUT FANFARE. ONLY THE GUARDS on duty are present to see us off. Josef pauses at the top of the wall, waiting for me before descending. I walk past him, place my quivering feet on the steps without pause and descend without looking back. My heart thunders with each step, but I refuse my impulse to slow or even to lean into the wall. It takes only minutes to descend all two hundred and ninety-three steps—counting them keeps my mind busy.

Falling into pace beside Katherine, I let Kennard and Davion take the lead through the town and into the forest beyond. Josef takes up the rear with Isobel and Ayleth. The group is heavy with silence and the memory of last night's meal. Our packs are loaded with breads and salted meat that Carolus had packed for us.

"The troops are northwest; we'll have to walk through the night to meet up with them by midday." I'm more determined than ever to claim these reinforcements. Some battles must happen, and I'm tired of waiting on them.

"What's yer plan? Because I 'ave a feelin' ye've got one brewin'."

I force myself to not look at Josef even though everyone else looks back to him and then me for an answer. Continuing my pace, I walk through the tree line and into the dark covering of the forest, crisp branches and leaves snapping and crackling under my step. "We're going to take out Roarke's forces. I'm not waiting any longer. We'll move against Devlishire and Carling at one time." I spin to look at them, warning heavy in my voice as I look at each in turn, holding their gaze for several seconds before looking to the next. "And I'll not have my decision questioned. I am the queen, and, right now, I'm commanding the army. I secured it, and they'll answer my commands. If you don't want to go to war, you should head to camp now."

I turn without waiting for their responses, continuing toward where my new troops are in hiding awaiting my orders.

The small, swift footsteps of Ayleth are the first that I hear. She falls into step beside me, looking up with a wide, eager smile. Her cerulean eyes sparkle with the promise of adventure. A drop in my chest nearly stops me as I realize I've just committed a child to accompanying me into battle. But I can't turn away, and I can't imagine heading into battle without any of my team, nor would I trust unknown soldiers with the girl. I whisper to her as I continue. "Are you frightened?"

Her face flushes as her grin expands even further. "No"

I nod, and we continue through the undergrowth, her nearly skipping to keep up with me as my mind tumbles with how I will protect this girl while I rush recklessly into another kingdom with one goal: to kill my brother.

The others maintain a distance behind me, but they are following. I imagine a significant amount of silent discussion took place between them before they fell in behind me. They are with me nonetheless, as I knew they would be. The one thing I feared was that one would be sent to tell Jamis of my plan—a plan I know he will oppose. Jamis will want to be there to assure my safety and witness my victory when I finally kill Roarke. Jamis himself would take great pleasure in witnessing Roarke's death, but I can't wait for him—I'm doing this as much for him as for Esmond, Melaine—and myself. And Jamis isn't available. He's lying in a bed recovering, and I can't wait until he's healed to do this. The time is now. I feel Nithenia urging me, agreeing with this course of action.

We cross King's Road and return to Fairlee's dense growth before the sun shines its midday light to warm the open spaces. In the trees, the air remains frigid. Each breath explodes into a visible burst as I push on. With my cloak pulled about me, one hand clutching it closed at my waist, and the heat my body is creating with the constant exertion, I hardly register the cold surrounding me.

Josef catches up, falling into step beside Ayleth. I'm tempted to drop back and walk with Katherine but decide against it. I should be able to walk and fight alongside him without falling into my stupid inclinations to turn to him for comfort. Katherine is my friend and my lady; I vow to sit close to her should I need a comforting presence. *But I won't need one. I'm a queen and a warrior. I need only my king and victory.*

The sun has disappeared and reappeared again before I hear movement in the distance of my new troops. As we approach, we're intercepted by men on horseback, their weapons drawn on us. Behind them, a sea of men rise from the comfort of their bedrolls and grab their weapons, their attention firmly on my small band of woodland warriors and exiled court members—and a child. The camp stretched far beyond what I can see, men mingling in trees, voices periodically shouting to each other.

"Drop your weapons," Kennard growls, stepping forward. "Your queen commander has arrived."

"And which queen would that be?" The man who steps forward is nearly as large as Kennard and seems fully prepared to match blows with him if need be.

I quickly assess the men; it would do no good to announce myself to an enemy troop. Though they carry no standard and bear no emblem, the emerald of their tunics are visible beneath their armor—the leather as well as the metal armor. These most certainly are the men from Gaufrid.

Stepping forward, I let my cloak fall open so they can see the sword at my hip and my open palms. I am no threat, nor do I have to be—I am a queen. "You were dispatched the evening before last with orders to await my arrival. I am the High Queen, Malory of Allondale, and you are fighting for me on behalf of your king, Carolus of Gaufrid."

They drop to a knee, heads bowed, an action that carries across the sea of bodies gathered in the clearing. Ayleth takes two steps in front of me, watching the roll of motion as men drop into a respectful bow. She cuts a sideways glance my way, her mouth pulled into an appreciative grin before she begins to walk, winding a path through the men who offer her small nods of acknowledgement as well.

"Who's in charge?"

The man who rivals Kennard in size stands and removes his helmet. His dark hair has tight curls, and his ebony eyes are lined with thick lashes. A pale scar lines his face from the corner of his left eye along his cheek to the corner of his mouth. Another, this one pale, but with a thick rope of scar tissue runs from his right ear, across the front of his neck, dropping into the hollow of his throat.

My hand impulsively goes to my neck, fingering the thin scar at the front of it.

"I'm Weaver Arionde, Your Majesty. Second Commander of the King's Army in Gaufrid and a Knight of the House of Ballæter."

I cut my gaze to Kennard, who shows no reaction to the announcement that Weaver is also of the order that trained him. I know Kennard won't give me any information, so I decide to question the other knight. "The House of Ballæter. We're lucky to have such a skilled soldier on our side. It isn't often you come across a true knight from that house, is it?"

His gaze cuts to Kennard, but quickly returns. "No, Your Majesty."

"Have you come across any others from your house since the war began?" From the corner of my eye, I see Kennard's chin lift. Though Weaver is effectively *not* looking at Kennard any longer, Kennard's interest is now on him. I have no doubt they knew each other at some point, but is he worried Weaver will admit to knowing him? Again, I'm intrigued by Jamis's most trusted advisor's secret past life and the number of secrets the man holds.

"No, Your Majesty. No others."

Kennard's shoulders relax. He turns, again focused on the duty ahead. "We should rest and make plans. There's no need to delay."

The men begin to gather around, so I take the opportunity to address them all. "I know we're in perilous times. I appreciate each of you who have committed to the fight with Allondale. Though our war seems insurmountable now, our bravery will be rewarded in the end."

I turn to Weaver and issue my first order. "Gather your captains. We've got planning to do."

"You realize you're mad," Katherine says after I've explained my plan, and the captains of the guards of Gaufrid have left to brief their soldiers. "Jamis will be furious."

"Jamis is in no condition to fight, and we can't wait any longer." I've been silently praying to Nithenia to tell me if my plan is wrong, but she hasn't responded. I even sent prayers of guidance to Kūbialus, the god of force and compulsion—protector of armies. It seems they support my plan, so I am more certain than when I first considered it.

Katherine drifts away to sit with Isobel, Davion, and Josef. They've joined a group of soldiers near a fire and are exchanging hot cups of tea and sharing food.

Kennard is leaning against a tree near me, gnawing on a crusty end of a bread loaf. I sit beside him. "Do you think I'm mad as well?"

"Always have." He swallows and follows with a gulp of water from his skin.

A huff of laughter escapes from my chest. I shake my head, grateful for his brutal truthfulness.

"But not about this," he says. "There's been no better opportunity to get into Carling. And for you to settle up with your brother."

It's a strange sensation to have Kennard agree with me. Even though we've grown to trust each other more on the battlefield and in our journeys, there's still a wall of distance between us. Kennard is someone who doesn't trust easily and doesn't reveal himself. Even Jamis doesn't know what Kennard's life was like before he came to Allondale.

"All I know is Kennard despises your father and Lester of Carling, though he would never actually verbalize his feelings about either. I can just see it in him," Jamis told me once. "But I don't know anything about his childhood or Ballæter."

Kennard tears a piece of bread from his and hands it to me. I accept it, turning it over in my fingers as I survey the army around us. They are settling in as dusk gives way to night. The dark drape of winter's night drifts across the forest to cover us in darkness and the inevitable cold that accompanies it. "You know Weaver Arionde. From Ballæter." I know better than to ask because it's a statement of fact.

"Aye," Kennard confirms without elaborating.

"Were you friends?"

"That's not how things work in Ballæter. We were brought there for a purpose, and making friends isn't that purpose."

I tear off a small bite of the bread and pop it into my mouth. Kennard won't elaborate or offer any personal information, but his brow is pinched and his jaw pulses as he clenches it. The skin around his eyes is tight as he maintains control of his external reaction to the inner turmoil. I can't see the memories, but they're painful. I fight my curiosity, letting the matter rest. "I'm happy you're with me, Kennard. And I know that Jamis only trusts me on this trip because you are by my side. He trusts you above all others, you know."

He harrumphs. "He's a good king—and a good man. He should be with us."

A cold pit of longing burns in my chest. Jamis *should* be with us. He should be riding beside us to claim this victory. "He will be. There are many victories still to claim, and Jamis will lead us into every one of those battles. But this one—this one we'll have to bring back to him. It won't wait any longer."

"It won't wait—or you won't?"

I keep my gaze on Ayleth as she walks through the camp. She talks to the soldiers, asking questions and inspiring laughter. I don't answer him. We both know the answer, and to deny it would mean lying to this man when I've tried so hard to prove that he should trust me.

He nods in confirmation and pushes up from the ground. "Well, on the off chance that I'm going to die during this, I may as well spend tonight getting good and drunk."

Aytleth runs to him as he weaves through the bodies lounging on piles of armor. He reaches the fire, leans over, and says something. She runs off, returning with a bottle that he opens and takes a long pull from. Davion accepts the bottle and passes it to Katherine. *And so it goes*, I think as I watch my troop cement the bond they've built.

An empty feeling of isolation creeps over me, my skin prickling. I close my eyes and imagine Jamis sitting beside me as we used to, watching as our hodgepodge band of warriors celebrated each victory, bonding over their accomplishments. We would listen as they reveled in their heroic deeds, laughing at each other's foibles. It was a feeling of belonging, of family, that had been absent in my life for such a long time. A feeling I never thought I'd dare feel again. They are my friends, my family, and I can't bear to lose a single one.

Yet I continue to lead them into danger in pursuit of vengeance. I'm a horrible and selfish person, I chastise myself. I look to Ayleth, who I'm also leading into danger, and guilt washes over me.

Am I so selfish that I'll risk them all, these people who've come to mean so much, who've put their trust in Jamis and I, and fought without question for what we wanted? I think of Roarke and imagine what it would be like to let my vengeance go, to let him walk

away. Why can't I just let him wear the High Crown without ob-
jection? Would it be terrible to command the troops back to their
origin, take my troops back to Fairlee, collect my husband, and
retreat to Allondale to rebuild the home we have there?

Yes! I can't even force that vision into my head. There's no other
eventuality but for me to confront Roarke. Because if I don't, he
will continue to sweep across the kingdoms, murdering and terror-
izing everyone who opposes him. He won't stop until he's achieved
absolute rule.

We're destined to meet again. Only one of us will walk away,
and though it may not be me, it's better that I will be the one to
suffer at his hand than Jamis. Jamis is safe, recovering in Fairlee.
But if this confrontation brings about my death, Roarke's may still
come—at the hands of my husband.

I sleep intermittently, leaning against the tree. My body has
warmed the ground beneath me, so I dare not move to another
place. The revelry around the campfire continues, Katherine and
Josef sneaking glances my way to ensure I haven't snuck away, but
something in my demeanor keeps even Josef from coming to sit
near me.

The drunkenness has claimed most of the men and Katherine
as well. The deep navy sky turns bright with starlight, and I hear
a murmur of low voices just outside the fading campfire light. I
squint against the darkness, looking for the source.

A horse nickers and steps aside, revealing the shadow of two
sets of boots. I control my breath and strain to hear the words,
though the voices are too low to make out even a single word. A
moment later, Kennard and Weaver step into the light and find a
place to lie down. Though I'd had no doubt the two knew each other previously and had recognized each other, they've gone to great
lengths all day not to be seen together. I wonder what Kennard
and Weaver had to discuss. Why was it so important to wait until
nobody could see or overhear them. And though I'm comfortable
in the knowledge that Kennard is loyal to Jamis, a prickle of distrust once again lodges firmly in my brain again where the guarded
knight is concerned.

What are you hiding, Kennard?

CHAPTER

TWELVE

THE FOLLOWING MORNING HALF OF THE TROOPS LOAD up and head toward Devlishire. We plan to initiate coordinated attacks on Devlishire and Carling, which will prevent either from sending aide to the other. Although our troops are small, numbering just over two hundred men in each group, we'll be catching both kingdoms off guard.

Legion E spies have supplied detailed instructions for the most advantageous places by which we can sneak into Carling, and I've told Weaver all the ways his troops can gain entry into Devlishire, including the crumbled section of wall I used to sneak through to reach the river.

Weaver's men will have to make the ride quickly. I've given them just enough time to make the journey. "We attack at dawn in two days," I reaffirm before they ride away. The remaining troops will spend one day here. Tomorrow night, we'll approach the western edge of castle Carling through the forest. Using the night as our veil, we'll surround the castle and position troops at the hidden entryways to await the sunrise.

The wait is excruciating, each minute longer than the previous. Carolus's troops have no trouble resting as they wait for the fight to come. They aren't as invested in this moment as I am. I spend the day familiarizing myself with the knights from Gaufrid, dividing them into troops, and confirming each troop's entry point.

"I'll enter through the dungeon," Kennard volunteers.

Davion points to my crudely drawn map in the dirt. "Katherine and I can—"

Kennard interrupts him. "Katherine will be with me. It's a dark, long passage. There are too many places for someone to hide. We've fought together the longest, and I'd prefer her at my side."

Katherine offers a nod to Kennard, and her look tells me it was already established that she'd be with Kennard. I wonder when they discussed this and why. But I can't fixate on it. Kennard's rationalization makes sense. Katherine has fought at his side since the Battle of Allondale. He has been her primary instructor in the manner of war, and she's proven an apt pupil. It's only right that he would trust her by his side, though I also imagine he wants her nearby so he can look after her.

Davion is noticeably irritated at having his attempts to align with Katherine thwarted—by Kennard again.

I try to soften the blow and ensure his worth is appreciated. "I was hoping you'd go with me. We'll enter here," I use a long stick to point to the eastern wall. It's the one secret exit closest to the royal suites, thereby making it the most logical exit point for the royal family—and Roarke—when they come under attack. If the Legion E spies' information is correct, it also leads directly to my brother's chamber. "We'll have twenty men with us. We secure the passage and clear the royal suites."

I raise my voice to ensure each knight gathered around hears me. "Your objective is to secure the royal family. You can kill Lester, his queen, Phoebe, and Prince Oliver if you'd like, but Prince Roarke is mine to kill. If he eludes me, you're to do nothing more than hold him for me. Anything more will amount to treason, and you *will* be dealt with immediately."

I look around the troops, meeting the eyes of those closest and scanning the men further back. The rise of their brows and the appreciative glances they cast to each other show they understand my message, the threat of failing me, and that they appreciate my command. My manner in managing my army is everything they've heard, and they're eager to see if my performance with a sword will hold up as well.

More important, though, a hint of fear has crept into their view of me. I'm not just a young girl with a title who has the authority to command them. I'm vengeful and blood-thirsty, they can see that now, and if the rumors of me are even slightly true, I am someone to fear. "One last thing, there's a baby. I want him. Whoever brings me the child alive can rule Devlishire in my name."

They look at each other as though they've heard wrong. "That baby was born to Melaine Alphonse, daughter of the Earl of Cavesdale. Once Roarke is dead, the child will be my ward." I have no qualms about giving Devlishire away. It holds nothing for me any longer. Perhaps, when Henry is older, he'll want to return there, though once he knows how the entire kingdom betrayed his mother, he may want nothing to do with it either.

With our tactics planned and the sun descending again, the men prepare their gear. Blades are sharpened, gear packed, and bellies filled.

"Which troop will I be with?" Ayleth plops beside me as I tighten my boots.

"You'll wait in the woods where it's safe."

"But I want to fight. You wouldn't know it by sight alone, but I'm quite good. I've killed before you know."

I sit up, cock my head to the side, and offer my most disbelieving expression. "When was that?"

Her blue eyes are wide and emphatic. "Well, it's been a long time, and I'm sworn to secrecy about the circumstances."

I laugh at her bravado. "I'm sure, young one. I'll tell you what, you'll take up a position just beyond the east passage. If my brother slips past me and gets from that door, you alone have my permission to kill him."

"I'll do it, and you'll owe me your gratitude forever." She slides a narrow blade into the leather rope that's tied around her brightly decorated tunic.

I smile as she saunters away then I look over my troops. Days ago, I'd never have imagined I'd be standing here preparing to raid Carling so soon. Certainty floods me, and I know this is the right decision.

While my father betrayed me, he also prepared me for this very moment. I wish he were alive if for no other reason than to see every belief he sowed in me about being a strong ruler and calculating warrior come back to topple what remains of his empire. Because even though I was cast from Devlishire, cast from the den of wolves who raised me, I haven't forgotten what it means to be one.

The words of our family motto dance on my lips. I whisper them into the dusk, letting the frigid breeze carry them throughout the lands. "Should he breach my walls and threaten those who stand alongside me, he will find me at the head of my own pack."

I nod as I scan my army, my pack, assembled to rise against those who dared to breach my walls and harm those who stood with me. "And I shall devour him whole and turn then on those who stand beside him."

"It sounds terrifyin'." Josef's soft voice startles me. "I din't mean ta scare ye. I just wanted ta offer ye this." He holds out a bowl, meat and root vegetable steaming in what appears to be a water broth. It looks inedible.

I cringe and lean away.

"Ye 'ave ta eat, Mal. You'll be needin' strength."

He's right, though I won't admit it out loud. I throw him a sneer, grab the bowl, and sit on a stump.

"I was hopin' we could talk a minute." His eyes are sincere and his voice soft, not urgent, but bordering on pleading.

I use the spoon to indicate the knights around us. "I'm busy preparing for a battle. Can we discuss it here, or can it wait?"

He takes in the close quarters, the men sleeping at our feet and talking in groups. He nods. "It'll wait."

"And whoever said you could address me so informally? I am a queen."

He smiles. "Aye, but yer not my queen."

I glare up at him as I take a spoonful of the soup. It's horrible. Just before I can complain about it, Josef leans in my direction, mischief sparkling in his dark eyes, and whispers one last retort. "And I'm never formal with girls I've seen almost naked."

I nearly choke on the food. When in all hells would he have seen me nearly naked? But after months on the run, living in caves, bathing in streams, and tending to each other's superficial wounds, we'd all seen each other nearly naked numerous times. At least he didn't say he'd seen me truly naked because that would mean—no, that's too creepy to imagine. And though Josef pays me attention, he doesn't seem the type to creep about and spy on a girl and her husband's private moments.

I force the remainder of the soup into my body, then move to sit against a tree as the stars twinkle in the night. I gaze up at the brilliant cover of lights placed in the heavens by Omnilus—the great creator.

Carolus's question comes to mind, about the God of the Heavens and the God of the Earth. I never questioned the origin of the gods when I was young—nor do I recall anyone else having done so. The gods were accepted as fact, though I admit their stories don't seem as richly developed as the origins of the Elyphesian gods. Why did the great kings of the past, who were so prescient in establishing a unification between the seven kingdoms to bring about a centuries-long peace, be so lacking in the details of the religion they practiced?

Once again, I'm confident in my own decision to pray to the Elyphesian gods. Their stories are far richer and more relatable than the lessons preached about the others. And I've felt the presence of the Elyphesians more than I've ever felt the spirit of another deity.

Ayleth brings me a blanket, then curls beside me. She falls quickly into a slumber I hope is filled with brilliant fanciful things, things that are proper for a child her age, and that they are not filled with war.

The crinkling of dry leaves underfoot and the snapping of the campfire bring my attention back just as Josef eases into place beside me, leaning against my tree. "I feel as though ye'r avoidin' me."

"We talked earlier. You brought me soup. It was awful."

"Right. But we din't really *talk*."

My focus has to remain on this war, on conquering everyone who opposes me and avenging those who perished for standing with me. At my core, I've finally rediscovered the Malory who opposed her father, who helped prepare Allondale for an attack. She's strong and not prone to capricious emotion. "I'm not avoiding you. I'm thinking about what lies ahead. Imagining the look on my brother's face when I finally drive my blade into him."

"Ye've waited a long time fer this. Ye've earned this moment, the chance to settle up with yer brother. I'll do all I can ta make sure ye find him and 'ave yer vengeance."

Emotion threatens to overtake me. I've existed on a precipice for so long, waiting for the right time to jump or for someone to pull me back from the edge and tell me that it's over, that I lost my chance. But it's finally time to jump, and I can't wait to finally launch into the depths of a hell where I spill my own blood, my mother's blood, onto enemy soil. "What if I can't do it? What if I finally have the chance, and I'm too afraid to kill him?"

He leans into me, bumping his shoulder into mine. He turns his earnest eyes to mine; his voice is soft, confident. "Ye'r no' one ta be afraid, Mal. Yer heart's forgotten what it is to fear."

I look ahead, at the dark sky, the people who trust my orders, the little girl asleep at my feet, and all the possible ways this plan could end. "That's not true. I'm afraid of two things."

"And wha' are those two things?"

My voice falters and threatens to not carry the words beyond my lips. "That Jamis will die…and that Roarke will live."

He leans closer, his shoulder pressed against mine as his eyes take in the scene in front of us—and perhaps the one I imagine. "All ye can do is pray ta yer gods and hope yer in their favor."

I whisper yet another fear. "And what if I'm not?"

"I 'ave no doubt the gods favor ye. Ye're brave, and ye're fierce in a way the gods admire. But ye can't demand an outcome. The gods decided long ago how the world would evolve. They foretold who would be born, who would live, and who dies. The stories 'ave been written—we just 'ave to wait ta see how they end. The gods rarely change their minds."

A huff of air escapes my chest. *Who is Josef to tell me about the gods?* While I spent my days hunched over dusty books reading everything ever written about the Elyphesians, Josef ran about the forest learning to hunt and fish. Sure, the Fairleans told tales of the same gods, but from memory. "You're warning me as though you've spoken to them, and they already told you how this is going to end."

He smiles and pulls his feet under him as he prepares to stand. "I just don't want ye thinkin' all yer prayers are ta be answered just because ye offered them." He lifts Ayleth and carries her closer to the fire, laying her beside Isobel before he walks further into the shadows.

I fume as I watch his retreating figure. How dare he think me so simple that I believe the gods will answer all my prayers? *But I do think that, don't I?* How long have I convinced myself Nithenia will grant me favors simply because I'm the only person in the Unified Kingdoms to pray to her anymore? Does she owe me for my faith? *No.* And what if I'm not the only person who prays to the long-forgotten gods? Is there someone out there who prayers more fervently than I? Someone who opposes me?

Are you even praying to the proper god? The one who has the most to offer? Jumping as the whispers fill my head, I scamper to my feet, scanning the periphery of the clearing, though I know the voice came from somewhere else. I clench the leather-wrapped grip of my sword, prepared to draw and strike. My voice is a fierce whisper cutting through the darkness. "Who are you?"

I'm waiting for you, mortal. Kill your brother. I will ensure your success. And then you will come to me, for I have everything you want, and you possess all I need. We are destined.

My heart thunders, fear coursing through my veins, burning its way through my body. More whispers invade my ears, conflicting tones that fill my every thought. There are so many. This must certainly be what madness is like.

My heart quickens. Just as I feel I'm stepping off the ledge into a panic, a firm voice calls above the others, *Shut us out. Now!* I close my mind, slamming an imaginary door that leads into my consciousness. The voices end, and only the hoot of an owl overhead and the crackling of the fire sounds in the darkness.

I lean against a tree, willing my heart to slow and my mind to clear. *Who was that?* I have no doubt it was a god, but which? And what do I have to offer?

My legs are shaky as I make my way to the fire. I lower myself next to Katherine. Her brows pull taut, and she reaches for my hand as I ease onto the ground. "What's the matter?"

"Nothing, I had a fright, but I'm fine." I offer her a sincere smile and squeeze her hand. "Probably just tired." I lean against her shoulder, my eyes searching the darkness, but Josef doesn't return.

Exhaustion finally triumphs over my determination to stay awake, and I lay back in the dirt and pull my cloak around me as I embrace sleep.

CHAPTER
THIRTEEN

WE SNEAK DEEPER INTO THE THICK OF THE forest hours before the sun hints at its presence below the horizon. The sky is slate freckled with brightly colored stars, but the forest floor is dark, readily concealing our presence and our progress as we sneak into thick tangles of ivy and danailor rods that have invaded the pristine forest.

Josef and Kennard flank me, Isobel and Katherine behind us. Ayleth moves with those at the rear and is under strict orders to remain at the back. Our trek is slow and cautious. I won't risk being detected. I've waited far too long to see this plan come to fruition. Each of my steps is soft and accompanied by the anticipatory thudding of my heart, which I'm certain is echoing through the night. A mist hovers at the base of the trees. Somewhere in the distance, an owl has taken notice of us and is commenting on our progress. Is anyone else paying him any mind?

"This is far enough," Kennard orders the troops. "We'll wait here until dawn." He distributes half the remaining soldiers into groups of twenty to cover the five hidden doorways to the tunnels leading under Carling. They'll gain entry just before dawn and be waiting for anyone who tries to flee the castle through them.

When we invade, the front gates of Carling will eventually be flung open. Either by the armies of Carling attempting to flee or by our troops who've made their way through. Either way, the enemy will be met by our remaining forces, who are following the stream to assume their positions under the bridges leading into Carling.

Davion and I, along with our twenty men and Ayleth, pick our

113

way through the darkened forest to the easternmost entry. At the passageway, we find only a wooden door, warped and misshapen from years without use. Using our fingers, we dig away the accumulation of rotting leaves and damp soil that prevents the door from opening freely. My nails dig into hardened dirt beneath the surface. I nearly whimper as three of my nails break away from the quick. Sharp pains shiver up my arms and deep into my shoulders as I bite against my natural impulse to cry out.

Davion kneels beside me and pulls a short, thick dagger from his belt. "Let me," he says.

I sit back, clenching my throbbing fingers to my chest. "Thank you."

It's only moments before Davion has cleared the debris, driven his knife into the space between the door and the frame, and pried an opening large enough for him to grip the ancient door. The hinges screech through the darkness as he pulls it away from the frame.

We stop, each acutely attuned to the dark, listening for the sound of anyone coming to investigate the origins of such a hideous sound. For nearly twenty minutes, we sit still, but nobody comes.

"Slowly," I whisper as Davion returns to pulling the door far enough to allow us entry. As the sky lightens, I notice a recessed ledge in the wall above us, a bird's nest intended for a guard to sit and monitor for trespassers. Judging by the overgrowth of vines, it's been long forgotten, as has this passageway. "Ayleth," I call for the girl, then point to the ledge. Before I say another word, she's scampering up the wall and onto the ledge, disappearing behind the stone façade. "Stay there and keep a look out," I order, hoping that an official duty will appeal to her sense of purpose and keep her safe.

With the door wide open, Davion and I peer into the dusty corridor. It's dark and obviously hasn't been used in years. The sky has lightened enough that I can see spiders scampering across a vast network of webs and vines that cling to the gray stone walls. A shudder runs its course along my spine, but it won't be the first time I've been surrounded by creeping crawling things while lying in wait for our enemies. The only difference is that this time I'll be walking through them instead of lying still as they crawl over me. *This is better*, I try to convince myself. My brain can't convince my heart, though. It thunders at the promise of what lies ahead: the spiders as well as my brother.

I pull a small blade from the leather strap that hangs across my chest. With my fingertips still throbbing, I use the blade to carve the symbol of Nithenia into the dirt. Davion is accustomed to this habit of mine and ignores me as he scans the trees for threats. The other knights look from the symbol to one another and shrug, nobody willing to ask the question until I hear Ayleth's whisper.

"What is it?" She climbs from her hiding spot and stands beside me, staring at the symbol.

"What are you doing down here?"

"What's that?" She whispers, ignoring my question as she drops to her knees, tracing the engraved lines with her finger.

"It's a symbol for my patron goddess."

"You have a patron goddess?"

I almost shoo her away without an answer. *Isn't it presumptuous of me to assume that just because I prefer Nithenia, she has some affinity for me as well?*

"I do. She's called Nithenia. She's the goddess of bravery and victory. My sister and I made the symbol."

Ayleth stands and looks at the symbol from a different angle, walking around it as she considers it. Then she looks up. "I like it." Without another word, she scampers back up the wall to her hiding place.

What a strange child.

The sky turns from gray to lavender. A peach glow begins to reach above the trees, taunting me with the promise of what's to come once the glow turns golden: the culmination of a year's worth of betrayal and vengeance.

My heart thunders, and my fingertips tingle. I wriggle them to keep them agile in the cold morning. Each of my breaths explodes in a white puff in front of me. I force my mind to still. I have to put fear and my past behind me. Though it's all driven me here—to this very moment—I can't allow thoughts to cloud my mind and distract me from what's happening around me. I need a calm mind to be in tune with everything.

I avoid looking in the others' eyes. I can't let their fear or emotion affect me. I focus on the still respite I've created in my mind and breath deep, willing my heart to calm as well. It's time for war; emotion has no place.

A golden glow creeps above the sky overhead. It is time. I look to Davion, and he nods. We file into the dark hall, sweeping blindly as we go to knock away the webs, but our efforts are in vain as the cobwebs are too thick. They dance around, tickling our necks and brushing along our faces as we walk.

The darkness in the tunnel deepens, light from the day far behind us and growing dimmer with each step. My boot catches, and I nearly tumble. Davion grasps my thick cloak and pulls me upright until I can steady myself on both feet. "Careful," he warns as though I don't already know that I hadn't been.

Though the dark has fully enveloped us, we can sense each other's movements, and we continue along, deeper into the cavern.

Davion stops suddenly, and I crash into him. *Oomph.*

"Stairs." His voice is low.

His shadowed figure moves with great caution as the rest of us follow his dark ascent. Boots are shuffling through the dark. There's no railing, and my mind returns to the narrow steps leading up the wall of Gaufrid. It's almost better to have no idea what lies below—or how far.

After several minutes, a glow appears before us—a thin band of light peeking from under a door.

"Shh," I command as we approach. I put my ear to the door and listen to the familiar sounds of daily life in a castle. Shutters are being thrown open to welcome the sun, dishes clatter as they are carried past on trays, and small groups of people deep in conversation as they pass. And then a loud crash erupts—and a scream. The time has come.

I stand back as Davion kicks open the door. Light floods the hidden corridor, stinging at my eyes. I squint as I move swiftly into a hallway of Castle Carling, blade drawn and ready to fight. Maids scream and hurry from the hall, and knights pour into the area in response.

I haven't time to count them, and it would do no good. Another follows each.

We draw our swords. I plant my feet in a ready stance, letting them come approach. Davion angles off at my right, and others take a rear defensive as our troops move from the passage and further down the hall. The clatter of steel meeting steel and the animalistic growls of men at war echo from somewhere deeper in the castle.

The knights advancing on us seem stunned to realize Carling has been invaded. They catch sight of me, then throw a look between themselves. They know who I am. Fear flickers in their eyes, but they are trained to carry on. They swing at us, Davion and I stand side by side, meeting their blows. We are easily outnumbered three to one, but we've faced worse odds. I focus only on my fight, trusting my troops to do the same.

I return one strike immediately with three others. My opponent is stunned, but he manages to block each of my strikes. His last one is powerful enough to throw my sword back against the stone wall. The reverberation jolts my body, and I nearly lose my grip. I recover and drop my sword at an angle, aiming for the skin between his armor and helmet.

The knight turns a shoulder. My blade slides along the metal armor, the scraping sound of metal accompanied by a spark. He quickly raises his arm, swinging it back and over my blade, trapping it against his torso. He moves with a jerk, using his weight to drive me into the wall. All the air is driven from me, and my lungs struggle to draw life back into my body. He moves as though he'll shake me from the blade, but this isn't the first time a man has tried to overpower me. What he doesn't know is that I meet strength with determination, and only one of those factors is subject to exhaustion.

He angles off and jerks again to pull me from my weapon, but my hand is trapped under his arm, pressed around the grip of my sword. I'm unable to release even if I wanted to.

He slams me against the stone wall again, then a second time. He finally lifts his arm and moves to grab me around the head, releasing my hand. But his arm snakes around me and he pivots, throwing a hip into me, which pulls me from my feet. I'm flung over his hip, airborne for only a second before being slammed onto the cobbled floor.

Bursts of yellow light erupt in my eyes, and the stones in the floor press into my joints. Heat flushes through my body in response to the injuries.

He raises his foot to stomp on me, but I roll aside at the last possible moment. I scramble across the floor, but he grips the back of my cloak and lifts me to my feet in one swift motion.

My fingers fumble for the belt at my chest, tips slipping from the ivory handle of the dagger before I can pull it out. He slaps my fingers away from the blades, bending my left arm behind me, trapping it as he leans against me with my face pressed to the wall.

His weight holds me firmly in place. He's panting into my ear, trying to catch his breath as he speaks. "I heard you were a feisty little bitch. You aren't getting a blade in me, though. No little girl's going to best Ridgely Runwick."

"Oh, I didn't know I was fighting Ridgely Runwick," I fill my voice with as much false awe as I can muster. I tug at the belt purse with my right hand, freeing it from under my weight, digging my first finger in and pulling the hidden item out. I relax my body. "Fine, I give up. Take me to King Roarke."

The knight bursts into laughter as he eases up on me, though his hand remains under my arm, trapping it with the pressure of his hand to my back. "I'm not stupid enough to bring you to the king."

He steps back, pulling my left arm. I resist, so he pulls harder to get control of me. As he does, I use the momentum to spin myself around, burying the long, narrow blade in my right hand deep into his neck. The crimson substance of his life pulses out over my hand twice before I withdraw it, letting the flow pour out unencumbered.

His eyes are wide, fear replacing his bravado of moments ago. When he sinks to his knees, I stand in front of him, looking him in the eyes with contempt. "You were only right about one thing, Ridgely. I am a feisty little bitch."

I turn away and grab my sword, leaving the knight to bleed out on the stone floor as I join my band.

We move through the hall, throwing open doors as we clear the castle and search for our troops. Rooms that hold women and servants are cleared, their occupants sent into the main hall between suites. Katherine is there with ten men and has assumed charge, forcing our captives to sit in a close group as we move through the rooms.

As each of the royal suites turns up empty, my fury grows. "Where are they?" I demand of a group of maids. They cry and cling to each other. "Get her," I demand of Davion, pointing to the girl who appears the most terrified.

"Malory," Katherine's voice is a low but firm reminder that they are not my enemy. That I've made every effort to avoid hurting innocents, and, if I fail to uphold that decision, it'll be an additional weight on my soul. One I may never be able to shed. But maybe I have more of my father and brother in me than I ever imagined and will be able to sleep fine when this is all over. I focus on the maid—on my goal.

Davion pulls her up by the wrist. I grab her from him, holding my sword to the back of her neck as I push her toward one of the chambers. A tray sits at an angle on the bed, and I push her toward it. A quick touch against the warm plate confirms my suspicions. "Where are they?" I growl. "They were here. Which way did they escape?"

"I can't, miss. I'll be killed."

With each moment, I feel Roarke slipping from my grip. I can't give him time to escape.

Tremors roil through the girl's body as I force her into the hall and into the passage I entered through moments ago.

Ridgely Runwick lies still on the floor. The stream of blood has crept away from his body and is pooling in the crevices between the floor's stones. "I did this," I hiss. "And now *you* are at the tip of my blade."

"No, miss, please," she cries.

I pull her to me, my blade pressing now along the front of her neck, against the bob in her throat as she swallows her fear. I whisper over her shoulder. "I am no miss. I am Malory of Allondale, and everything you've heard about me is true. Now, where did they go?" Her shoulders crumple under further sobs as she leads me into the chambers and points at a panel. "Through there."

Davion pulls the thin cover aside. We scramble into the passage, followed by several of our troops. The corridor is empty, and we rush, slowing only at each intersecting hall.

"Mal!" My name echoes through the hall. Josef has found the passageway as well though he's far behind us.

Davion and I reach a series of doors just as one swings open and knights from Carling flood in. We draw and engage without hesitation, meeting each blow and delivering our own. Davion spins, his lightweight sword in one hand and a dagger in the other. Carling's formally trained knights have no experience fighting in this manner, and they fall quickly to him.

I dispatch two knights quickly and step over their bodies into the adjoining room.

The throne room is plush, plum-colored velvet with crisp

white details hangs from the walls and the windows. The colors of Carling have been draped over every possible surface. Even the floor is stained plum except for the large black raven painted on the floor. The bird is in the center of the room, its head just below the steps leading to the throne of Carling.

A sound to my left draws my attention, and I catch sight of someone ducking through a door. I follow without delay, sword at the ready.

The door leads into an alleyway outside the palace, and I know the man running away from me. "Roarke!"

He stops and turns, a sardonic grin crossing his features. "You *are* alive. I'd hoped the stories of your continued existence were nothing more than lore."

"You knew I'd come looking for you, whether in life or death, I was always coming."

He steps backward to maintain his lead as I take three steps toward him. Roarke is fast; he always has been. Even as a child, he was swift as a doe. If he runs, there's no way I can catch him.

I take two more steps, adopting a subtle limp. Not too great, Roarke is no fool—or perhaps he is a fool, but one with a strong survival instinct. I let my ankle wobble as I stop. He takes two additional steps back, but he's watching me closely, noting every weakness.

"Your knights are well-trained—or are they Lester's?" I lower my sword so the tip of the blade rests on the ground, my right hand—still covered in Ridgely Runwick's blood—balanced on the pommel. "But they were never going to stop me. You know that."

Roarke's eyes are on my hand. I can see him processing, wondering just how injured I am. But I can't act as though I'm giving up—he'd never believe that. The only way to draw him in is to be myself, to be unrelenting. I take another step toward him, letting my torso waver slightly as I lift my sword, the blade barely higher than my knees.

A priggish grin curls one side of Roarke's mouth, and he lifts his blade in my direction. "You are stupid, Malory. What makes you think you can walk into Carling and ever walk out again?"

I fix a maniacal grin on my face and stagger once more toward him, though he remains too far away for me ever to catch him if he runs. "I will gladly die in Carling if I do so with your blood on my blade."

He rolls his eyes and smirks as he angles toward a barred egress in the narrow alley. He's assessing me, checking for my weakest side, wondering if he stands a chance—he could still bolt through the passages between the castle and the buildings lining the inner ward.

"That's just like you to think yourself so much greater than everyone else. How foolish you are to believe still everything Father said about you being a great warrior. You're just a vessel for the heirs of true kings. A sharp toy and an overly confident manner don't make you a warrior."

I lift the sword briefly, pointing the tip in his direction before I set it heavily back to the stone. "I'm going to get your son. After I kill you, I'm taking him and raising him the way Melaine would want."

His face pinches in fury. "You'll never have my son."'

I laugh confidently. "I'll get him. And when he's old enough, I'm going to tell him how you slit his mother's throat as she professed her love for you."

"You bitch," he growls and runs for me, lifting his sword as he does so.

"Mal!" Josef and his troop exit into the alley behind me. "Leave her!" he yells, and the footsteps stop as Roarke reaches me.

Roarke proves within moments that he's gotten no smarter about war or strategy. He attacks me full-on, obviously believing my ruse of being in a weakened state.

I step aside, evading his blade, and his momentum carries him into Josef, who throws him off and back in my direction.

Roarke lifts his sword in Josef's direction. "Don't touch me, forest rat!"

Josef raises his brow at the insult. "Ye'd better hope she kills ye fast, or I'll rip yer tongue out and feed it ta the dog's."

Roarke turns back in my direction to find me at a full ready stance. The corners of his mouth pull up in self-satisfaction. He whips his sword about in his right hand, cutting through the air. He's trying to cause me to doubt my skill. "I've trained since we last met, sister."

I hold his gaze, not letting emotion invade me. I have to be practical even with Roarke. "Your left arm hasn't recovered, though."

Anger flashes across his face at the memory of the injury I left him with the last time we clashed. During the Battle of Allondale, I drew a blade into the muscle on his torso beneath his left arm. Judging by the way he's underused it so far, the muscle hasn't recovered. His arm moves, but it lacks the strength and control of his right.

Roarke roars and lunges. He clutches his sword in both hands, driving it overhand toward my shoulder. When I deflect and spin away, he blocks my counterstrike and comes back.

The clatter of our swords striking each other echoes through the abandoned alleyway. My body screams in protest, each of my joints that were slammed into the walls and floor of the hall threaten to give out under the added exertion I'm demanding. With each blow, the weight of my sword grows heavier.

More soldiers run from the castle into the narrow corridor—Carling's troops. They barely pause long enough to recognize that neither of the fighters is their sovereign before running the other direction.

"You bitch. Whore. Bastard!" Roarke curses with each blow, and I feel myself weaken further.

Do I have the drive to see this to the end? I call on the fury and emotion I need to weather the fight against my brother. Flashes of Melaine and Esmond fill my mind, as well as Jamis. Each person who has suffered because of Roarke's greed and evil deeds floods through my mind, and I embrace my fury.

An audience of knights stand about in the alley, watching the heirs of Devlishire yell and trade blows, the clatter of our blades echoing along the long stone corridors. Davion and Josef hold them with drawn swords, though they are all too entranced with the battle playing out to interfere.

I lift my blade, and the fury I've carried since Roarke first betrayed me escapes from me on a primal yell. I swing away, Roarke reacts wildly and instinctively to block each blow. But I focus most of my force on his left, and he weakens quickly. His arms are shaking, and fear fills his eyes as he realizes I am gaining the advantage. I swing high and then low, then high again. Just as Roarke settles into the rhythm, I drop and roll, swiping behind his knees and drawing my blade across both.

Roarke drops to his knees with a scream. Blood soaks his pretty silk breeches where my weapon bit into his flesh.

He looks wildly to the gathering crowd of knights, though my troops continue to hold his off with their blades—though nobody seems to be trying too urgently to save him. "Help me!" he demands, and they only cast their glances at the ground, ashamed to realize they are incapable or unwilling to risk themselves for him.

Roarke collapses onto his hands, his palms pressed against the stones as he tries to maintain some semblance of pride, but he quickly gives up, rolling onto his side.

He glares at the knights watching dumbly as his sister bests him. His face rages red, spittle flying from his mouth as he screams at them. "I am the High King. Defend me!"

I smirk as my troops lift their weapons, daring the royal knights to do so. As a group, they take one step back, not willing to engage in a battle that's so nearly over.

"You will defend your leader!" His words may reach their ears, but not their hearts.

I circle him. "Perhaps they have no leader. Perhaps they have only a petty tyrant with stolen a crown on his head."

I place the finely-honed edge against his throat, and he glares. "I have a secret, brother. There are no heirs to Devlishire. Grayson was the last."

His brows draw together, scowling. He is defiant even when faced with death.

"I'm not the only bastard in our family." I lean forward, my blade sliding easily into the hollow of his throat and watch as the life evaporates from his terrified eyes, and his blood washes against my boots.

A knight with the red tunic of Devlishire approaches slowly, palms up to indicate that he poses no threat. He kneels at my brother's feet and places his sword at his heels. I kick it away. "He doesn't deserve a warrior's death," I say through clenched teeth.

My brother was no warrior. He betrayed his family, his kingdom and the unification that bound seven kingdoms together. He planned for my death, and it was because of his actions that Esmond was killed. He murdered King Eamon, our father, and Melaine—all in his quest for the High Crown—something that was never intended to be his.

The man holds his hands up and backs away, then turns to run down the alley.

"Malory?" Josef is beside me. He turns toward me, placing a hand on the low of my back as he tries to get my attention. I set my jaw and cast him a side look before returning my attention to my brother. Josef nods once and retreats to wait with the rest of the men.

I stand over Roarke and watch as the flow of blood slows then ceases. The crimson fluid spreads, finding its way into the crevices between the stones lining the small path and seeping into the soil beneath. His glassy gaze is fixed on the sky overhead as the sun hovers behind hazy clouds that threaten to rain showers to wash his blood from the lands of his ally—his queen.

One more devil dispatched. The thought is immediate and overwhelming. I shove it from my mind. This has nothing to do with Nemii or his devils. It is simply my brother and the realization of my vengeance.

But where is my relief? My sense of completion? Each time I'd imagined the moment I would kill my brother, there was a sense of finality, a reprieve from the oppressive weight of vengeance. But I feel no relief, and nothing feels complete.

Because he wasn't alone in his actions, I reason. Just as it wasn't only my father who betrayed me. Lester and Phoebe are guilty—as well as King Brahm. My retribution is only partially complete. A twinge of sadness sparks in my chest as I look upon my brother's lifeless body. I've taken my mother's son and my nephew's father.

I remember Roarke as a child. Giggling as we'd run about the castle playing hide and seek, and I'd leap from my hiding spots and chase him back in the direction from which he'd come. Emotion stings behind my eyes, but I know that boy with whom I laughed and played died long ago. I swallow it away and tuck my deceitful memories—and my sadness for my young brother—into the empty chamber that used to house my zest for life.

I pull the cloak of vengeance across my heart again and turn to my troops. Drawing my blood slickened blade through a fold in the corner of my cloak, I wipe it clean before sliding it into my belt. "Find Phoebe—and the baby."

CHAPTER
FOURTEEN

JOSEF CATCHES UP AS I ENTER THE HALLWAY leading to the throne room. "I should stay with ye. The castle 'asn't been cleared yet. We don' even know where—"

I spin on him. "Find my nephew. That's all I need from you right now, Josef."

He's still standing, his mouth open to argue, when I storm into the darkened hall. Davion scrambles alongside me, casting a sidelong glance but reluctant to say anything.

Katherine is with her troops in the throne room. Maids and house boys are all sitting in tight groups, some still crying. "There were too many. We had to move them in here while we keep searching."

I nod as my eyes travel over the servants. "What about Lester and his family?"

"Isobel's troop intercepted Queen Filomena as she was escaping over the south bridge. Three men are holding her in her chambers, and two are positioned outside each of the doors from the queen's suite."

"And where is Isobel?"

Katherine shrugs. "Gone to help elsewhere, I imagine." It isn't uncommon for Isobel to assign someone else guard duties. She prefers to be busy and engaged, sitting watch over a queen would quickly drive her mad.

"And Kennard?"

"Don't know. We were supposed to be together, but he's looking for something. He came through a while ago. Asked one of the pages about the dungeons. Perhaps he's gone there."

I pull the sapphire encrusted dagger Jamis gave me from the belt across my chest and continue to make my way through Castle Carling.

Bodies litter the cold stone hallways, men bearing the insignia and color of their kingdoms while bleeding the color of the one that brought about their deaths: the scarlet color of Devlishire.

Crystal shards of broken glassware crunch under our feet as we walk through the halls meant to show the wealth and power of Carling. Tapestries bear slash and splatter patterns of our invasion and the fight that was waged against it. One tapestry catches my eye as I pass. On it, three kings stand over the body of another who lies bleeding on the ground, a blade protruding from his chest. In the clouds overhead, the gods are peering over as they move pieces on a chess board. The image is troubling, but I have no time to linger.

Davion and I descend the stairs making our way ever lower. The troops who accompanied us have slowly peeled away to cover other passages and have yet to return. We are alone as we reach the lowest level of Castle Carling—the dungeon. It's cool and damp as expected. The heavy stench of mildew and urine permeates the air. Distant plinks of water echo from the stone walls. My eyes strain against the dark for several minutes before finally adjusting.

In the middle of the dungeon is a large alcove with three corridors leading further into Carling's depths. A thick door beside the stairway stands locked. Iron bands around the door would prevent it from being breached with any ease. Whatever is locked behind that door is secure—for now.

Narrow slits are cut deep in the stone at the edges of the room, allowing a faint stream of sunlight to taunt the darkness with its presence, but not enough to flood the rooms with a functional amount of light. The fire has long burned out, indicating that no prisoners are currently housed here. Any prisoners who were here were likely offered release in exchange for fighting for King Lester.

At the center of the main area looms a rack and an iron chair with sharpened spikes and leather straps. Along the walls, various implements of torture hang from over-sized hooks.

The subtle scuff of a shoe against stone comes from one of the corridors. My skin prickles in anticipation as I make my way past the rack. I turn to Davion and hold a finger to my lips, indicating for him to be silent—though months of sneaking about the Ar-gralands has caused silence to be our natural impulse.

As I approach the center hall, I can see that four cells line each side of the corridor, each separated by a wide stone wall and guarded with the iron bars thick and rusted with age. With soft steps, I creep closer to where the noise came from. The unmistak-able sound of breathing draws me closer. I press my back against a wall and steal a glance down the hall. The cell directly across from my position is empty, and another stolen look confirms that the one behind me is as well. Without thought, I quickly roll from the wall, and with three swift, silent steps, I'm in the first cell, Davion immediately at my side.

I peek around the corner of my new position and notice a flick-ering glow coming from the opposite side's furthest cell. Whoever is in there is carrying a torch.

What are they doing?

The cell is open, there's no reason for anyone to be there, and yet they've been there several minutes already. As I prepare to move again, a clatter erupts in the direction of the entry.

Davion and I rush back to the main room as the iron-banded door swings open, and knights of Carling enter torches held high, flooding the room with an orange glow that assaults my eyes. I squint and turn my head as my hand reaches for my sword. Beside me, I hear Davion unsheathe his weapon, and then there's a body moving from behind me into place at my left with a sword directed at the knights. *Kennard!*

We are too late, though; the knights have filled the room. Be-fore I can pull my sword free, my arms are restrained, and I'm being jostled about then driven to my knees. I thrash against the arms securing me, kicking wildly in the hopes of contacting anyone and any part. All I need is an opportunity.

The dull thud of blows being rained on Davion and Kennard echo in my ears. They grunt and curse, fighting their way against this sudden onslaught. But soon, their sounds subside, replaced with the labored gurgling that accompanies the fight for breath against gathering blood—a sound I've become far too familiar with.

"Lock them up," a harsh female voice commands. Through my racing thoughts as my mind tries to process what's just happened, I know I've heard the voice before.

I struggle again, trying to stand and launch myself from the grip of these knights of Carling. A blow to my temple drives me back to my knees as ringing explodes in my ears.

"Touch me again, and you'll draw back a stump," I snarl at the man beside me.

He holds a dagger up, ensuring I can see it before he flips it and drives the hilt into my temple.

Nausea swells in me, and my stomach joins my body's revolt. Acid and winter berries force their way out of my body and onto the floor. I continue to wretch until my stomach is empty, and then again, until I worry I'll expel my innards.

Nausea subsides, and the hem of a silken gown stops just in front of me, just beyond the reach of my sickness. The gown is light gray and trimmed with dark fur. "If it isn't my sister-in-law. Come to pay your respects?"

I spit thick, acidic saliva directly in front of the skirt and struggle to my feet. Phoebe's dark eyes and pinched face seem more severe since I last saw her. Her hair is pulled tight, a pearl tiara in place though slightly askew—her narrow head as unable to bear the crown's weight as she is ill-suited of bearing her title. Fine gowns and jewels can't turn her from the silly, mousy girl she's always been into a queen.

I pull myself up tall, fighting against the pain and exhaustion to meet her like a queen. My back screams in protest, and my head swirls against the change in position. A trickle flows from over my eye, and I wipe at it, my dirt-covered hands coming away with fresh blood, in addition to that which has dried in the crevices of my fingernails. "That would require me to have some respect to spare."

She offers a demure smile as though unaffected by my lack of respect—or even manners. "Your brother will be so pleased to find that you're alive. We've heard differing accounts."

"Roarke's dead." I smile, leaving no doubt as to how that came to be.

Her smile falters for only a second before she recovers her composure. "Well, then all things move forward. Put her in a cell."

Two knights grab my arms, and I shrug them off. "Don't you even care? Your husband's dead. You're no longer a queen."

She smirks and walks closer, confident now that her knights have regained control of me. "Oh, but I am. I'm Queen Regent of Devlishire and Queen of Carling."

"Queen of Carling? Your father—"

She *tsks* and gives a shake of her head. "An unfortunate fall from his horse, I'm afraid." She holds my look, and I understand the undercurrent. Her father fell just as my own, and Jamis's before, took ill—all to advance someone else's aspiration. She can have Carling, but she'll lay no claim to any other lands in the Unified Kingdoms if I can prevent it. Devlishire technically belongs to no one but my mother now.

I grin at Phoebe. "You're not Queen Regent. You're the widow of a bastard. A false king who sat on a throne of lies. But I'm willing to overlook it all. I'll let Henry serve as heir to Devlishire—I'll find him a suitable custodian to raise and educate him so that he can one day rule Devlishire as it should be ruled. And I'll leave you to rule Carling as you wish."

"You'll *allow* that will you?" She guffaws and then leans toward me, her face pinched and upper lip pulled back to reveal misshapen teeth. "I will kill you if you ever threaten to take my son again. I should have you strung on the rack simply for making the threat."

She pulls away, and I laugh at her misplaced show of force. "He isn't your son. He was born of Roarke and Melaine."

A succession of three slaps strikes across my cheek, causing me to waver in surprise. No doubt shocked by this demonstration of fury between two female monarchs, the knights release my arms and step away.

I catch my balance and lift my eyes to meet Phoebe's. Where there should be pain, I feel only satisfaction spreading its warm path across my cheek, throbbing deep into the bone. The satisfaction she is making this move to clash with me, that I might finally have a chance to exact some vengeance on Melaine's behalf.

I smile as I stand, my tongue lingering against my upper lip, tasting the copper tinge of the blood that's gathered along my newly split flesh. I'm determined to cause Phoebe pain, and while I could quite easily mete out physical punishment, I prefer a more direct route. "You're the reason Melaine is dead. You made him choose between the crown and love for Melaine and his child."

Phoebe's eyes widen in rage as she points a finger in my direction, stabbing it into the air as she yells. Her pale skin flushes with fury as an unfortunately pronounced pair of veins bulge from her temples to her brows. "Your brother was weak, and he was a fool. His only useful characteristic was the greed that drove him."

"And you used that greed to make him murder Melaine. You couldn't bear that he *loved* her. That he kept her in the castle, kept her as his lover."

Phoebe clenches her fists and lets out an enraged shriek. She paces a few steps one way and then the other. The knights look to each other, their wide eyes silently begging the other to make some decision as to how to act in the face of a maddened queen.

Spittle accompanies the words that fly from Phoebe's mouth. "She was a peasant and a bastard. I don't understand why the heirs of Devlishire were so enraptured by that little beast."

I maintain a calm demeanor, smug in my ability to have brought her to this level of fury. "Melaine was the mother of Henry, the only heir to Devlishire. Which is a blessing as you turned out to be barren."

"Barren?" She shrieks the word then steps closer, her finger once again jabbing in the direction of my face. Her facade of regal composure is long forgotten. "I am not barren, a fact which may have become apparent had my husband ever lain with me. Had he fulfilled his husbandly duties, then I would have an heir in my belly. Instead, he pined away for a bastard, peasant, chamber-maid."

I strike without thought. The rush of warmth as my knuckles crack across Phoebe's cheek is nearly as satisfying as watching Roarke's life seep from the slit I made in his throat. I draw back to strike again, and as my clenched fist cracks against her face, the guards finally come to their senses and grab me, pulling me back as I launch one last kick directly into her abdomen, driving her from the bottom of my foot across the room. She crumples against the stairway.

I'm still bucking against the grip of the knights as she pushes herself to her feet. "Lock her up," she commands. Two drag me backward. Like a mad animal, I buck against them, determined to break loose, although I have no idea where I would flee if I did manage to get away.

They lead me into the same corridor they took Davion and Kennard. As I'm thrust into a cell, I see the bodies of my friends lying motionless in the cell across from me. I grasp for the bars, my fingertips clinging to the roughened iron as the two men push me through. Their arms are extended as they try to push me far enough away that they can pull the bars across the opening without me slipping past them.

"For the love of the gods," another man says. He pushes through the other knights who've gathered to watch me battle. I see the armor-covered foot break through the space between two bodies only a moment before it slams into my abdomen, driving me away from the door.

I tumble backward, my heels catching against the stone floor and causing me to fall back. My head cracks against the wall, and laughter erupts from my captors as my head spins. I struggle to one knee, reaching one hand behind my head to feel for the tell-tale moisture of a bleeding wound. My fingertips pull away dry and free of fresh blood.

The knights grow quiet, and the scuff of slippers on stone alerts me that Phoebe has come to gaze upon her caged animal. I pull myself up again—wondering how long I'll have to endure this time.

"This is a good look for you," she says. She's scrunched her face into a contemptuous look, but the confidence has gone from her eyes. It's all a show now. Phoebe knows that if it weren't for the bars, I would best her physically and verbally. "It's a shame, though. I almost thought we might work together."

I spit blood, this time directly at her, but Phoebe maintains a cool demeanor bolstered by—I can't quite tell, but it's no longer a naivete about what I'm capable of. "I would never align with you."

"That's a shame because I think you underestimate me, *sister*. You see, when I called your brother weak and a fool, I was generous. He was just a means to bring about unrest within the Unified Kingdoms. With the Unification fractured, I'm bringing more to the deal my father brokered on my behalf—of course, he assumed he'd be the benefactor—but he was only ever meant to arrange the deal."

I can't imagine what she's talking about. With unrest permeating the Unified Kingdoms' remains, I can't imagine a single alliance within them that would assure her an advantage.

"What deal?" I ask. "There isn't a place within the kingdoms that will give you power."

Her mouth purses as though looking upon an orphaned puppy. She leans forward. In a whisper, she says, "If you manage to escape this cell, you can have Allondale—for now. My aspirations don't end in these crumbling domains. I've sworn allegiance to King Travión. I bring Carling and Devlishire with me. The rest of the

131

kingdoms can *submit* to Traviónian rule or *fall* to it. And I'll take great pleasure watching *you* fall to King Travión." She shrugs and turns to leave.

I'm stunned. All this time, Phoebe has had a grander plan than marrying the man who held the High Crown or even claiming it for herself? Travión is a kingdom of far greater wealth and force than any of the Unified Kingdoms. The only thing that kept us from being absorbed into Traviónian rule was the unification a hundred years ago that bonded the seven kingdoms together in peace and as allies against invasion. With the realms at war now and each alone in their battles, we are all at risk to fall.

My mother fled from a conquered nation as a girl, barely escaping before it fell. Now that the Unification has been destroyed, seven realms are at risk.

"Phoebe!" I don't know what to say, but I can't let her walk out with the last word.

She comes back but says nothing, just stares with her brows raised and mouth pursed.

"You have to kill me," I say. "If you leave me, you risk that I'll be found and released. And then I *will* come for you."

Her smile is a sweet threat. "I hope you do. I'll take great joy in watching my new husband destroy you further than my former one did." She turns again, and her knights fall in behind her.

Venom fills me as I study her and consider the depth of her betrayal to all seven kingdoms. Not only will each kingdom fall, but innocent people will die, her people included. When I think of Melaine and how she died, my chest roils with a vengeance again. I may be trapped in a dungeon, but I won't let her walk out of here with the last word."

"You're his second choice, you know."

She stops but doesn't turn.

"King Travión's. He wanted my sister, offered her the throne to his right. I wonder if he'd have kept his word had she made it to Travión as planned?"

She flinches, then straightens her shoulders and walks from the corridor, leaving only the echo of footsteps on the stone steps in her wake.

CHAPTER

FIFTEEN

EXHAUSTION CLAIMS MY BODY, AND I CRUMBLE TO the stone ledge. "Davion. Kennard?" Neither man answers, and I strain my ears for sounds that they are alive. The subtle rasps of breath carry across the narrow hall between cells.

I lean back against the wall, resting my head and allowing my eyes to close. My mind whirls with revelations of the day. As horrible as I've thought Roarke to be, it's even more chilling to realize that all this time, Phoebe was a greater threat, lurking and waiting for her opportunity to advance her agenda. She's far from the mousy and unimpressionable girl I always imagined her to be. *How could I have been so unaware?*

My mind slows, dwelling on details until I fall into dreams laden with threats and pain. I'm woken by a deep moan, one I recognize from far too many mornings after far too many drunken nights. I stand and cross the small cell to the bars, leaning against the cold iron. "Kennard? Are you okay?"

Rustling sounds from the dark cell as he moves, and then the large shadow of his figure rolls and lifts as he stands. He's rubbing the back of his head and moans again. "Who do I have to kill for this?"

"Phoebe," I answer.

He leans against the bars, and I can see his eyes in the soft light coming from a slit. His brows are raised in surprise.

"Well, her knights anyway, but at her bidding."

He nods. "Fair enough. I'll add the little twat to my list."

A heavy silence settles around us in the dark. We are far too deep into the castle for sounds to reach us, and it'll do no good for us to call for help. "Someone'll come," Kennard assures me.

I nod, though I'm not sure he's even paying attention. I ease my aching body onto the uneven ground. My joints submit against the firm earth's pressure underneath me, and I allow my muscles to relax finally. I roll my head from side to side, stretching my neck and shoulder muscles, then sink against the wall. "What were you doing down here?"

Kennard pauses for only a moment. His voice is smooth when he answers, the usual gruff and steel of his demeanor absent for only a moment. "Just looking for something. But it's not here."

"What was it?"

"Just a shadow as it turns out."

Davion moans then, and his shadowed form rolls and pushes upright. "What the—"

Kennard's gruff voice has returned. "You can blame the queen for that headache."

"The queen?" Davion holds onto the bars as he shakes off confusion.

"Phoebe," I clarify.

An apricot glow lightens the hall between the cells, and the shuffling of feet on the steps fills the space between us. My heart races, unsure if Phoebe has reconsidered and sent one of her men back to dispatch with me. This would be the easiest opportunity they'll ever have to best me. I'm an animal in a cage, ripe for poaching.

A small group moves through the main room and into one of the other halls. I remain quiet, angling myself to see them when they turn into our bank of cells. They are swift and silent as they clear the other halls. My heart thunders with the certainty that they are heading to our corridor next and that this could be the end of my fight.

The shadow of a bow comes into my view first. The hand clutching it is small, the wrist narrow. The archer angles around the corner, prepared to loosen their arrow at any threat. They clear the first cells, and I hear the familiar tinkling of motion.

"Isobel!" I press against the bars, leaning so that I can better see her. She rushes to the cell, one of her knights holding up a torch to peer into each as they pass.

In the light of the torch, I see Kennard and Davion for the

first time. Kennard's nose is swollen and off-center. Blood has left a path from one brow, across the bridge of his nose, and down to his collar. Purple dusts the surface of the areas that are swollen.

Davion stares back from one eye. His left is swollen shut, and his lip is split in several places. His usually handsome face mangled and horrific, though he seems unaware of what effect the sight of him has on others.

Isobel looks from the men's cell back to me, her mouth crooked in a half-smile. "There was a time I'd have been happy to see *this*."

I smirk. "Take a good look, and then get us out of here."

"Just one more moment," she says with a self-satisfied smile. Her eyes linger on every detail of my imprisonment. One of the knights returns with a brass ring, keys jingling as he moves. He slides the largest of the keys into the lock and turns. The door screeches against the movement as he pulls it open. I step into the corridor and accept a torch that's offered by one of the Gaufridian knights.

With Davion and Kennard freed, the group turns to move from the hall. Kennard lingers in his cell as I cast a glance over my shoulder. He lifts his hand to the wall, his fingers lingering on something for several seconds before he hurries to meet up.

"Phoebe was here." I update Isobel and point to the door, once again locked. "They must have escaped through there. She's going to Travión."

Isobel leads her troops up the stairs, Kennard and Davion at the lead with her as they discuss Phoebe's escape. I linger, retrieving my weapons from the floor and then make my way back to the cell Kennard was in. When I hold the torch up to the wall, the light plays across the shadows of cracks and etchings in the stone. The lingering evidence of the prisoner's past is etched into the surface. The marks they scratched into the stone to both pass their time and mark its passage remains. Small etchings in other languages declare allegiance to gods and kings of faraway lands. But I'm most interested in the large word chiseled deep into the stone, the word that—based on its position and location on the wall—I'm certain Kennard had lingered at. It is one word—a name really: I'awn.

CHAPTER
SIXTEEN

THE SUN HAS FINALLY BROKEN THROUGH THE CLOUD cover as we walk through the gates of Carling and into Fairlee. I have to think the sun's appearance has more to do with the fact that Roarke is no longer in this world, casting a shadow of greed and deceit across the kingdoms.

I linger with Josef and Kennard as our troops pass through the gates, walking across the bridge and toward the depths of Fairlee. Fifty of the Gaufridian knights will remain in Carling to hold it in my name and await the two hundred men Weaver Arionde led to reclaim Devlishire. I task an eager young soldier with delivering my orders to Weaver.

Ayleth walks alongside Isobel at the head of the group, gazing up as she speaks seriously, though Isobel's eyes are trained on the path ahead. They both catch me watching. Isobel offers a curt nod before continuing. I imagine she's exhausted to have finally found herself the object of Ayleth's attentions. A youthful exuberance overtakes Ayleth's expression when she sees me. She offers an enthusiastic wave before falling in behind Isobel.

Our progress through the forest is slow. The troops are weary and our royal prisoner unaccustomed to hiking through the forest. Each branch that snags Queen Filomena's finely shod feet elicits a cry of fear from her. After only an hour, she stops and refuses to take another step. "This is an undignified way to treat a queen!"

I'm already bored with her royal sensibilities and complaints. I lift one brow and shrug as she turns. "Apologies, Queen Filomena, but I find myself without a chariot to offer you. I believe your *hus-*

band's men burned mine."

"I will not take one more step through this dreadful forest." Her proper, erect posture and the set of her jaw do nothing to mitigate the effect of her frizzy silver and ebony hair sprouting at all angles from a collapsing updo and the streaks of color from smeared makeup that now appear more garish than aristocratic.

I shrug and turn away to continue my trek. "Kennard."

He lets out a sigh, but heads back toward the queen as Josef falls back in step with me.

"W—what? Don't you touch me you—" Queen Filomena's screeching is interrupted by a grunt from Kennard as he undoubtedly heaves the small woman over his shoulder. I don't look back, but in my mind, it's a very undignified manner she's being carried in.

"Ye shoulda left 'er. She's goin' ta be more trouble than she's worth."

"Her husband is dead, and her daughter is on her way to make her alliance. I can't risk leaving her in Carling to build an army of sympathizers. And she isn't safe there."

Josef looks over his shoulder, a smile forming of equal parts disbelief and humor that we've taken a queen hostage. "She's still goin' ta be more trouble than she's worth."

I cast my glance back to Kennard. The queen tossed over his left shoulder continues to curse and pound small weak blows into his back. Kennard meets my gaze and rolls his eyes. "I have no doubt."

The queen quickly determines that walking is far more comfortable—*or is she concerned still for her dignity?* —and she falls into step with the rest of us, though her pace is slow.

I'm eager to get back to Jamis. I'm both concerned for him and eager to share the details of how I was able to finally get vengeance against Roarke. Of course, his death has been overshadowed by the realization that Phoebe remains a greater threat—and perhaps was all along.

Our return to camp will take longer than the trip here if we are forced to maintain Queen Filomena's pace. Perhaps I did make a mistake in bringing her.

The Queen finds more things to gripe about as we make camp, though all the knights have now grown accustomed to the constant flow of complaints from her mouth and hardly notice any longer.

Katherine—ever the court raised lady—tries to appease her. Still, Isobel remains as far away as possible, unable to tolerate the constant talk, much less the negativity the words contain.

Our group gathers around several small fires, the knights settling into rest as small game is roasted in the flames. The musky scent of campfire and damp forest undergrowth surrounds us as the aroma of meat slowly drifts across the troops with the promise of a hearty meal to end a long, hard day.

I accept a handful of berries from Kennard as I join him, Josef, and Davion at one of the fires. "How long until Weaver catches up?"

"Three days. Maybe two at the pace we're keeping." He casts a hard look to where the former queen of Carling is tied to a tree and remains under four guards' watch.

"The baby wasn't at Carling," I sit, my attention focused on the dancing flames.

"There's a chance she left him in Devlishire. If she isn't his mother, she wouldn't be as inclined to keep him with her. She might have left him for someone else to care for—in his kingdom, where he'll be protected."

I nod, hoping that is the case and that Weaver's men didn't inadvertently hurt him when they raided.

The sunlight vanishes, and darkness reclaims the distant depths of Fairlee. With my cloak pulled tightly about myself, I watch as knights from Gaufrid mingle with my small band of Allondalian and Fairlean warriors. Before I know it, Katherine, Isobel, and Josef leave the fires and are foraging in the dark.

"What are they doing?" Ayleth is on her knees, peering over the fallen tree that we've been leaning against. Her eyes pinch tight as she squints into the night, trying to keep track of the others.

"They're looking for stygialas. They're going to use the root to tattoo those knights." I point to the three men who are scraping ash from under the fires into wooden bowls.

She turns and plops beside me again. "Do you have one?"

A laugh leaps from my chest. "A tattoo? Me? No."

"Why not? Haven't you proven your bravery? Are you not a skilled warrior who has proven courageous and honorable in the face of great challenges?" Her bright eyes are wide, and brows raised as she awaits my answer.

A response catches in my throat. "I—I am a brave and proven warrior. But I am also a queen."

"Can you not be both?"

I laugh again at the thought of a tattooed warrior queen. Can a woman be equal parts warrior and queen? *Why can't I be both?*

Ayleth is watching me as I turn the idea in my mind. The way she studies me causes me to realize that everything this girl will think about queens or female warriors could be shaped by what she sees in me. How would I want her to one day relate her impressions of me to others? Will she find me to be strong and capable, will she say that I shaped my path or that I remained bound by the conventions of the courts that I fought against?

I watch as Katherine grinds the stygialas root and dark ashes into a paste then adds water to smooth it. This craft has become normal to her as though she had been mixing ink for the entirety of her life, and not simply over the past several months.

Twelve soldiers are tattooed, the session spreading later into the night than any other I've witnessed. I lean against a tree watching as Katherine finishes a symbol over the heart of the last knight.

"She's a natural artist," Josef steps from the dark and leans against my tree just in front of me.

"She never ceases to impress me. Her abilities are far greater than she would have ever discovered in courtly life." Warmth spreads through me as I gaze at my friend. She's so much more than a lady in waiting, and while I'm often regretful that I led Katherine into a life of war and risk, she has blossomed since she first picked up a blade. She can excel in any setting, and joy seems to pour from her each day she tests her abilities and discovers new challenges to overcome in our new world.

Josef crooks his forehead in the direction of Katherine and the knight she's painstakingly marking. "Ye know, ye've earned it. If ye want."

I meet his eyes, and my heart rushes at the thought of having my bravery declared through this ancient Fairlean tradition. To have a mark on my body that confirms I am indeed brave. Would that quell the doubts that still creep into my mind periodically?

"Ye are brave, Mal. Despite yer own doubt, yer braver than most."

I swallow against the surprise and self-doubt that have gathered in my throat. My head is nodding before I even realize that I'm ready to commit fully. There's a pull in my chest. It's leading me toward Josef, to this opportunity. I've wanted this all along, haven't

I? For someone to recognize that I am brave, that I'm worthy. Isn't that what I felt the first time I saw Josef tattoo Katherine? It *was* jealousy that she'd been recognized for her bravery when I had not. I hadn't even had the opportunity to decline the honor, and that was what had bothered me. I'm certain of that now. But I don't want to decline the offer. I nod and walk toward the fire with Josef.

The knight Katherine was decorating nods, pulling his tunic in place as he walks away with his new symbol. She makes way when she sees Josef and me approach. Josef leans close and whispers in my ear, "Ye don't 'ave to."

I gulp again and sit beside the fire. Katherine offers a smile. Pleasure dances in her eyes, sparkling in the dancing ochre and gold glow cast by the fire.

I release a deep breath as Josef sits in front of me, stirring the bowl. His eyes hold mine, then cut to my top and back. His brows are raised. He doesn't want to say the words, but he also doesn't have to. I understand his silent message. My fingertips release my cloak's clasp, then fumble for the pearl buttons, pushing them through the slits in the material. My chest constricts in anticipation as my gown loosens. I hold Josef's eyes, afraid to see his reaction as I bare the skin over my heart—the traditional location for the first mark of bravery—and afraid to miss it.

Prickles form along my shoulder as the cold winter air assaults my exposed skin, the fire doing little to negate the effects of the cold. Josef scoots closer, then brushes a loose tendril of hair over my shoulder. A shiver rises up, tickling my back as the hair falls in place.

Josef considers my bared skin like an artist visualizing a blank canvas.

I clutch my dress's material to maintain as much decency as possible, but my skin flushes with heat the instant his skin comes in contact with my own.

As Josef lifts the sharpened quill, his hand brushes the skin over my sternum, and a small gasp leaps from me. He's startled, his eyes questioning as they meet mine.

I nod that he should continue.

The first sharp poke of the quill into my skin jolts me from my haze. I pinch my brows, opening my lips to offer a silent, *Ow.*

Josef sits straighter, pulling his hand toward his own chest. His voice is a whisper. "Should I stop?"

I shake my head and he leans forward again, his focus on his work. I sit still as he pokes and scratches into my skin. The heat of scratching turns to a numb pressure. I watch his face as he works, his brows pulled together in concentration, the tip of his tongue darting out to brush against his lip periodically as he considers his design from one angle or another.

He's so near that each of his breaths warms my skin, chasing away the gathering cold of the night. It's nearly an hour before he sits back, considering his artwork. I watch his face as he considers it for several seconds, his gaze intense. Then, slowly, his eyes raise to meet mine.

Against the darkness, I swear that he blushes before he shakes off the moment. He nods toward my still bared skin. "What d'ye think?"

I look down and gasp. There, across my heart, reaching from my sternum to my shoulder and from my clavicle to the top of my breast, is the symbol of Nithenia. It's the symbol created by Laila and me. "Now ye can carry it into ev'ry battle. Ye don't need to draw it anymore."

The thumping in my heart is pure joy. Both for the fact that I have this symbol etched into me forever as well as the fact Josef chose this as my first Fairlean tattoo. I'm not surprised he's noticed me drawing the symbol, but that he has paid so much attention that he can recreate it and recognizes that there could be no better symbol to tattoo me with is touching.

"It's perfect." My cheeks ache from the smile as I look down at the ink again. Though the surrounding tissue is red and swollen, I have no doubt the tattoo will be beautiful when it's healed and settled into my skin.

Katherine approaches, and I stand to show her. She offers her confirmation of the work. "It's perfect. I swear sometimes you know her better than anyone else does, Josef." She turns and adds, "But as perfectly suited as it is, I'm exhausted, and we'll certainly set out early." She walks to the larger fire where her bedroll lies between Kennard and Davion.

I turn toward the fire again, taking one last look at the symbol. I can feel the symbol left in the wake of Josef's hand, permanently etched into my skin.

Josef is standing close. I quickly regain my sense of decency and pull my dress back over my shoulders, but I realize he wasn't looking at my bare skin; he's looking intently at my face. I smile. "Thank you." The words whisper against the night, dancing between us, swaying on the shifting breeze before being swept away.

He leans his head closer, his lips nearly close enough to brush against my temple. He breaths deep, drawing in my scent, and whispers. "Anything for you, Mal."

Before my breath has a chance to catch in my chest, he turns and walks into the dark.

CHAPTER
SEVENTEEN

QUEEN FILOMENA IS ONLY SLIGHTLY LESS IRRITATING THE second day. She nearly keeps up with us as if determined to keep whatever pace gets her out of the forest fastest, though she remains prone to sudden shrieks when roots take hold of her shoes or small animals burst from the underbrush.

Josef and I fall back into our usual progression, side by side but without conversation. The throbbing of my new tattoo remains, a lingering effect of having it etched into my skin providing a constant awareness of its presence.

Or is it Josef's hand that's now branded there? I shake away my self-doubt and focus on the rationale. Josef is my friend, my ally, and he has fought at my side for months. He's one of the few people who has proven himself trustworthy. I feel comfortable with him, that's all. We are all bonded.

Would Kennard elicit such a reaction?

No! I shudder at the thought of Kennard touching me in such an intimate manner.

I chance a look at Josef. He's surveying the terrain ahead of us, his eyes scanning for any hint of threat. He notices me looking and raises his brows in a quick gesture, asking if something is wrong. But there's no hint of any deeper meaning—no deeper feelings toward me.

I offer a quick shrug, glancing back at Queen Filomena. "We should probably make camp before she starts complaining."

We find a clearing large enough for a few fires for our group of over one hundred. Josef, Isobel, and Kennard disappear into the trees with a hunting party while Davion and Katherine collect our skins to refill them with water at a nearby creek.

"You are everything they say," Queen Filomena says as I secure the rope that will bind her to the tree.

All of my interactions with the members of Carling's house have consisted of seemingly kind words followed with barbed tails, and I have no interest in falling victim to another member of their family.

"And what is it specifically that you're referring to? Because I'm not dead, and I'm not mad."

She shakes her head. With a deep breath, she begins to pull her updo apart, letting the long strands unwind over her shoulder. She faces me as she talks, her expression resigned, no obvious sign of deceit or bargaining apparent.

Even in the absence of her usual surroundings, she is a queen again and has firmly pulled the cloak of royalty over her shoulders. She speaks as she would any other queen during times of peace: as though we're on the same level, as though we share a bond that few can ever experience. "They say you're fierce. And that you may be far better prepared to wear the High Crown than any other monarch before you."

My gaze snaps to hers even though I maintain a controlled expression. I'm looking for any sign that she's deceiving me, playing on my ego to advance her agenda. But her expression remains open and earnest, her chin held high in the way of royalty. Her naturally bronzed skin is aglow with sunlight, and her cheeks rosy with exertion for which she's unaccustomed. Her sable eyes are calm and thoughtful as she takes me in.

My jaw pulses as I clench my teeth to control my response. Although she appears earnest, I can't allow myself to be taken in. My voice is even and controlled as I respond. "I am fierce. But I didn't have time to prepare, did I? Grayson and Lester made sure I wouldn't have time to offer any opposition. They conspired to murder Jamis and me before we even had a chance."

"Yes." When she nods, I think I see regret in her eyes for the first time. A heavy silence sits between us. Queen Filomena clears her throat, her lashes fluttering as she looks off at an angle and then back. "I would like to enter into an agreement with you."

An incredulous burst of air escapes from me. I'm amused at this woman's gall. "An agreement?"

She meets my look of doubt, but her aspect remains earnest. She nods.

"And what sort of an agreement would you and I enter into?"

"I'll do whatever you ask to ensure my son's life." Her voice cracks, her eyes filling, but she blinks away the moisture before it can spill over.

I hadn't even thought of Oliver of Carling, Phoebe's twin brother, older than her by minutes, but with a similar small, dark presence. Oliver should be the reigning king of Carling. The way Phoebe declared herself queen, I assumed she'd dispatched of her brother as well as her father. I'm burning with questions, but I doubt she'll be inclined to answer. I decide to proceed with the information she's offering freely. "Where is he?"

"He was sent away. I convinced him to abdicate for his safety. He's—not *delicate*—but he is no match for his sister's voracious aspirations."

At one point, I thought Phoebe and I to be in similar predicaments: both pawns in the games being played by my men. As it turns out, maybe I have more in common with Oliver. "You expect me to leave Oliver alive to avenge his sister? Because I do intend to kill her. It'd be shortsighted of me to leave someone alive to seek vengeance. Certainly, he'll feel the need to retaliate and claim Carling as his own."

Her eyes are wide, and she leans forward against the bindings as she shakes her head fervently. "No! He'd never seek to retaliate. Oliver is a gentle soul, more inclined to music and the arts than politics. He isn't a threat to you, I swear."

I sit on a stump across from her, leaning on my knees. "And you are so easy to choose one of your children over the other?"

She purses her lips, rolling her eyes. Her voice drops as she admits the heinous thoughts she's having about her child. "That girl is of her father more than me. Perhaps she's got more of her grandfather in her than anyone imagined."

I perk up at this new information. Phoebe's grandfather, Edward of Carling, was once the High King. He'd successfully manipulated the King's Council into bestowing the High Crown on him after my great-grandfather died, leaving a nine-year-old heir who was ill-prepared to accept such a responsibility. King Edward was responsible for betrothing my mother to King Alexander, and Grayson after that. But his enduring legacy was that he went well and truly mad. The High Crown was stripped from him and grant-ed to Eamon of Allondale—Jamis's father. "She's mad?"

Queen Filomena sighs. "She's mad with her quest for power. I fear she'll do anything."

I think of the story Laila relayed, of how Phoebe, driven by jealousy, had demanded that Roarke kill Melaine. Had she been driven by jealousy after all or simply recognized an opportunity to dispatch one more person who stood in the way of her goal?

The queen continues, a flush of humility spreading across her cheeks as she relays the actions of her daughter. "She's secured a proposal of marriage with King Travión. Now that Roarke is dead, nothing is standing in her way. If she aligns with him, the entirety of the Unified Kingdoms will be brought to ruin. If all the king-doms fought together, we could perhaps stand a chance. Divided, we cannot withstand a war with him."

I nod.

"And she will ensure her brother is dead before this is all over. She won't risk an heir of any realm surviving. She plans to rule them all—even Tiernan."

I stifle a gasp. I hadn't even thought about Tiernan, the realm furthest from the rest, and the most difficult to reach. It's loca-tion, surrounded by steep mountainous passes on two sides and the Great North Sea with a narrow and heavily guarded inlet, has en-sured it remains resistant to invasion thus far. Still, with the armies of every realm at their control, Travión could easily sack Tiernan as well and claim the entirety of the lands.

"What is it you want from me?"

"Assurance that you won't harm Oliver."

"That's all?"

She nods, picking away dried bits of leaves that cling to her skirt.

"And what do you offer me?" I can't imagine that the former queen has anything left to offer. Her husband is dead, and her daughter left her behind to be claimed by their enemies.

She swallows. "I haven't anything. We both know that. What I can promise is that I will go with you willingly. Wher-ever you plan to take me, I will remain your prisoner, and I will praise your treatment of me while I remain captive."

"You're assuming that I will treat you fairly."

Her gaze is steady on me, reading me then nodding as though confirming her impression. "I think we both know that you are far more ethically inclined than either my daughter or husband. You have an idealistic vision of what it means to be a ruler, and no matter how driven you are to right the many wrongs done to you, you will always hedge toward the side of goodness."

Fury lights in my chest. How dare she assume to know me! She has no idea how driven I am by vengeance, how many lives I've ended in my quest for retribution. But I can't deny her view of me either. Part of the reason I seek vengeance *is* for the wrongs that have been dealt me and the people I love.

Her voice is soft, smooth as she makes her final plea. "I will remain in your control for all my days if need be. I will tout your beneficent qualities and endorse you as High Queen. When we arrive wherever you'll hold me prisoner, I'll tell you where to find Oliver. He won't resist you if you deliver my message. And he will also endorse you. He has no thirst for war or power. He isn't a threat."

When I left camp for Gaufrid, I never imagined I'd be returning with a prisoner, much less a royal one. I haven't even considered where I'll house Filomena. I stand up, thoughts spinning in my head. Filomena is an experienced queen, and I can't risk that she'll perceive any doubt or incompetence in me. "I'll consider your pledge."

She simply nods as I walk away, four knights assuming post around the queen, though I'm certain she won't leave—and not just for fear of being alone in the forest.

A starless night descends over Fairlee. The knights fall into their usual campsite routines, dining on a large buck and several pheasants as well as roots and berries foraged by Isobel and Ayleth. With full bellies and journey-weighted muscles, they settle in for boastful stories of women and war.

Kennard joins me as I once again sit on the periphery, watching everyone. He tips his head in Filomena's direction. "What's the plan?"

I tell him about her offer to endorse me in exchange for Oliver's life. "Whatever it takes to get the old cow through the forest on her own two feet," he says, chewing on a narrow twig. "I'm too feckin' tired to be carrying people anymore. Or maybe I just care less if I leave 'em to die of their own stupidity."

A grin pulls at my face. "I find myself caring less if you leave them to die."

Kennard casts me a cautious glance to see if I'm serious. Realizing that I am, he offers an almost imperceptible nod and turns his attention back to the large fire in the middle of the camp. "Almost left *you* a time or two."

My smile spreads tighter as I try to control it. This is the closest I've ever felt to Kennard, and I know it's driving him mad to be softening toward me, no matter how slow the process has been. "I know."

A companionable silence settles over us as we sit sentry over our group. The soldiers are in groups around the fires, some lying on their bedrolls, eyes covered as they snooze, but the boastful tales will continue until far into the night when exhaustion and good sense finally claim them all.

Ayleth sits beside Katherine as she sharpens her arrows and inspects the quills. Ayleth says something and points to the arrow, as though instructing Katherine, who rolls her eyes, but patiently endures the little girl's input.

"Who are her parents?" I look to Kennard.

"Don't know." The corners of his mouth turn down, and his brows raise as he considers the little girl. "She just showed up at my hip one day, and I couldn't get rid of her."

I offer a wide-eyed look and conciliatory nod, though my voice can't conceal that I'm teasing him. "You're very paternal."

His response is gruff. "Was easier to let her stay about than to try to chase her off all day."

"Mm-hm." We both turn our attention back to the girl as she finally bores of Katherine and makes her way through the sleeping knights. She peers over them, speaking to some before moving on.

I want to ask Kennard about the name I saw him looking at in the dungeon. Clever openings come to mind, but then disappear the moment I try to voice them. Maybe I should just forget it. It was likely nothing more than curiosity. Kennard has proven loyal to Jamis and me. If he has secrets, he should be entitled to them. He doesn't owe me the right of baring his every thought. But I can't help myself. "Who is I'awn?"

I nearly flinch as his head snaps up. The words burst out, but now I'd give anything to shove them back into my mouth and erase the memory of this moment. I'm once again that new princess to Allondale and terrified by the large man guarding my future husband.

Kennard pulls his feet closer, resting his elbows on his knees. He drops his head as a long breath escapes. When he lifts his head again, his eyes remain fixed on the fire closest to us, though he's seeing images from a different life.

"I was nine when I was brought to Ballæter from the Candor Islands. My family was dead from the plague, and I'd been on my own for months, stealing to survive, sleeping in woodpiles and trash heaps to stay warm and to avoid being seen. One night I made the mistake of falling asleep on the docks, behind stacks of supplies that were to be loaded the next day. A Venbrúid pirate found me and offered to take me on board. He promised the life of a pirate, a life of adventure. I just had to be willing to work hard."

I swallow the tension gathering in my throat at the thought of a young Kennard without family and at the mercy of pirates.

"I knew I was strong, and I didn't understand how working on a ship could be any more difficult than trying to survive on my own. So I went." His mouth turns down as memories absorb him for several moments. His brow pinches as he takes a breath to continue. "It was worse than anything I could have imagined or anything I've seen since. When we arrived in Tiernan's port, I was given a choice to commit to the Venbrúids and spend the rest of my life at sea or be sold to the Knights of Ballæter. I didn't know anything about House Ballæter then, but I figured it *had* to be better. And it was—but only marginally."

I remind myself to breathe, but Kennard transfixes me. His deep, usually gravelly voice is smooth and echoes with the pain of his boyhood memories. I want to sit up, turn toward him, and get lost in his story, but I fear that any movement on my part will pull him from his reverie and that he'll stop—returning to the stoic, closed Kennard I've come to know.

"I was trained to fight. I could barely lift the sword I was given to train with. It was made of wood, and the splinters dug into my blisters. I tried to smooth the wood to reduce the splintering, but the brothers only replaced my sword with another, which was heavier and more warped than the previous. Brother Fitzpatrick lashed me twenty times before he said, 'Our goal isn't for you to learn to do your duty more easily. Knights of Ballæter endure what they are given. The pride you seek in your heart comes from overcoming all obstacles. Honor is not simply in winning.' We spent our mornings training, our afternoons working the land, and our evenings studying the kingdoms and in worship."

"Who did you worship?" This question comes far easier as late.

"We were allowed to worship as our families did, but we had to study the God of the Heavens and the God of the Earth as the kings do."

I nod. "And I'awn?"

Kennard takes another deep breath. "I'd been at House Ballæter for a year. By that time, I'd far exceeded the expectations of the brothers and everyone else my age. Some of the brothers returned from an auction in Oberstedt with twenty new boys. I was to manage the new boys, make sure they knew what was expected. They were frightened; we all were when we first came to Ballæter. But I'awn was different. I saw the terror in his eyes, but he hid it behind a calm demeanor. He did everything that was asked of him, but one thing the brothers of Ballæter could never do was instill in him an impulse to kill. He had one thing none of the rest of us possessed. He was brilliant. His father had been a scholar and his mother a singer. Had he been given a chance, I'awn could have become a great teacher. It was what he wanted more than anything. But the brothers had purchased him for a purpose—like all of us. We were products to be sold to kings."

Kennard shifts, dusting some unseen annoyance from his pant leg before he continues. "I'awn and I were the largest, and we were often paired against each other in sparring, but I would easily best him. One day, I was so mad I shoved him to the ground after a training session and demanded he give me the fight I deserve. I yelled that by being such an easy target, he was robbing me of the opportunity to develop the skills that would one day save my life. He cried, and I felt horrible. I wanted him to be my match, to be someone I could rely on. I'd never had that before. He said he didn't think he'd ever be able to kill—that it would be easier to succumb in battle than carry the stain of someone else's blood on his soul for life. I swore to help him. I would help I'awn learn to separate his sensibilities from the job that would keep him alive. In return, he would teach me to read and about everything else he knew. We were fast friends, a team. As long as I'awn and I were paired together, he didn't have to hurt anyone. I took that burden on myself. I protected him, but his fear never truly went away. I'awn was kind and brilliant—and beautiful. He was the light that

150

overshadowed my darkness, and I loved him. But I also failed him because I never imagined we'd be parted. I never imagined that everything I did to improve his skill, to save him, the brothers would use against us. They used our equal abilities to drive the price up between two kings, and we were separated so neither king would feel better armed than the other."

Anger pulls one side of Kennard's face into a tight grimace as he finally turns to face me. "Your father almost claimed us both. But in the end, he let Lester of Carling take I'awn. He wouldn't pay the one additional piece of gold that would have ensured I'awn served Devlishire at my side. He let I'awn be dragged away, lurching against the iron cuff that was secured at his neck at the brother's instructions. There was nothing I could do. Everything the brothers had taught me was so deeply entrenched that I did nothing to stop him from being dragged away. I stood there, behind my new king, as I'awn screamed and grasped in my direction, his eyes begging me to help."

A solitary tear spills over Kennard's lashes. He swipes it away immediately, pulling his stoic veneer back into place.

I can't speak. So much makes sense now—how Kennard could have so easily sworn allegiance to Jamis after being sent from Devlishire, the venom with which he spoke about my father.

"Your father used I'awn to keep me in line. He knew where I'awn was. The brothers had told him that they long suspected the bond between I'awn and I was more than friendly. He assured me if I failed him, he would ensure I'awn was tortured most excruciatingly. I lost track of I'awn. It's been ten years since I've heard anything. But Weaver said he'd seen I'awn in the dungeons just months ago when he returned an escaped prisoner who'd sought refuge in Gaufrid."

I let the breath I've been holding out into the night air. It bursts into the cold air and dances in front of me before drifting away. "He was there."

Kennard nods, but remains wordless, lost in his thoughts—perhaps his fears.

"That's who you were talking about. Before we left, you told me that it was easier to imagine the one you loved had died."

He nods. "I didn't keep my promise, didn't keep him safe. I did everything to make him an ideal candidate for a king, and then I let one drag him away. It's been easier to imagine him dead than to consider that he's been treated badly all this time—at least that's what I've told myself."

My words are only a whisper on the breeze between us. "How long has it been?"

Kennard's lids close. The skin around them tightens, clenching against his memories. He blows off the past, his memories, and turns. "Twenty-two years."

"I'm so sorry, Kennard." There's nothing more I can say. Kennard is one more person who was betrayed by Grayson and tossed away. It breaks my heart to think he was in so much pain that it was easier to imagine the person he loved dead than to imagine the truth. Poor I'awn, wherever he is—or was—was at the mercy of people who likely cared less for him as a person than what he could offer them. From what little I know about I'awn, if he didn't rise to prove himself a warrior, his course in the kingdoms may have been far more horrid than Kennard's imagination can even embrace. Even whatever horrors he endured amongst the Venbrúid pirate ships would likely pale in comparison to I'awn's certain fate. "If he's out there…"

Kennard offers a sad smile. He reaches to squeeze my hand for just a second before he pushes himself up and walks into the darkness.

I sit alone, stunned at last to know some private thing about Kennard, and what that thing is. I didn't even ask him if Jamis knows about I'awn, although I'm fairly certain he doesn't. There's a sudden sense of overwhelming isolation amid a large group of people and the realization the bonds between us are few and some of a gossamer thickness. I rise and join my companions at the fire, feeling the presence of people who know me and trust me, though they don't actually love me. Few people do, and I'm bathed in yearning to see my husband and my sister.

With Queen Filomena in tow, we are still days away from camp, but I vow that once I return, I won't leave again until Jamis is ready to ride again. Solitary wars aren't for me. I need my husband by my side to strengthen me and ensure that we are always fighting for right. The weight of decisions is too heavy a burden for me to bear any longer.

Just a few more days, Jamis.

CHAPTER

EIGHTEEN

PREPARE TO RIDE, GIRL.

The voice is a collection of whispers, insistent and paired with a shock of energy that reverberates through my sleeping body, alerting my mind that this order to prepare to ride wasn't part of a dream. I sit up, looking about for any signs of threats. Birds have begun to wake, their quiet songs just beginning to ring through the trees.

Crisp leaves crackle as they roll by, pushed by an increasing wind. The cold gathers around, forcing its way in through gaps in my cloak, causing my skin to shudder in response.

Ayleth is awake, sitting up, legs crisscrossed in front of her under her cloak. Her eyes are on me, watching calmly as I struggle to sit up against the sleep clinging to my bones and the urgent whispers that are dissipating with wakefulness. "Did you hear that?" I ask.

She says nothing. Instead, she looks over her shoulder as I hold my breath in anticipation.

The breeze picks up. Isobel jumps to her feet, angling her ear to the wind as the trees sway above us. Her eyes widen. She taps Josef and Katherine, turning to face the same direction Ayleth is looking.

"What is it?" Though I'm trying my hardest, straining my ears for the message I know is there, I can't hear anything.

Isobel's brows furrow. She looks to Josef, who turns away, shoulders low and head down.

Katherine is beside me in an instant, and Isobel addresses her.

"You'll ride with the queen."

The queen? It's been far too long since Isobel has referred to me by my title. I grab her wrist as she turns away from me. "Tell me!"

She tries to look away, but three riders burst into view. Their horses run at a demanding pace as they spot us and turn toward our direction.

All around us, knights shove to their feet, certain of an attack. I reach for my sword, pulling my belt about my waist, but Isobel's hand on my wrist stops me from drawing. Concern pinches her eyes. She tries to hold my gaze. Still, it's drawn to the approaching riders. "You won't need that, Malory."

Suddenly, I know. These are no knights nor vagabonds who mean us trouble. I watch as they grow nearer, the deep blue of Allondale evident under the cloak of one of the riders. The other two are likely from Fairlee accompanying their new ally. I will this moment to stop: the horses slowing, the men elevated slightly above the saddles, their unspoken message forever trapped on their tongues.

But I have no such power. *Albati, goddess of love, I implore you to intervene on my behalf. Stop these men, make their message a mistaken one. Let Jamis live.* I look to the sky, gray again in the relentless grip of a winter that refuses to cede.

A tiny hand slips into mine, and Ayleth peers up. Her eyes are wise beyond years, and she nods once as the horses draw in front of me. The riders command them to stop as heavy breaths burst from the animals.

I step forward, chin up, hands clenched at my waist. I pull the High Queen's countenance firmly about me to conceal my quivering fears behind the practiced performance of royal countenance. Fear and grief churn inside. If these men deliver the words I fear they bring, I will crumble under their weight right here in front of everyone. And I will not apologize. Losing Jamis won't just cause me to show weakness, it will *be* my weakness. Everything I have accomplished, everything I've become, is because of Jamis—if he is gone, I can't bear the thought.

The man in the blue tunic kicks one foot over the horse and slides to his feet in front of me, then drops to one knee, head bowed. "Your Majesty."

The other riders follow suit, bending before me even though I am not their queen, as Fairlee has no ruler. I recognize this as a show of respect—for Jamis or me, I don't know.

I take a deep breath. "What news?"

He stands, reluctance slowing his tongue and drawing his eyes from mine. He focuses instead on Ayleth as he relays the message. "The king has taken a turn, Your Majesty. He isn't expected to last long."

A burning pain drives into my chest, clutching at my heart and driving the breath from my lungs. My lips part, trying to draw air into my body, to inhale through the pain, but the muscles required to draw in breath stutter, refusing to cooperate. I double over as an ache explodes throughout my chest, pain and numbness battling for dominion over my body.

Ayleth's tiny hand falls from my grip as my knees quiver. Someone is beside me, their arm weaving over my back and around my waist, preventing me from falling. I'm bolstered against their body, giving me the moment I need to regain control. "Ye need to go, Mal. Ye don''ave much time."

I stand, nodding though I can't make sense of any words and couldn't verbalize them in any case.

I look at the crowd gathered about me as Josef leads me to a horse. My allies and knights regard me, eyes wide with sympathy. Fury tries to quicken in my heart. I don't want to be pitied. That would mean that the message is correct, that Jamis is dying, and I can't have that. I won't stand for it—can't stand for that to be true. Josef holds the horse and assists me to mount. "Come with me," I beg. I have no strength for this; I cannot bear this burden alone.

"Katherine's with ye. I'll be along as soon as I can. Tell him—" He grimaces, unable to find an accurate message for the friend he's had since boyhood. He shakes his head and steps back.

"Your Majesty?" The Allondalian knight is back on his horse and eager to ride.

Katherine angles her horse alongside mine. "We need to go, Malory."

I look at the knight and nod, casting one last glance at the troops before I drive my heels into my horse's belly and offer a commanding, "Ha."

The horse leaps into pace, and I cling, leaning forward against the wind, falling into rhythm with the motion of the great roan animal. Within minutes, we are angling through the forest, the horses deftly weaving a path through the trees.

Each hour that we ride, Jamis feels even farther away from me. I grow more convinced he will pass before I've had the chance to see him one last time. Desperation gripss me, and I drive the poor horse to go faster, although she's certainly already met her limit. Although I understand when we need to stop to rest the horses and let them drink, the lost progress is nearly unbearable.

My mind reaches out, trying to send Jamis messages to wait for me while also running a constant stream of prayers through my mind to Nithenia and Albati. I include the other gods in my prayers as well: Rūvolo, Liræmor, and Kūbialus. Each the patrons of bravery, masculinity, wars, and men in their own way, certainly one recognizes the strength and honor in Jamis and will intercede on his behalf. I even offer a prayer to Nemii, because if death has come for Jamis, I will gladly offer my allegiance to any god who opposes death, including Nemii.

It's dusk before I smell the permeating scent of campfire drifting among the trees, and we angle hard to the north. Within minutes, I see the first signs of camp. It feels as though it's been months since I left.

I draw my horse short at the tent and leap from her back, running to the doorway. But Laila appears and I smack directly into her, both of us nearly tumbling to the ground.

I push past her, but she clings to my arms. "Malory, stop! Listen."

I shove her, trying to break her grip, tears burning at my eyes. "Is he— I have to see—"

The tent is dark, silence hovering in the air. Jamis is lying in bed, blankets heaped upon him, his gray skin damp with perspiration, dark hair pasted to his forehead.

Florie is seated beside him. She seems startled as I barrel into the small space, but not so that she doesn't scold me. "Hush! He's sleeping."

A cry leaps from my chest as I drop to my knees beside him. I reach under the blankets and grasp his hand, dropping my head to his chest. The tears flow, fear I wouldn't see him alive again turning to liquid relief and pouring from my eyes. "I'm here," I whisper. "I'm here, and I'm never leaving you again."

Laila brings a stool for me, and I sit beside Jamis to observe him. None of his breaths go unobserved, particularly the raspy sound as he draws each new breath. Despite the perspiration moistening his ashen skin, his lips are dry and cracked. "He needs water," I whisper to Laila, looking about the tent for something to offer.

She shakes her head, pity filling her eyes as she responds. "He rarely wakes. We can't give him water if he isn't awake to swallow."

"It isn't the water." Florie's voice is biting, uninterested in coddling my denial of Jamis's condition. "It's an infection. It's too deep to drain, and it's spread. We can only keep him comfortable."

"Florie—" Laila's voice is beseeching, her sweet nature coming out again. She wants to comfort me, to let me have some hope, even though she knows it's misplaced.

"I won't lie to her. Queen or no, she needs to face the truth. No gods are intervening." Florie emphasizes the point by drawing her brows up and nodding pointedly toward me.

They didn't answer me, but they've let Florie know. And she's as in tune to them as I am.

"Jamis..." My voice is low, but I won't be silenced any longer. I won't have him die without knowing I'm by his side. "Jamis, I'm here, my love."

I sit beside him, telling him everything I'd hoped to. I detail my time in Gaufrid, that King Carolus is my father, and that we've secured four hundred additional forces. I relay every detail of the invasion of Carling and how I killed Roarke. His breathing is slower, as though he's listening, so I continue.

"Phoebe is on her way to Travión, but with Queen Filomena and Oliver in our control, we may have a chance. I'll trail her to Travión if I have to. We *will* reclaim the High Crown, Jamis. I will make sure you wear it again."

Laila joins in, periodically asking questions in a hushed voice. "What about Henry?"

"Weaver Arionde led the troops who were to invade Devlishire. If he finds him, he'll bring him to us."

"What are you going to do with Queen Filomena? We can't keep her in a camp."

She's right, and it's something I've been mulling over. "We have to open the towers in Allondale. We'll put them to use housing prisoners."

"When will you go back? To Allondale?"

I squeeze Jamis's hand and brush a stray lock of hair from his brow. The gold-spun highlights in his dark hair are harsher now, brassy. "When Jamis is ready."

"Malory," she cautions.

"Not now, Laila. Give me this."

She nods and slips from the tent. I stoke the fire, removing my heavy cloak as the heat from the fire effectively warms the small space. The fire and my exhaustion conspire against me, and I feel dizzy from the heat, lack of food, and constant battery of events. I pull my gloves off and unbutton my gown to dab at my perspiration, lest I later catch a chill. At some point in the night, just as I'm about to give in to sleep, Jamis stirs. His voice croaks, "I knew you'd back, My Queen."

A joyful cry escapes me as I lean down to kiss him. "I'm sorry to have taken so long."

His smile is weak, his eyes rolling under half lids as though he's drunk too much wine. "You're here."

"Yes," I whisper.

"Did Carolus agree?"

Sighing, I relay all that's happened since I left. I begin with Carolus sending the troops and how we invaded Carling. "We are still waiting for the troops that invaded Devlishire to join up with our troops. But our friends are safe."

He nods, pleased though he doesn't have the energy to verbalize it. When he reaches a hand to cup my cheek, I press my shoulder and cheek to his hand, trapping it against me long enough to lock the feeling into my mind. I've missed his touch, the warmth, and the love that Jamis gives me is like nothing I've experienced before. Despite the rough roads we've endured on our journey, we came together and have proven to be each other's greatest allies and most loyal champions.

"You are so brave and beautiful," he says before he grows too weak to hold my hand any longer. When his arm quavers, I grasp his hand between mine, holding it to my chest.

"I am brave for you and because of you," I whisper, leaning to kiss him. His lips are dry and rough against my own, heated with the flames of a thousand fires. I look deep into his eyes as I pull away, the gold flecks no longer sparkling. They are only flecks of light color against brown. Around the irises, the whites have dulled to the color of aged parchment.

His gaze travels from my eyes, to my face, lingers on my mouth, which he reaches for, his thumb brushing along my lower lip. His gaze then travels down, following the path of my neck to my chest.

His brows pinch, and he lifts his head. Reaching his hand out, he hooks a finger at my neckline, pulling at my gown. "What is that?"

I sit back sharply and gasp, embarrassed to have been so careless. Heat floods across my skin as I stammer. At some point, I would have had to explain the mark. At some point, Jamis would have seen it, but I'd never even considered how I would tell him—or how he would react. "A—a tattoo." I draw the neck of my gown down farther, letting him see the entirety of it. "It's Nithenia."

My heart slams against my chest as his eyes pass over the symbol etched into my skin. His jaw pulses, and his eyes narrow beneath his brows as they draw tightly together. "Who did it?"

The answer catches in my throat. "Josef."

Jamis rolls his head away from me. I reach for his arm, trying desperately to explain myself. "It's only a symbol of bravery, Jamis. It doesn't mean anything more than that."

Eyes averted, he speaks quietly, but his tone carries a dangerous edge. "I know what it's a symbol of. And you're wrong, Malory. It means everything. More than you'll ever understand."

He's wrong; it's only a tradition. It means nothing more than a Fairlean finds me brave. *Then why didn't I tell him? Why does shame burn through me when I think of Josef's hand brushing against my skin as he marked me?*

I say nothing. I can only sit silently in shame until he falls asleep again.

It's early in the morning when a din arises across the camp. I stand at the entry to the tent and watch as hundreds of warriors on horseback pour into camp. Kennard, Davion, Josef, and Isobel each ride with a knight of Gaufrid and dismount before the horses have come to a complete stop.

Josef seeks me out and holds my gaze until I turn from him, ashamed to have even entertained paying any attention to his return while my husband lies dying only yards away.

Someone hands Ayleth to Kennard as he passes, headed directly for me—and his king. He eases her to the ground as stops in front of me, Davion and Isobel joining him. I shrug, unable to say the words, and step aside so they can pass and pay respects to their king, their ally, their friend.

Josef is loosening a saddle belt. Katherine approaches and says something I can't hear. She places a soft hand on his shoulder, and he nods and turns away. I watch as he disappears into the trees, once again walking away from Jamis. And now, when Jamis needs him most.

"Your Majesty?" Kennard's voice cracks as he approaches, and my heart shatters.

"He's only spoken once since I got here." Shame heats my core at what happened when he woke. I can never admit to them that Jamis awoke only to discover I'd let another man mark me. Even if it was intended as a mark of bravery, Jamis didn't see it as such. Perhaps he'd have taken it differently had he been present to take part in the decision.

Our friends join me at Jamis's bedside throughout the night. Only Josef is missing, and I'm conflicted. I want him to be here for his friend, to show his support and loyalty. But I also don't want Jamis to have many reminders of my tattoo, of the fact that Josef gave it to me. *You're ridiculous*, I chastise myself. *It's just a Fairlean tradition. It meant no more than when Katherine received hers.* But the shame that swells up every time I think of it tells me it was more.

In the early morning, Isobel slips from the tent. Within minutes I hear her voice as she sings a song to the forest. I can't hear the words, but I imagine she is asking for mercy for Jamis, be it life or painless death.

"Your Majesty." The low voice of Sir Walter, Grandmaster of Allondale, reaches me from just outside the tent. He shuffles his feet when I wave him in, obviously resistant to enter. I squeeze Jamis's hand and tuck it under the blankets. Katherine assumes my position beside Jamis as I duck through the tent opening to face the knight.

"What is it?"

"It's about the Queen, Your Majesty." His ruddy complexion is bright pink in the cold morning air, his white hair so thin that it barely masks the skin beneath. He hooks a thumb in the direction of a large boulder, upon which Queen Filomena is perched.

Her cloak is pulled tightly around her tiny frame, the hood pulled low, concealing her unkempt hair. She sits with her hands clasped in her lap, shoulders back and chin high. She is a queen, despite her circumstances.

What am I going to do with her?

Her expression is calm as we near her. "I apologize, Your Majesty. I wasn't prepared to host a royal prisoner. I'll ensure a tent is secured for you until we can transport you to Allondale, where you will be properly housed."

Filomena offers a nod. "I am at your will, My Queen. I shall be grateful for whatever kindness you bestow on me."

I don't like having a royal defer to my own rule. It feels far too awkward. This is more than having the title of High Queen. She is declaring me *her* queen. It's far too great a responsibility and far too great a target.

Arrangements are made for Queen Filomena to have a tent—and an entire troop of guards. But I can't house her in a tent for long. "Where is Mereck de Grey?"

Sir Walter points to the fire. There, listening to a band of warriors argue about the best methods for separating a man from his head, sits the diminutive treasurer of Allondale. He's seated on a fallen tree amid the men, his head rotating from one side to the other as he listens intently to each speaker. His eyes are wide and his open grin evident that in his mind, he's right there on the field taking part in some glorious battle with his own sharpened blade, not simply hearing the tales. I approach and wait quietly as the conversation dwindles, then clear my throat to get his attention.

"Ahem."

He leaps to his feet and drops into a bow. His brilliantly colored tunic has dulled from months of nomadic living, but unlike many of his counterparts, he has yet to adopt the more functional wardrobe of the Fairleans. "Your Majesty."

"I need your assistance, Mr. De Grey."

He nods, eager for someone to make use of his talents.

"You're to take two hundred of the knights from Gaufrid and return to Allondale. The towers are to be opened and prepared to house royal prisoners and guests of Allondale. Ensure the chambers within the tower residences are properly furnished. Queen Filomena is a guest of Allondale, but she isn't free to be from her chambers unless accompanied by guards. Do you understand?"

"Yes."

"I want you to begin renovations with the towers first to ensure the wall is sound. The loss of any prisoners will be inexcusable. Those who cannot tend to the repairs of the tower and wall are to be used to replant the fields. The animals are to be brought back to pasture, and the villagers informed it's safe to return to their fields. It will be an effort for all of us to ensure Allondale is restored and prepared to serve as the seat of the High Crown one day. All knights of Allondale are to return to the castle unless they are on a mission with or at the orders of the king or myself. Then you can solicit masons to repair the kitchens and the chapel."

"And the castle, Your Majesty?"

My heart gallops at the thought of returning to the castle I shared with Jamis. We fled in the dark of the night when my brother's and King Lester's men invaded us. After the Battle of Allondale, we stood outside the gates, watching as smoke danced along with the tattered remnants of our home. But we've never been able to bring ourselves closer than that. After all that happened, Allondale no longer felt safe, no longer felt like a retreat. There was too much left to do, too many scores to settle before we could find comfort there again. And now Jamis may never return.

"Do what you will with it." I spin on my heels and head back for the tent.

I'm surprised to find Josef just stepping from the tent. His eyes are red, swollen, and his expression pained.

"Has he—"

He reaches for me. "No, he's awake."

I push past him, driving my palms into his chest, "What did you say to him?"

"I said nothin', Mal. Nothin' he don't already know."

The fire crackles. The orange glow from the stone hearth can't chase away the pallor from Jamis's skin. He holds a hand out for me as I enter.

I clutch it to my chest for only a second before lowering it to my abdomen, unwilling to remind him of what lies under my gown, what's seared forever into my skin.

"Get him some water," I command Florie, who sends me a withering glare, but complies, handing me a carved bowl no larger than my palm. It holds only a small bit of water, no more than would fit in one cupped hand, but it's far more than Jamis can tolerate. He takes one sip, swallowing hard and grimacing at the pain it causes him.

"Try another," I encourage, slipping my arm under his shoulders to ease him up for a better angle. He sputters against the liquid, his coughing the only thing that's brought any color to his cheeks. The redness dissipates with the passing cough. He pushes my hand away, struggling to regain his breath.

I ease the cup to the floor, setting it beside my feet. Tears burn at my eyes, the shadow of guilt I've been just ahead of since the day I came to Jamis hitting with full force. I entered his life intent on robbing him of the High Crown for my father's benefit. The shadow threatening to encroach on my happiness since I vowed to stand beside him finally eclipses me. The treachery of Devlishire is fully realized now, and Jamis is about to fall victim. A tear rolls over my lashes, its warm path following the rises and hollows of my face until it drops from my jaw onto our clutched hands. "I'm sorry. For everything. I failed you."

A weak smile pulls at his mouth, and he shakes his head once. He pulls his hand from mine, trying to reach for my face, but the effort is too great for him to endure. "You did everything. *We* did everything—*together.*"

Jamis's eyes redden, and moisture gathers. A sob escapes me, and I turn my head. I don't want him to think I've given up on him.

"Malory." His voice crackles against his dry throat, fighting to be heard. "This was always going to be. I've known for years. I fought it—" He's drifting, his lids fluttering, body growing lax. With a deep breath, he jolts awake again, or as close to awake as he can be. He starts again as though he never stopped. "—wanted to be there. But...sf...l...*love*...vr..." He nods as though making a definitive point, but I can't decipher the jumbled words.

Love, he said love. I drop to my knees, whispering in his ear. "I love you, Jamis of Allondale. Now and forever. I love you, My King." Sobs erupt from the tent. Perhaps it's me sobbing, but I don't know, and I don't dare stop whispering to him.

Footsteps scuff throughout the tent, followed by whispers and more urgent steps. Jamis's breaths slow, every few breaths stuttering as he draws in. Soon, the breaths are slower, each one more difficult.

Laila approaches the opposite side of the bed, lifting the blankets aside. "What are you doing?" I demand.

"Looking at his skin color." Her eyes are wide under furrowed brows, and her lips pressed tight—the only answer I need. I stand, drawing my sword from my belt. It takes all the dignity I can muster to walk the three paces to the end of Jamis's cot. I kneel, lower my head, and lay my sword at his feet. "Please, gods, be with him, guide him into Elyphesus and secure him a seat at the table of warriors. Assure him a kingdom amongst you that befits a king of such honor and esteem."

I stand, though the ache in my chest threatens to drive me to the ground. The cavity in me threatens to expand until I am fully engulfed in emptiness.

Kennard steps around me and kneels, placing his sword beside mine. Davion, Isobel, and Katherine follow. I try to stand tall, but my body is weakening, unwilling to bear this grief. When I sway, Kennard moves beside me. With one arm around my back, he supports me as a procession of Fairleans and knights of Allondale pay their respects and leave behind their weapons.

Resigned sadness taints Ayleth's blue eyes as she lays her small dagger at Jamis's feet before running from the tent.

"Someone should see to her," I whisper.

"She'll be fine," Isobel replies. I'm shocked at the callous comment. Does she not realize Ayleth is just a girl? That she may be frightened?

I retake my place on the stool at Jamis's side. Only those closest to us remain, sitting vigil as their friend and ally slowly dies in front of them. Exhaustion claims us slowly. First, Isobel and Katherine collapse against each other, then Davion—sitting beside the fire—drops his head in sleep. Kennard has been standing sentry at Jamis's head, and his own head drops once. I fear he may collapse on Jamis. He shakes his head, resuming his guard.

Darkness takes hold throughout Fairlee once again, and a heavy silence descends in the tent. Even the sound of the fire fails to penetrate the ominous silence. I wipe a hand over Jamis's marbled cheek. It is cool and damp. I focus on his face, absorbing every detail of him and locking them into my memory. My breath stutters behind a cry as I try to hear his voice only to find it's already fading. I want to shake him, demand him to wake up one more time to tell me he loves me. And I want the opportunity to tell him the same. Despite the doubts that lingered so long in my mind, I really do love him—I've come to love him even though I may not have come to it easily.

Yells erupt from outside the tent, along with a clattering sound, though I can't decipher where it's coming from. I glance at Kennard, then cast my eyes to the door, an order for him to check it out.

As he steps through the entry to the doorway, there's a thud and an *Oomph*, followed by another thud.

"Get out o' me way." Josef's voice carries a threat I'm not sure he can carry out if directed at Kennard.

"You're drunk," Kennard growls. "Sleep it off."

Josef's whisper carries in on a light breeze, finding a path through the dense silence. "There's no time. Is there?"

I hear a deep sigh before Josef enters the tent, Kennard on his heels. Josef's head hangs low. He glances from under the hair that's fallen across his brow, then looks to Jamis. He steps behind me, studying the pile of swords at Jamis's feet before dropping to his knee and adding his own. Josef's shoulders heave, his sobs echoing in the tent.

I watch him from the corner of my eye for a moment before I turn my attention back to Jamis. His lids lift slightly and my heart surges, thinking he's awakening again, but the irises remain still behind his lids, unmoving and unseeing.

"No!" I shake him gently, my animal mind thinking if I just jostle him, he'll remember to breathe. "Jamis!" I shake him again, but there is no response.

He draws no more life into his body. The silence that's hovered for hours drifts away, taking with it my husband's life.

I drop to my knees and lay across him, my head on his chest and arms around him as I sob until exhaustion finally claims me. Then, Kennard lifts me from my husband's lifeless body and carries me away.

CHAPTER
NINETEEN

WE BURY JAMIS JUST BEYOND THE WALL OF Allondale. His body is placed overlooking the lake beneath the tree where he first kissed me, the one he once told me he'd sat under for three days as a boy.

Villagers, knights, and Fairleans gather as he's laid to rest under the canopy of trees. Pink blossoms dot the delicate branches, as though the trees themselves are welcoming their king home and embracing his eternal rest.

As bolstered as I am that so many people have come to pay their respects, I'm also awash in bitterness. For all my life, the passing of kings was met with the respect of the others. Knights were dispatched, and the Conclave of Kings held to show respect for the fallen sovereign.

But for Jamis, nobody has been dispatched. There is no consolation from the other kings. Jamis was the first king in over a hundred years to give his life in defense of the Unification of our seven kingdoms, and he will pass into history with no commemoration. There isn't even a scribe to note his accomplishments into a book for future generations to read. The reign of Allondalian blood has ended.

I've no more tears to spare as Jamis's body is interred in the land he was born to and died defending. I am flesh stretched tightly across a gaping void. My mind no longer functions. I can't decide if I am distraught, brave, or angry. I feel them all and nothing at once.

Katherine's voice is hesitant. "Will you stay in Allondale?"

The castle looms behind me. I keep my back to it, though I can feel it's pull. Taunting me with memories of times when I assumed my life to be troubled and dangerous. How little I knew then. How carefree those early days in Allondale truly were compared to what has come to pass.

"No. I'll stay here. With him."

Katherine stammers. "H-here? F-for how long?"

"Until I'm ready to leave him." I walk nearer, standing at the foot of Jamis's grave as the last of the earth is replaced.

The grave diggers bow as they walk away, heads down, uneasy being responsible for such a somber moment in the kingdom.

I kneel at Jamis's grave and run the tips of my fingers over the freshly turned soil, imagining he can feel my touch.

Sir Walter takes one knee beside me, clearing his throat. "Your Majesty, certainly you'd be more comfortable in the castle. You'll be near enough to look over h—"

My voice is venomous, and I make no effort to stifle it. "I will remain right here. Perhaps those of you who would be more comfortable in the palace should go. Please feel free to take my old chambers. But I will remain here until I am prepared to walk away."

"Y-yes, Your Majesty." He rises and steps backward, remaining beside those who have taken up guard around me. It's only moments until he walks away, in the direction of the path that will lead him from the lake to the comfort of the castle.

I don't turn to pay attention to anyone else. I focus all my energy on Jamis, reaching out with my mind. I imagine him being welcomed into Elyphesus. Nithenia's recent silence explained by her need to adequately welcome a brave king and warrior.

I close my eyes and lie on the cool soil as I embrace the vision of the warrior goddess, her porcelain skin in contrast with her deep wine-colored locks, in tightly woven tendrils, pulled away from her face. Brilliant blue eyes shining from under black lids that seem to emit deep plumes of smoke and the slightest hint of flames as she blinks. Her deep-cut gown, the color of which gives the impression that it's simply an extension of her hair, gathered at her waist by a belt of diamond arrows. Nithenia—as she was portrayed in my book *The Wars of Gods and Men*—reaches through the mist, into the great between, and grasps Jamis's hand. He's making his way through, trying to orient himself to his new world, his just rewards.

The sun descends, and nobody approaches me. Kennard, Josef, and Davion take turns standing guard at the head of Jamis's grave as I remain there, unmoving. Unwilling to walk away from him, I lie on the fresh soil, dwelling in my sorrows and clinging to each last moment I'll ever spend with him.

Katherine and Isobel alternate trying to coerce me into drinking or eating, but I don't feel it if I'm hungry. I only feel the gaping space that Jamis occupied in my life.

As determined as I am to escape reality and linger on the edges of the world with and the world without Jamis, the cold bites into my skin. The trees covering the grounds of Allondale don't offer the same coverage as those in Fairlee, and the wind whips about, burning at my ears and cheeks.

Nearby, Kennard has gathered firewood, and the promise of warmth—and perhaps companionship, silent though it may be, draws me from the freshly turned soil. We are near enough I can continue to oversee Jamis's grave. What is my fear exactly? That someone will disrupt his grave or that by leaving it, I will relegate Jamis to an echo of my past like so many others?

Kennard barely acknowledges me as I ease into place beside the fire. He passes me a skin of water without a word, and I wonder if this is at Katherine's direction. Soon, he's pulled bread and dried meat from his pack, and the days of being without food causes my body to take over. I eat as though I'll never stop, filling the void in my body with crusty bread and salted meat.

The silence that exists between Kennard and me has always been slightly awkward, our initial interactions difficult to overcome. But he has always been loyal to Jamis, and Jamis is what brought us together. Even the awkward distance between us has become comfortable.

But with Jamis gone, can I expect Kennard to remain aligned? Doesn't Kennard have his own life—one that was denied him as a boy and young man—his own desires he'd like to address? How can I hold him to a duty he didn't willingly choose? Especially when he still so clearly yearns to find I'awn. I can't deny him that freedom. Kennard isn't obligated to remain in my service.

I clear my throat. Swallowing past the bubble of emotion and dry bread, I say, "I know my father thought you under his control, and he treated you as property to be traded."

Kennard eyes me wearily from an angle, one eye constricted as my soft words flutter between us before being carried across Lake Allondale on a breeze, but he says nothing.

"I also know you were loyal to Jamis, not to me." I gulp against a surprising swell of emotion that gathers in my throat. "You aren't beholden to me—or anyone—any longer. You're free to go. I release you of any duty to Allondale or Devlishire."

He nods as he turns his attention back to the small fire. "I never imagined I'd hear anyone say those words."

Silence settles between us for several minutes, but it lacks the uneasy quality of our previous encounters. Perhaps only *I* ever felt the awkwardness, and, now, having extended freedom to him, I feel more at ease with myself. Perhaps it was me all along who was the awkward one. Me and my privileged lack of awareness for those who were indentured to the crown.

Kennard finally breaks the silence as he stands, brushing the dirt and flakes of dried leaves from his trousers. "I'll take your freedom. No man in his right mind would refuse that."

I chance a glance as he stretches, peering into the darkness beyond our small fire. The idea of Kennard leaving so soon after Jamis pulls at my chest, tightening it further. My eyes burn anew with fresh tears, but I blink them away. I'll cry for nothing and nobody else. How can I even have the tears left in my body to so? Inhaling a deep breath, I prepare to watch him walk away.

Kennard turns as he adjusts the belt at his waist so his sword hangs properly beneath his cloak. "I *was* loyal to His Majesty. I admired him, and he deserves to be avenged—as does I'awn. So, I'm staying—at least until the Beasts are brought to their knees."

I offer a grateful smile, but my jaw quivers, threatening to disobey my vow not to cry again. Instead, I nod in acceptance of his decision and drop my head to my chest, hugging myself against so much loss and gratitude.

Kennard resumes his position at the head of Jamis's grave. But the days of uncertainty and sadness finally catch up with the giant of a man. He soon sits at the base of the tree that hangs over the grave, and though he remains upright, his body leans against the tree base and his lids engage in a slow descent until sleep has fully engulfed him.

I stoke the fire as Kennard's breaths slow into a rhythmic pattern. Through the low-hanging budded branches, the castle looms dark against a gray feathered sky. Pinpoint lights sparkle across the night above thin clouds as though Omnilus himself had commanded they be lit to guide Jamis to the great kingdom of Elyphesus.

I stand and walk a few steps away from the orange glow of the fire until the darkness surrounds me and the stars sparkle more brightly.

Fixing my eyes on the sky, I reach with all my senses as Isobel taught me, extending beyond my body. I feel Jamis's presence on the air—perhaps only because I'm willing it to be there. Perhaps there is nothing at all but my overactive imagination. I stride deeper into the trees. The sound of the lake lapping at the shoreline dominates, its rhythm seeping into my body, relaxing my muscles.

My voice is small in the vast dark. "Nithenia, I am your loyal servant. I implore you to welcome Jamis of Allondale into Elyphesus. He's an honorable king and brave warrior, beloved by his people. He is a king among kings, and he would be a loyal champion in the service of the goddess of war and bravery."

As the last words drift from my lips, brightness surges throughout the sky. From the corner of my eye, a bright light shoots across the horizon from over my shoulder, where Jamis lies to the southern ridge of the Gates of Tiernan, the mountainous region that surrounds Tiernan and long ago was rumored to be the path to Elyphesus. A spear of joy shoots through me. I do not doubt that light was the ascent of Jamis into the great beyond, beckoned by Nithenia and destined to serve at her side. I ease to my knees. With my finger, I begin to draw the symbol of the Great Goddess into the damp soil. I stop, remembering I now carry the symbol at all times. With a soft pat of my fingertips over my heart, I whisper to the great goddess, "Thank you, Nithenia."

Though I'm certain I'll mourn Jamis for the rest of my life, some of my sadness has been lifted with the certainty he's now being welcomed by the gods—and perhaps being greeted again by Esmond—in Elyphesus.

I survey the dark shadow of the castle. It no longer seems as foreboding, merely an empty shell that used to house hope and opportunity. Curiosity and determination overcome me, and I make my way through the canopy of trees, around the wall, and to the gates that lead into Jamis's castle—*my* castle now, though it still bears the deep wounds of the assault that was waged against it.

The portcullis has been lifted again, and two knights flank the entry. They startle as I approach, drawing their weapons. "Halt!" one orders. On the battlements, other knights peer over with arrows drawn and sites trained on me.

I lift my hands, but the words don't come right away. Do I want this? Am I ready to return? To claim Allondale as my own? My gaze sweeps over the men. Their eyes are hard, but the longer I stand without speaking, the more nervous they grow, uncertainty making them dangerous. My breath hitches as I draw it in to make my proclamation.

"I am Queen Malory, the true High Queen of the Unified Kingdoms. The sole sovereign of Allondale. This is my land, and you are holding your queen in your sights. You will only be forgiven this error once."

They release their weapons, the knights at the gate dropping to one knee with their heads bowed.

I clasp my hands at my waist. Despite my filthy, torn gown and muddy men's boots, I assume a regal countenance. "Stand," I command.

The courtyard is dark. Two small fires and several well-placed torches provide enough light that I can see men sleeping in clusters across the grounds. One of the guards seems uncertain what his role is when met with a returning sovereign. I wish I could offer him an idea, but I don't know any better myself. I'm acting on impulse.

"Tell me who is within the grounds and where."

He informs me that repairs have begun on the towers and wall. The masons and villagers—as well as the knights from Allondale and Gaufrid—are distributed throughout the grounds to ensure it isn't overrun during refurbishments. Members of the court have also reclaimed their rooms within the southern wing of the castle.

"Shall I get someone to accompany you, Your Majesty?" Eagerness brightens his face, preventing my initial impulse to scoff at his offer. His intentions are noble, but this young knight has likely no idea the amount of danger I've been subjected to—and overcome. He may even be appalled that the rumors of my conflicts are often vastly underreported.

"It won't be necessary. Thank you." My steps are light, hesitant, as I make my way over the threshold and take my first look from within the grounds since the night we fled.

His whispered voice cuts through the air behind me. "Your Majesty."

I turn and squint against the sharp light of the torch the guard is offering. I thank him and turn away. I don't want to wake anyone, don't want to draw attention to my presence, I just want to drift through the halls like the ghost of my former self.

Following the path I was led when I returned to Allondale as a princess, I step into the grand entry hall. The white stone that makes up the castle's exterior has absorbed the cold outside and efficiently transferred it to the inner sanctum. The large fireplace that burned both for heat and light stands dark and unused, soot clinging to the mantle and wall above. Torches that once lined this passage hang unused from iron hooks. Faint scratches sound as small animals scurry past me in the dark hall, the light of my torch insignificant to illuminate them.

I move forward, torch held high in front of me, it's orange and yellow glow dancing across the shadowed masonry. The inner castle's gray stone casts a dark pall around me, providing the ghosts of castle life more shadows to hide among.

The Queen's Suite is easy to find. The massive doors, twice my height, stand open, one askew on its hinges. The interior of the suite has been tossed about. Gone is the extravagant chamber that each new bride to Allondale has been brought to, the impeccably decorated suite in which I first discovered that instead of one day ascending to the throne of Devlishire, I had been promised to the new king of Allondale—Jamis. Most importantly, that I was to be used to destroy his claim of the High Crown.

The floor sparkles in my torchlight with the remnants of the crystal vases, bowls, and windows that once looked over the now-destroyed pristine private garden.

In the bedroom, I find the mattress has been turned from the bed and slashed, along with the bedding, which lies in tatters throughout the rooms. Two of the engraved posts from the bed have been hacked away and lie in the fireplace, nearly charred but still recognizable. "Monsters," I whisper as I continue, surveying the damage done by the invading troops in the short time they controlled the castle.

The Great Hall has suffered similar damage. Tables and benches lie strewn about the room, some stacked as though used to barricade the entries. Tapestries of the rulers of Allondale have been marred, some slashed while others bear the remnants of food thrown at them. Outside the Great Hall, the walls are scorched. An obvious attempt was made to burn the castle from the inside.

Tapestries and furniture are piled and charred by the flames that failed to catch.

In the throne room, most of the tapestries have been stripped from the walls. The thrones lie in fragments on the dais, their velvet cushions slashed, and the strong stench of urine permeates the pile. Had the invading soldiers relieved themselves on the pile before they set the fire, or as it burned?

I turn from the destruction, unsure if I can take any more or if I should flee this horrible remnant immediately. I gasp at the image that greets me on the opposite wall. With tentative steps, I inch closer, my free hand covering my gaping mouth as my eyes travel across the sole charred tapestry that still hangs from the walls. It is—or rather was—a massive representation of Jamis and me, highlighting our separate lives and then in the center our union. The detail and craftsmanship had stunned me when it was presented to us in celebration of our wedding. It was a gift from the king and queen of Claxton, and my first clue that Claxton was conspiring with my father. It was also my first clue that the plan to marry me off had been in place for at least a month longer than I was aware of the intent to destroy Jamis's rule.

Most of the gold and brightly colored threads have been burned. Dark, charred material hangs in limp tatters from the edges. But most shocking of all is that right in the center, where Jamis and I were once represented as ethereal and regal with sparkling, jeweled crowns and enveloped by soft light from the heavens, now only my scorched image remains. In the absence of Jamis's image, the expression on my face is no longer one of a benevolent and regal queen, but the piercing gaze of an accusatory woman with a plan for retribution. I shudder at the image, so representative of the person at my core, the girl evolved into a blood-thirsty warrior.

Don't let doubt fill you now—don't turn away. They created this in you. The whispers fill my head, but this time I welcome them, for they speak the truth. I haven't become this—they've created me. And now they will get that which they wrought upon the lands. The bangle hidden beneath my sleeve seems to pulse. I was certain when I first slid it on my arm that this was a fabled Nithenian bangle. And I'm even more certain now that Nithenia has been with me, guiding and guarding me ever since.

She isn't the only one, mortal. Though it's indistinct, I recognize the energy and tone of the voice. It's the one that contacted me in the tent that night, the one that drew Florie in. But once again, the others swarm to drown out the voice—perhaps demanding their messages be heard, though I can no longer distinguish one from the others.

Indecipherable whispers accompany me as I move from the throne room through a secret passageway into the anteroom between Jamis's chambers and my own. I push open the door to my chambers and am surprised to find them relatively undisturbed since the night Allondale was invaded. The nightgown that Katherine threw on my bed before slipping a dress over my head still lies in a crumpled heap next to the cloak Sarah Bainard left behind when we fled from the chambers.

Frost clings to the remaining windows, and my breath bursts in the air in front of me. The gaping hole in the wall remains along with the rubble of the mason work and boulder that had been launched over the wall.

Jamis's chamber is untouched. It escaped any damage from the initial assault or the troops that invaded the interior. The screen remains in place, hiding the secret door I fled through with my ladies so many months ago.

I lift the tapestry that conceals the door, then slip into the king's passage and onto the balcony overlooking the rear of the castle across Lake Allondale and far to the east.

A goat bleats in the paddocks along the southern wall, and a dog in the distance responds. Aside from the livestock and a symphony of night creatures, there is no sound. I'm engulfed in total silence, and I embrace the chance to escape war and strategy and heartbreak for even a few moments.

I let my mind drift and settle into a calm state where neither grief nor vengeance exists. I simply observe with no other demands or expectations. Much the same as when I was simply a princess and heir to a throne. There were no true expectations of me. I did whatever inspired me at any given moment, with no regard for how it affected others, for rarely did it affect anyone else. I long for that simple life again, the opportunity to simply exist and have nobody die or fall to risk because of it.

Images of my easier life revisit me—Melaine laughing in the gardens, Esmond's mischievous twinkle as he taunted me during our sparring matches, Laila chasing butterflies through the gardens, and Jamis. The kindness with which he first greeted me, and

the joy with which he introduced me to Allondale were unexpect-
ed, as was the love I came to feel for him. But it was too late, wasn't
it? I didn't love him when I should have, nor did I love him as truly
as he deserved. A tear forms as guilt gathers in my chest, burning a
path from my heart deep into my lungs. Both Jamis and Esmond
died because they loved me and were loyal. But did I do enough to
protect them?

What if they could walk the earth again? The whisper is soft. I
startle, peering over my shoulder, certain that someone must be
standing directly behind me whispering in my ear.

"Impossible," I hiss, though hope swells in my chest. Is it impossible?

Your gods would have you think so, wouldn't they? Again, I look
about, certain someone must be lurking in the shadows, whispering this idea. If this isn't Nithenia, or her brother and sister gods,
who could it be? Perhaps I have truly gone mad.

"Which gods?" Although I'll pray to the gods of my choosing, I
haven't quite been so brave as to admit to just anyone that I adhere
to the long-forgotten gods. That the God of the Heavens and the
God of the Earth never rang within my soul.

*The gods of the falling kings, as well as your secret gods. They will
all tell you it's impossible, but I can give this to you. I can give them back
to you.*

My heart thunders. This is certainly blasphemy, no matter the
gods. Even the Elyphesian gods only offer a kingdom for great
warriors, never to return them to a place among the living. But if
Esmond and Jamis could return...

"Who are you?" I whisper into the dark.

*You will come, Malory. I am waiting. Waiting to rule the world
with you at—*

A scream erupts, accompanied by a shout, and the buzzing of
a thousand whispers fills my head, drowning out the solitary voice.
The noise is nearly intolerable, and I drop to my knees, clasping my
palms against my ears to keep the noise out. But it's no use. The
sounds are coming from within my head. They grow louder until
the pain becomes intolerable, my head threatening to explode to
release the sounds. I clench my eyes tightly and cry out, unable to
endure it any longer.

"Mal!" Josef drops beside me, pulling at my hands. "What's the
matter? Are ye hurt?"

I open my eyes. He's directly across from me, pain pinching his own face as he searches me for injury. I shake my head to deny injury, but I can't deny the pain and that something is very definitely wrong. The voices dwindle. *Did I imagine them?*

Good people are dying, and I'm the cause. Pain, guilt, and loss explode in me, and I sob. I attempt to cover my eyes and turn away, but Josef pulls me against his chest.

"Ye're all right," he whispers into my ear as he holds me to him. My own body gives up, collapsing into the comfort of someone else. I sob until I've expelled every last tear in my body, every tear I'm willing to give.

Josef stands, pulling me up with him, then swings my legs up. My head falls against his shoulder as he carries me through the darkened halls in the king's passage and into Jamis's chamber. He's careful as he lays me on the bed and pulls the blankets over me to shield me against the cold.

"Don't leave me," I say as he stands. "I don't want to be alone. I can't...can't stand to be."

He nods and sits on the bed beside me, leaning against the opposite bedpost. With one foot on the bed, the other on the floor, he keeps watch over me as I drift off.

A fire is crackling in the fireplace when I awaken. Through the windows, the sky is still dark, and Josef is exactly where he was when I fell asleep, but he's asleep, too.

I roll from my back to my side, and his eyes open. Offering a conciliatory smile, I whisper into the space between us. "I'm sorry."

"What've ye ta be sorry fer?" His voice is also soft, as though we're both afraid that to raise our voices any louder would disrupt the spirits that linger.

"I fell apart. I lost control."

"Ye couldn' help it, could ye?"

I fall into thought for only a few seconds before I utter my confession. "He's dead because of me."

Josef's face pinches, and he turns his head from me. When he turns back, his eyes are reddened, brow still pinched. "It wasn't because o'ye. There was always greater things at play than the High Crown or you. Jamis knew fer a long time that—" He shakes his head, falling into silence.

I push up so I'm leaning against the opposite post, angled so I can see Josef. "That what?"

He takes a deep breath. "Did he ever tell ye how we met?"

I shake my head.

"He was six when 'is mother died. His dad was deep in 'is own grief 'n 'ad no time fer comfortin' 'is son. So Jamis ran away, as far away as a young prince is willin' to venture anyway."

I recall the time Jamis mentioned having spent three days in a tree. At the time, I'd wondered what could make a young boy do that, but he didn't elaborate. "To the lake," I confirm.

Josef nods. "I was feelin' a bit brave m'self. I'd come into Allondale ta fish from the king's lake. I thought there must certainly be bigger fish in a *king's* lake, and they'd be easier to catch than the ones from the Great North Sea. T'was certainly easier to get to the lake than the sea."

I smile at the image in my mind of a young Jamis sitting in a tree while Josef fished nearby.

"He yelled, threatened ta send his dad's knights after me if I din't leave."

I smile. "What did you do?"

"Told him I'd outrun any knight 'nd that none of 'em would be brave enough to follow me into Fairlee even if they did catch up. He was surprised ta find I's from Fairlee. Suddenly, he was interested in me." He laughs at his memory.

"He told me 'is mother died and 'is father din't care about 'im. He did spend most of those three days in the tree. But then 'e came down and fer three more days we'd fish, and we talked long into the night. We used tree branches as swords and fought until our arms felt as though they'd fall from our bodies. At one point, 'e was convinced 'e was goin' ta' join me and live in Fairlee. He swore we'd be like brothers and we'd fight anyone who tried to enter."

"Why did he go back?"

"I told 'im that 'e had to. That 'e had a path 'e had to follow. 'Twas written long ago, 'nd although we might change the course fer a while, we'll always end up back on our true path. Jamis's path was ta be High King."

Anger lights through me. "Even if that meant he'd die?"

Josef considers me, but he doesn't answer.

"Are you saying that he knew all along he was going to die before his time?"

Josef nods once. "'Twas 'is time. Was always goin' ta be."

After I jump from the bed, I pace a few steps before I stalk over to where Josef sits. I tower over him, angry and challenging. This is madness. How can Josef sit there and tell me that Jamis knew—from boyhood—that he would die young and willingly went along that path? That Josef had done nothing to protect him.

"That's madness. And how dare *you* allow him to follow a path that would put him in danger. You were no friend at all if you let that happen."

Josef grimaces, averting my eyes. "There was no other path, Mal. I thought I was helpin' by tellin' 'im what would come ta pass. He 'ad a chance ta fight fer 'imself…fer you. But we always knew—"

I'm nearly screaming now. What he's telling me makes no sense. "Knew what? How could you know?"

His voice is barely a whisper, as though the words themselves dare not be said. "The gods."

I'm slammed into silence, my raging mind numb as I try to work out what he means. "What gods? What are you saying?"

He scans the room as though someone might be hiding in the darkness, listening to some eternal secrets. He focuses on me, his expression somber. "The Elyphesians."

He stands and takes my hand, angling me so I sit on the edge of the bed. My mind and body are both numbed by his statement, so I don't resist.

"When the gods left the earth, one godling remained behind to watch over the humans."

I nod, familiar with the story of the godling son of Nithenia— an archer. The godling had fallen in love with the maiden Sadini. After escaping the imprisonment of the godlings in Targatheimr, he had been given the opportunity to return to Elyphesus with the gods. Still, he vowed to remain in Fairlee to protect Sadini and the other mortals from the anger of the god of the Great North Sea. "Forwon." The godling's name is a whisper on my lips.

Josef nods. "And his descendants remain in Fairlee to this day."
"You?"

He nods once, holding my gaze so I don't doubt the veracity of his claim.

"And they speak to you?"

He shrugs one shoulder. "Some of us hear their messages. Sometimes, they are sent by the trees or on the wind."

"And what did they tell you about Jamis? What did you tell him?"

He sits beside me and leans in, whispering into my ear. "I'm forbidden from telling what will happen to you. I was young and made a mistake in tellin' Jamis. He was my friend, 'nd I tried to prepare him for 'is role in the prophecy. I tried to prepare him, but the gods punished me and stopped talkin'."

I'm stunned. I don't even know how to ask him any more questions. If I were so intent on honoring the Elyphesian gods, how did I not ever consider the godlings? I know the stories. I've studied each one I could find. I only thought of the gods and gave no consideration to their descendants on earth. "You're a descendant of the gods?"

His gaze is even, but he neither confirms nor denies my questions any further.

"Are there others? Besides in Fairlee?"

He meets my gaze again without confirmation.

It's then I realize the gods I was so determined to adhere to knew Jamis would die. It was a piece of a greater plan. One Josef had shared with Jamis once, but that neither had ever shared with me. Not even hinted. "Will I die as well?" My question is whispered between us, so silent it can't drift, but so dangerous I fear what Josef might confirm.

He leans close, his words no more than a whisper. "I can say nothin' ever again lest the worst possible events come to pass. But know I'll be at yer side no matter what comes. Until ye send me away."

He looks about the room before he adds, "And that was foretold." He stands and walks to the door, glancing over his shoulder as he pulls it open. "I'm goin' ta 'ave a look around. I d'nt want ta rush ye, but we need to decide what we're doin'. We can't stand vigil forever. There's a war ta fight."

I nod as he pulls the door closed behind him. Alone in Jamis's chamber, I'm aware of the heavy weight of this war. It's the first time I've born the responsibility on my own, without my husband to fall back on.

My father, brother, and Lester of Carling are all dead. My original goal of taking vengeance upon them for the wrongs they served me is complete. But this war isn't over. If Nemii sent them, three of my devils are behind me. My enemies—my devils—remain plentiful.

King Brahm of Claxton conspired against us. And Phoebe

was a shadowed opponent the entire time. Driving my brother to kill Melaine and to continue my father's plot against me. And to what end? Phoebe had no true desire to wear the High Crown, but she's set her sights higher. King Travión will prove a greater threat to the Unified Kingdoms, and me, than anyone I originally feared.

If Phoebe is allowed to align with him, all the kingdoms will fall. I will be a queen in name only, a ruler amid the rubble of the kingdoms that fall in my wake.

No, my war is far from over. The time for mourning has passed.

CHAPTER

TWENTY

It's still dark when I climb on my horse and ride from the gates of Allondale.

Word has spread that the queen has returned, and people are gathered along the road leading from the castle into the village. Knights, farmers, and nobles line the route, reaching for me as I pass, calling my name and blessings for the king's memory.

I pull my shoulders back and assume a regal posture, though I try to meet the eyes of each, nodding to acknowledge them as I pass. A tuft of white catches my eye as we move through the main corridor in the village. An old man, his frame thin and wiry, meets my gaze without flinching. The nod he offers is slow, as though he knows me.

I recognize him as the vendor who placed the bangle on my wrist when Jamis and I walked in the village so long ago. My gaze remains fixed on him as I pass, I'm unable to turn from him and certain the bangle, still nestled beneath my sleeve, thrums against the skin of my arm. Something about him is familiar, as though I know him from another place, as if I'm more familiar with him than simply having seen him once or twice before. The familiarity is in his eyes...his expression perhaps.

But my horse carries me past him, and I find my attention being called back to the crowds who've gathered in the night to greet me. Children run along the road in front of my horse, calling for me and demonstrating their skill with wooden swords. I smile at them as I follow the turn of the road, heading toward Fairlee.

Before I lose the opportunity, I cast another glance back. The old man is standing in the middle of the road, his gaze cast sky-ward as his mouth utters words I can't make out at such a distance. Just as I'm about to turn, his eyes snap open and catch mine, a grin playing about his narrow lips, pulling his low-slung cheeks into a taut smile. He nods once and I return the gesture, unwilling to show how much this man has uneased me.

The moon casts a hazy light across the fields that lie between Allondale and Fairlee. Silence creeps across the land, enveloping the horses' plodding steps and the somber breaths of my group. Isobel and Davion ride at the head while Katherine remains beside me, casting uneasy glances my way every few minutes. She's no doubt concerned that I'll dissolve into emotion again, but I have no need to do that. I've spent all the sadness one person could house, I'm an empty vessel; war is the only thing that will replenish me. And my body craves to be filled again—to have purpose.

Laila is behind, riding pillion with Josef, who has taken up the rear of our group, along with Kennard. Though I'm surrounded by Fairleans and knights from Allondale, the sensation of being alone in the world hangs heavy on my shoulders. Where I once felt so heavily connected to my family and my lands, it now seems that I have no real place in the world—nobody and no person to which I belong. With so many people looking to me to lead them, my isolation is even greater. Might it be easier if I were to ride out and wage this war on my own?

We near the tree line. As I feel my distance from Jamis grow, my eyes catch a solitary monument under one of the trees. The stones, piled waist-high and packed with mud to hold them in place for generations, mark the place Esmond was buried months ago. My brave friend will forever look over Allondale and Fairlee, the two places he fought to protect—for me.

I tear my eyes away; I cannot allow emotion to weaken me any longer. I am stronger, more focused, and more successful when driven by rage than by love. Every kingdom I am heir to lies in ru-ins: Allondale, Devlishire—even my mother's realm of Glynnairre. But I am a queen. I was born and raised to rule, and I will rebuild my kingdom from the stones my enemies have thrown. I won't let Esmond and Jamis's deaths be in vain. If they won't let me have the lands—and the crown—I'm owed, I will take them all.

Morning casts a hopeful glow across the land when we final-ly reach camp again. With the horses tended to and most of my group slumbering, I stand alone outside the tent Jamis died in.

"Take mine," Isobel whispers, though I hadn't heard her approach. "I'll sleep by the creek."

"Did you know this was going to happen?" I can't turn my eyes from the drab coverings on the simple cot upon which my husband died. A pile of faded and tattered, patchwork blankets remain, as does a single sword at the foot of the cot—Jamis's. I'd intended him to be buried with it, but in overseeing the preparations as he was enshrouded and placed on the cart, I overlooked it.

Isobel's sigh is heavy, resigned. "He has a bad habit of telling you more than he should. He's far too weak where you and Jamis are concerned."

I turn my head, jaw pulsing as I study her.

She nods once and swallows before she draws breath and answers. "We knew. We've known many things. Not all come to pass, and not all of what we know is clear. We can only recognize it after the fact."

Her ebony eyes fix on me, narrowing, and a feeling of unease comes over me, one I haven't experienced in Isobel's company since I first met her. "We recognized *you*. When you rode into Allondale in that carriage, we knew who you were, and that one of the prophecies was to be fulfilled."

"Which prophecy?"

Her mouth pulls tight, jaw set as she rolls her eyes and turns her attention back to the tent. "I am not my brother, Malory. I won't recklessly disobey the gods to satisfy the curiosity of mortals. I won't risk my connection to them, or my brother's life, for you."

I open my mouth to argue, to assert I'd never risk her life or Josef's, but aren't I risking their lives by asking them to fight beside me for my war? And would I not want to know everything she knows of the gods and their plan?

"We will fight beside you. I'll guide you as well as I can, and I will share what I'm able. But there are things you must do for yourself in order to win this war. You must decide your own path. The prophecies aren't set. They're fluid. Should you fail, they will fall to another. Perhaps you're only a factor to bolster or supplant someone else's prophesy. I don't know. But I can never tell you what course you should take, and you can never ask Josef."

"I would never knowingly put you or Josef at risk."

Her smile is sad. "Your presence does that. But we welcomed

you, knowing the risks."

She turns from me before I can respond, following the creek, into the thickening tree line and the shadows that cling there. I lose sight of her as birds begin to wake and call throughout the forest in response to a rising breeze. The happy chatter of spring has suddenly arisen, while inside me, the cold isolation of winter remains.

With resignation, I enter the tent and climb into the cot, pulling the blankets over me. I close my eyes, shutting out the sun and the new day, letting my mind dwell in the past.

Jamis's scent lingers on the blankets, the musky, spicy aroma that I remember of him as a king and warrior, as well as the sour smell of his fevered sickness. As the smells envelop me, I fall asleep feeling his presence—as well as his absence—one more time.

My dreams are a troubled and scrambled mix of pleasant memories and terrifying possibilities. Jamis and Esmond sit at Nithenia's side, a mist drifting around them as they gaze down upon a battle. Fires and charred plains stretch across the kingdoms; bodies litter the earth. I am in the midst of the fighting, sword in hand, when I hear my name, a whisper across the battlefield.

Come. Join me. And as I survey my surroundings, I understand in my gut that answering that call is the only way. *I will spare them.*

As I turn, hideous creatures, dark and indiscernible figures with black eyes and gaping mouths, hover over a field of white roses, their delicate blossoms bow under the weight of thick, crimson blood.

The monstrous forms undulate in the haze and smoke, but in each's grasp is one of my friends: Katherine and Isobel looking terrified, Davion screaming in pain as Kennard does so in a fury. And Josef, hanging lifeless as the specter lifts him into the air, then drops him.

As Josef's body plummets to the ground, the voice becomes a demand. *Join me now. Save them!*

Thunder explodes—the shouts of the godlings trapped in Targatheimr—shaking the earth and sky alike. I shout my answer, but it's veiled in the rolling boom and even I don't know what it was.

How did I answer?

Clouds in the sky drift apart, opening to a downpour, saturating me thoroughly while the fires surrounding me continue to burn. I look to the heavens. As the mist swirls about, slowly engulfing them, I see the saddened faces of Esmond and Jamis looking upon me as the tears of the gods rain upon the earth.

Only Albati spares me a glance, though, the glow of her hair, like a fiery sunset whipping about her face as she hovers just below her brothers and sister, her amber eyes piercing as they meet mine. *He'll lie as certainly as he walks beside you.*

I yell to her, desperation griping me, knowing this is something I need to know. "Who?"

Him! She chokes and points behind me.

I spin.

Another crash rattles the ground, followed by the roar of someone yelling as the world goes dark.

"Wake up, girl!" The sting of a slap explodes across my cheek.

I startle and sit, gasping as my heart thumps against my chest. Fear has set my senses tingling, and my body is prepared to leap from the cot and flee for safety.

Florie is standing over me, one hand clutching the neck of my cloak and the other drawn back to slap me again. The heavy haze of a late afternoon storm casts a dusky pallor over her translucent skin. Seeing that I'm awake, she releases her grip on my cloak. "Never let 'em linger in your dreams."

I'm still fighting to regain control of my breath and slow my heart when she turns from me. I toss the blankets aside, determined the old healer won't brush me off so easily this time. I reach for her as she shuffles toward the door, grasping her by her narrow wrist. She pulls against me, rheumatic joints rubbings against my firm grip. "Let go of me, girl."

"What do you know? You hear them. You know what they are saying. You listen to them whether you want to or not."

Her face constricts in anger, upper lip pulling into a snarl as she pulls again. This time, I let her hand go. "Tell me."

Her shoulders drop as she sighs. "Your legend will be spectacular, whether you win this war or choose the other path."

"What other path?" I'd hoped the old lady could offer some insight, some clue as to if I truly do have the favor of the gods and will be successful. Now I fear she's been stricken with some feeble mindedness I hadn't recognized before.

"The gods themselves have old conflicts not yet resolved. Your presence in the world could finally resolve those old wars. But that means a winner will be decided after thousands of years of conflict among them. If you choose the wrong path—believe in the wrong promises—the end may come for all the others."

A low rumble echoes in the distance, thunder gathering like a warning. "You will be the salvation of mortals, or the end. You've pledged to all the gods at some point. They all have plans for you, but Nemii's call is strongest. His voice lingers in your mind and heart, preventing the rest from reaching you. Open your mind to them all or prepare to linger with your devils."

I'm stunned as she pivots and hurries from the tent. How can the crazy old lady think I would possibly be so pivotal to the gods? Or that I would ever choose anything that would harm my friends and my people? Have I not risked everything for my people? For Jamis's? Images from my nightmare flash through my mind as the thunder rumbles nearer.

Florie stops and turns in my direction, but something in the sky above catches her attention. Panic fills her eyes. "Don't believe—"

Crack!

An ear-piercing snap paired with a flash of light explodes through Fairlee. I turn from the assault of sudden brightness and cover my ears, my back to the explosion. My teeth jar, and a force jolts me to my knees. It's over in moments, and a brief silence is interrupted by ringing in my ears. I push to my feet, my legs shaky as they try to find stable ground. Urgent voices cut through the high-pitched ringing. Slowly, I'm able to make sense of the jumbled voices, able to discern words and distinct voices. My first steps are tentative as I walk from the tent, legs still wobbling to the point that my inclination is to simply give up and sit on the ground. But I push forward, drawn to the gathering group of people.

"What happened?" Katherine is at my side, but I can't answer her, only push on dumbly toward the crowd.

Davion appears, placing himself in front of Katherine, examining her. "Are you okay?"

She nods and they embrace, but I push forward, weaving through the people who stand looking down at the body on the ground in the center: Florie, her green eyes staring blankly toward the gods she just warned me about.

I'm stunned at the loss I feel that this lady I hardly knew but shared a secret bond with has been stricken down.

She was stricken, wasn't she?

I nearly stumble as I pivot to watch the grey feathered clouds slip together across the slate sky and whatever lies beyond them.

As I cast one last look at Florie's body, the whispers erupt in my head, their words lost among the volume of their message, but the urgency apparent as I force them all from my mind.

CHAPTER
TWENTY-ONE

THE FIRES ARE ALIGHT THROUGHOUT CAMP AS NIGHT settles. The elderly and youngest are the hardest hit by Florie's tragic death. The healer had saved lives, brought new ones into the world, and tended to everyone's great and minor injuries in the forest. One would think she'd lived a hundred years by the tales of her life, and perhaps she had. I hadn't known her well enough to say. I only know that the person who heard the gods as I did is gone. Likely because she tried to warn me.

I shudder, thinking that such a fate might await Josef and Isobel should they try to tell me anything the gods deem wrong.

The benches around the fires are filled though nobody sits beside me, leaving me alone with my thoughts—horrid though they may be.

A rustling of cloth from behind me precedes the crisp voice of Queen Filomena. "May I join you, my queen?"

Pulling my own ratty and war-worn skirts aside, I nod to the bench. She sits primly, ever the queen even when imprisoned and held in uncultured surroundings. "I'm sorry for the loss of the healer. She seemed quite kind. It's apparent she was thought of highly here."

The crackling fire provides us both something to focus on so that we don't have to endure the discomfort of acknowledging our awkward circumstances: me unsure how to be a captor, and she uncertain how to behave as a captive. Two queens, side by side, but holding vastly different persectives.

"The towers have been prepared for your arrival," I say.

She smooths her skirts and pulls her shoulders back. "I told you that I plan to go willingly, and I will keep my word. What about you? Will you return to Allondale?"

I shouldn't tell her anything. She's my prisoner, not a confidant. Even so, I find myself confiding—though without proffering specifics. "I'll ensure you're well cared for, but I won't be there. There are matters I still have to attend to."

"My daughter." Her voice lacks emotion. She understands, perhaps even embraces the path we are all on. She has already made it clear that if forced to choose between her children—which Phoebe has forced her to do, has she not? —Queen Filomena's loyalty lies with her son.

"She may prove to be less of a threat than others, but she will be dealt with."

"And Oliver?"

"I can't return him to you if I don't know where to look."

She stiffens at the realization that she will have to tell me where her boy is if I'm to liberate him from hiding. "He is in Landyn under the protection of Margaret Saint-Léger."

I snap my attention to her as a gasp escapes my chest. "The heirs of Landyn fled. Why would you think it safe to place your son in the care of Margaret Saint-Léger?"

Her expression is solemn as she holds my gaze. "Because I alone know where her heirs are hidden. Should she put Oliver at risk, Prince Castriel and Prince Zaugustus will both perish. Margaret and I go back a long time. She is the woman who is most true to her word that I know, and most fierce—until I met you, of course." A small laugh flitters from her. "Even Margaret knows she's no match for you."

Margaret Saint-Léger accompanied King Herrold to Allondale shortly after I married Jamis. He was invited as Jamis and I tried to establish alliances among the other kings. Though I wasn't completely honest with Jamis at the time, there was already a risk to Allondale that I knew of, one I'd been sent to help set in motion. But I'd defied the plan set in place by my father and Queen Filomena's husband to plot my own course. Although King Herrold left Allondale as a supporter of Jamis, I always felt that his lover had been no fan of his decision—nor of me.

I consider the queen of Carling for several minutes before I respond. "Perhaps it wasn't the kings of the Unified Kingdoms that should have been feared all along. Perhaps the true danger was standing at their sides with matching crowns."

She offers me a girlish smile—full of mischievous delight—and raises her brows. "If only they'd known."

Although I don't trust Queen Filomena, a life of wary alliances and political shifting can't be forgotten, I do find that I like her. I watch as she moves—under guard, of course—through the crowd. She accepts a bowl of food and sits alone to eat though her eyes follow me throughout the evening. Whether we grow to be true allies or not, we will always study each other and tuck away our observations should we need to call upon them later. Arming oneself for future betrayals is an integral aspect of royal life.

As dusk transitions into an inky night, the sound of horses carries through camp. The crowd scatters: men, women, and children grasping their weapons and then disappearing into the dark cover of the trees. They scamper into the treetops and among the bases, blending into the forest as they move about it. The knights and remaining villagers from Allondale retrieve their weapons and stand their ground, swords and arrows at the ready as the riders approach.

"They aren't invading," I say to Kennard, who stands beside me. "The pace is too slow."

"Or they're cautious. It's difficult to navigate the forest in the dark," he counters.

Davion swings onto a horse, then rides into the dark. I control my breaths to hear into the night.

Isobel's head angles as she also listens. She relaxes her stance, lowering her bow and turning. "It's the troops from Gaufrid. They're going in circles." She shakes her head as she returns to her bowl of food, setting her bow at her feet.

Kennard isn't so quick to drop his guard, nor am I. We remain vigilant until Davion rides back into the light of camp, Weaver Arionde riding beside him.

I slide my sword into my belt as I recognize the knights from Gaufrid. Several men, bound at the wrists and tethered to the horses, walk behind them. Exhaustion colors the men's faces. They've just walked from Devlishire to Fairlee after certainly being defeated in the invasion. I imagine they must be stunned and tired.

I greet Weaver as he climbs from his horse. Kennard offers a curt nod, but still won't let on that he knows this man from Ballæter.

I survey the twenty men that Weaver has taken prisoner. They are barely outnumbered by the men who rode in with him. "You were successful, then?"

"Aye," He pats the neck of his charcoal mare as one of his men leads her away to tend to her. The prisoners are corralled near one of the fires, tied together, and made to sit on the ground. They comply, sitting back to back to relax against each other. Each is dressed in my homeland's black tunic, the scarlet wolf on their chests the emblem of a pack that no longer exists. It now represents only me—a lone wolf, never truly a member, forced to live on the fringes and now cast into a solitary existence—and Laila.

I watch as Laila tends to the blisters and wounds of the new arrivals. She has so easily assimilated into this new life, but I crave for her to have a kingdom again. A life of ease, without turmoil, one in which she wears pretty dresses and plays chess in the gardens.

But that life never really fulfilled me, did it? Would she prefer it if given a choice?

My sister speaks kind words and tends to wounds, her skin aglow with purpose. Perhaps *this* life is Laila's destiny.

Weaver interrupts my thoughts, Ayleth at his heels, listening intently. "We lost a hundred men, I'm afraid. Devlishire mounted a vigorous opposition."

"I'm sorry for that," I answer. I scan the returning troops. There are still far fewer men than I sent out. Did they decide they would no longer fight on my behalf after all and return to Gaufrid? Did they abandon their posts and flee into the Argralands or book passage across the Great North Sea? "And the rest?"

"A hundred remain in Devlishire to hold the castle in your name, Your Majesty." He offers a bow of his head. "The rest returned with me. Most are posted within the boundaries of the forest awaiting orders. We stopped in Carling as we passed. My men are still holding it in your name as well."

Emotion swells in my chest. While I'm still appalled at the realities of war, I'm thrilled to have conquered Carling and reclaimed Devlishire. The lands that were meant to be mine initially, my homeland—though it turns out not my blood land—is finally under my control. I am the truest queen of Devlishire, no matter its current state. My father and brother drove me out, denied me the lands, yet I am here. I am victorious while they have been remitted to memory and legend.

"And your prisoners?" I look to the men. Many faces are familiar. Perhaps they are men I passed in the halls when I was a princess in Devlishire, men who once swore an oath to protect me and then vowed to kill me when my brother was their ruler.

"They are all titled men who maintain their allegiance to Devlishire but refused to swear allegiance to you. And there is one other." He gestures to one of his men, who disappears into the mass of Gaufridian soldiers relieving their horses of their packs.

A man comes forward, his clothing, once exceptionally fine, is now soiled from the dirt of hard travel. As he nears, I see golden threads, tattered and poking at angles from the hem of his scarlet surcoat. A once-white blanket is tied at an angle across his chest, now a pack for carrying something. The man is older, perhaps my father's age and the bright blue eyes that frame his bulbous nose are familiar. His hair is soiled, darkened with dirt and oil, though I can see that it was once the lightest blonde, now graying, and if it were any longer might curl about his ears and his collar. I gasp and stiffen as I recognize Favion Alphonse, the Earl of Cavesdale—Melaine's father.

He approaches and offers a shallow bow. "Your Majesty."

Laila has taken notice of him as well, and she makes her way to my side. The earl offers her a nod as well.

I'm entirely uncertain how to greet this man. He's a member of my father's court, which makes him a likely enemy—but he's also Melaine's father. I've always detested him for ignoring his daughter and relegating her to a life of poverty. But while he did nothing more for her than ensure she had a position in court—as my maid—the possibility remains that he may be angry at how his daughter met her end.

"My Lord," I greet him, then turn to Weaver for an explanation.

He holds a hand to the earl, indicating he should offer his own explanation.

In response, Earl Alphonse shifts and reaches into the blanket secured across his chest. His pack squirms as he does. From it, he withdraws a tiny body. The sleeping baby calls out as it's pulled from the warm cocoon.

As soon as I see the blond curls, I understand—this is Melaine's baby—and my brother's. Laila claps and rushes forward, pulling the baby into her arms. She runs her hand over his hair and the chubby flesh of his thighs.

"We found him, Your Majesty. The earl was shielding him in a crypt."

I pull my shoulders back as I turn my focus from the baby to the earl. "Shielding or secreting?"

"He is my grandson, Your Majesty. I only want the best for him. I was keeping him safe." The earl drops his gaze from me to the ground before him, his head bowed and shoulders slumped. His expression is of someone sufficiently shamed and docile, though I don't know that it makes him any more trustworthy. He never took such care for his only daughter.

"Where were you when your daughter needed sheltered?"

He looks up sharply, but drops his gaze instantly, a flush creeping across his marred skin. "I failed Melaine, Your Majesty. I don't wish to do the same to the boy."

I step forward. Beginning a slow circle around the earl, I consider him as Jamis and I used to do those we captured after battle. I ensure he sees my eyes travel slowly across his face as I consider him from head to foot. I stop directly in front of him. My tone is low, only those directly near us would overhear, but my voice won't travel beyond our small group. "Perhaps your interest in Henry is as the heir of Devlishire."

He shakes his head in vigorous denial. "I assure you that I only want to protect my grandson. He is the only blood in my line, and I will see him into adulthood."

"And what if I told you the baby has no claim to Devlishire? That my brother was, in fact, a bastard who also had no true claim on the kingdom?"

Surprise stiffens him for the briefest moment before he shakes it off. He looks to where Laila holds his grandson, his expression soft. He stands straight as he faces me. "I hope only to be allowed to pass my own title to the boy, with the queen's permission. I should name him my successor now if it pleases Your Majesty. But he isn't safe in Devlishire—nor anywhere in the Unified Kingdoms—right now."

"The Unified Kingdoms have fallen. There are seven separate kingdoms now, each scrambling to survive this war. And larger ones poised to move against us."

He nods in agreement. The unification is indeed irrevocably broken. "I only wish for a future for my grandson. And those who despise his father may seek to harm him."

"I despise his father, my lord. Do you imagine I would harm the child?"

The way he meets and holds my gaze tells me that he *does* fear I might destroy the baby to maintain my own claim on Devlishire. The idea causes a jolt in my chest.

My only desire as queen was to be benevolent to my people and defend my lands. Have I become a queen people fear? One they believe would kill a child to ensure my own claim? Perhaps the rumors of my dark vengefulness have traveled further and been more widely relayed than I ever imagined.

Even Laila seems to await my answer, unsure if I am a threat to the plump, giggling babe in her arms.

I release a breath; I cannot mend a reputation by reinforcing it. At some point, I'll have to display the benevolence I want to be known for. "I am no threat to my nephew. But I do intend to protect him from any who would seek to use him to their advantage. Including you, Lord Favion."

I watch Laila bounce the child in her arms, her fingers trailing along his arm and cheek. "My sister will tend to the prince. You're welcome to remain with him, but you will be under guard. I won't have you stealing into the night with him."

He bows and offers a smile at Laila. "Of course, Your Majesty."

Laila leads the earl toward her tent, where she has fresh blankets and her own ladies to whom she has begun teaching the healing arts to. I lift my chin in Kennard's direction. He nods and points to four knights, gesturing for them to follow the earl.

I call to the old man before he's out of earshot. "Know that if you attempt to abduct my nephew, I will come for you. And I won't stop until I've found you and made you pay for the slight."

He offers a deep bow before scurrying to catch up with Laila.

I sit with Kennard, Katherine, Davion, and Josef by the fire.

I'm relieved to have the baby in my care, but I know he can't stay with me. "He isn't safe here. So long as this war wages on, he's at risk. He'll have to be sent away."

"Where will he possibly be safe?" Katherine asks. "Isn't it better where we can protect him?"

Davion's voice is soft as he responds. "She's right. They'll come for her, and the baby is in danger if he's here."

There doesn't seem to be a perfect plan, nor can I think of one on such short notice. "I can have someone take him across the

Great North Sea. To the Candor Islands."

"No!" Josef's voice is urgent, and he nearly leaps from his seat as he says it. His eyes are wide as he looks about the startled group. He stammers, trying to come up with a reason for his outburst. "It's…the sea…you can't…"

I interrupt his stammering, certain he's implying something the gods would prevent him from saying. The fear in his eyes tells me that sending Henry to the Candor Islands is an unfavorable plan—perhaps even dangerous.

"What about Tiernan?" Kennard's voice is hesitant, and he is staring into the fire instead of looking at anyone in our group.

"Why Tiernan?" Katherine considers him, her brows pulled together and eyes pinched as she tries to work out his thinking. "The king's done nothing to help. He's closed off Tiernan to all travelers."

"He'll take the boy," Kennard says. He finally looks up. Focusing directly on me as he takes a slow breath, he pulled the air in deeply before releasing it. "He'll take the baby, and he'll protect him if I bring him. He's done it before."

My mind spins faster, working out what Kennard is about to say. Feeling that I know exactly what his revelation will be.

Kennard holds my gaze. "Twenty years ago, I carried another child through the Gates of Tiernan and left him with the king."

When would Kennard ever have taken a baby to Tiernan? He's been in my father's service for—

The conversation with my mother and King Carolus comes rushing back. My mother's first-born child to a king of Devlishire. My words come out on a breath. "My brother."

He confirms my statement with a single nod. "I can take the baby to him. He'll protect him and hide him as his own bloodline. Tiernan is built on the bonds of hidden bloodlines. So many hidden heirs in one capital, each unaware of their true genesis."

My eyes burn with tears that I refuse to shed. "You took him from my mother?"

He nods.

Without thought, I leap from my perch on the old log and shove at Kennard with both hands. He barely moves under the entirety of my force. His eyes remain cast aside, refusing to meet mine.

Furious heat floods my body, my head throbs in anger and awareness. All this time, not only has Kennard known I had a brother; he also knew exactly where he was—because he'd robbed my mother of her child and spirited him into the shadows of another kingdom.

"Leave us!" I demand of everyone else, glaring at Kennard, who remains planted in his seat, attention fixed on the fire.

Davion holds a hand out to help Katherine rise. She slows as she passes me, trying to catch my eye, seeking some sort of confirmation I'm okay, but I refuse to meet her gaze, keeping my attention firmly and intently on Kennard.

"You too," I growl at Ayleth, who has slipped behind a nearby tree. She steps slowly from the dark. With her head low, she follows everyone else. But where everyone else seemed eager to avoid this conversation, Ayleth wants to hear it.

I cast a withering look that I hope will hurry the child along. This is no conversation for a young girl. Much less one I barely know and who knows even less about me.

"You stole my mother's child from her," I hiss at Kennard once I'm certain we won't be overheard.

His head bobs slightly in confirmation. "Aye, under your father's orders. Under *the king's* order."

"How could you? You're a Knight of Ballæter. Aren't you supposed to be honorable?"

His eyes snap to me. For an instant, I see pride and irritation that his honor has been brought into question. His brows pinch and the skin around his eyes wrinkles under his scowl. There's a low rumble of fury as he responds. "We're loyal and honorable *to our kings*. That's how we're raised, how we're trained. We aren't expected to make judgements of our own—we're expected to *not* make any."

I'm furious as my mind turns to Kennard's seemingly shifting allegiance. He swore to protect I'awn, then was commissioned by my father and aligned with Jamis—now me? Who truly holds his loyalty—or does anyone?

"Who are you loyal to, Kennard? Because it wasn't my father—the king you were commissioned for. And if you never told Jamis or me about my brother, I wonder how loyal you ever were to us."

At that, he jumps up and towers over me. He's menacing and angry, and my body responds instinctively, shaking in fear as my breathing becomes constricted.

Just as I register that Kennard is looming over me, a blade

appears over my right shoulder, pressed into the lump at his throat. "I'll 'ave ye sit down, mate. I know ye'r not intendin' to threaten yer queen, but ye'r givin' that impression."

Kennard's withering gaze slides from me to Josef. I can sense his body twitching, eager to reach for his sword and fight, just as I can feel Josef's energy preparing for that possibility.

Kennard snarls as he takes one step back—but only one. He holds Josef's gaze, daring him to command more of him. "I was loyal to King Grayson even though I detested him every day I was in his service. He was disgusting and foul to his core, but I did my duty. When he sent me to Allondale, I remained loyal for years, but only because he reminded me that I'awn's life was in my hands. At some point, though, I decided I'awn was likely dead and that Grayson was to blame for whatever wretched life he'd lived until then. King Eamon was kind. He spoke to and tried to know the man who watched over his son. And Jamis—" Kennard's voice cracks at his name. He turns from me, hiding any emotion that threatens to make an appearance. He won't allow anyone to believe that, despite his appearance as a mountain of a man, he is a human at his core, with emotions and bonds as any other man.

"He trusted you," I say. "You more than any other."

Kennard nods, but offers no words.

It tears at my heart to see how the loss of Jamis affects Kennard, as does my doubt of his loyalty to him. Regret washes over me that in my anger and frustration, I lashed out at Kennard. But a spark of anger remains that despite how much we've come to rely on and trust in each other over the past several months, Kennard never told me about my brother.

"Is my brother a prisoner?"

Kennard looks to Josef, who remains behind me, before he answers.

"Not a prisoner. Nor a servant. His life's been comfortable. He's had everything an heir to a throne should have."

"Except his family," I add with the raise of one brow. It's difficult to imagine this boy I don't even know—the true heir of Devlishire—being raised away from his family and his countrymen. Sent away to protect him from something he may never know he's entitled to. His life being saved from a very risk he might never know exists.

"Or to protect him from them as well." Kennard casts a knowing nod before growing silent again.

He isn't wrong. Perhaps Erik was better off far from the creeping shadows of Devlishire. He would have only become one more victim of Grayson—or Roarke—would he not?

The baby cries out, a soft breeze carrying his voice to where I stand—contemplating the same course for his life. Doubt swirls in my belly. Will Henry truly be safe with King Kyste? The reclusive king offered protection to my own mother when Glynnairre was sacked. And has he not shielded and protected Erik for twenty years?

But why? What does he gain from housing secret bloodlines?

I can't keep the baby with me, though. He's at certain risk if he remains anywhere near me or one of my strongholds. My initial impulse was to send him across the Great North Sea to the Candor Islands—my grandmother's lands. But Josef's reaction to that frightens me. He knows something he's unable to tell me. Does it have to do with prophecy, or does he know of something else?

He'll lie as certainly as he walks beside you. That's what the whispers said, but who were they referring to? Josef? Kennard? Someone else?

It's all nearly too much to struggle with. So many decisions to be made and me alone to make them. Me alone to bear the weight of each choice I make, the good and the bad. But they need to be made, and my mind can turn over a thousand outcomes of each decision, or I could become lost in them. Such is the price for wearing the crown.

I look to Kennard. "You'll take the baby to King Kyste in Tiernan. Lord Favion will accompany you and remain with the baby. He's to be left as the boy's ward."

Kennard nods once. "And then?"

I hadn't thought beyond Kennard safely delivering my nephew to Tiernan. Part of me is still angry that he's kept such an egregious secret from me, but I also can't imagine fighting without him at my side—and we *will* come to battle again. Perhaps bigger than any fight we've imagined or endured. I need him at my side, but I won't beg him. I pull my shoulders back, clasp my hands at my waist, and calmly meet his eyes. "That's up to you, Kennard. I can't imagine going into battle without you at my side. I've never been forced to. But you're a free man. After you deliver the baby safely, where you go and what you do are at your own discretion. Whatever you choose, you do so with my blessing."

I turn and walk into the dark, weaving through soldiers sleeping against saddles and tents. It pains me to think that I may never see Kennard again—that he might very likely take this opportunity to leave. He'll be free to search the world beyond the kingdoms for I'awn, or retire to a quiet life, perhaps farm a small bit of land and live a quiet existence.

I had considered him a friend, but as desperately as I want him by my side as I move into certain danger, nothing would make me happier than to know he was gifted with long life and the chance to make his own decisions finally.

As I near my tent, I hear the mumbled voices of Kennard and Josef. I cast a glance over my shoulder. Their heads are angled together, and they are both watching my retreat. Though my impulse is to turn away quickly, I reinforce my resolve and hold the gaze of each for several seconds before I turn and duck into my tent.

CHAPTER

TWENTY-TWO

"SHOULD I TAKE HENRY TO TIERNAN?" LAILA AND I sit at the great fire in the center of camp, watching as Kennard prepares his pack and horse.

The thought has crossed my mind, one more decision that I've struggled with. Is my sister safe in camp, or would I do best by her if I sent her to a kingdom? "Kennard won't let anything happen to him."

"But can we trust the earl?"

I shrug. I hope that the old man will take more care of his grandchild than he ever did his daughter. But I also know that where wealth and power are at play, nobody can be trusted. "I'm trusting in the king more than anything—and in Kennard's history with him. But maybe you should go with Henry. The king will protect you the same as he offered to do for Mother."

She swallows hard and nods, though her expression is more one of resignation than agreement.

"What is it?"

"I'll go if you think it's best. But…I'm a healer now. If anyone at court were to know—"

She doesn't have to finish the thought. Most of those in court—nobility—still view healers as heretical. Laila would be at greater risk in the halls of court than in the forest should anyone discover what she's done to survive—to help others survive. "You're right. It may be safer for you to stay here. If you're sure this isn't too hard for you, living this way."

She takes a deep breath as she scans the camp. Her smile is

earnest when she refocuses. "I thought it would be. Hard. But it turns out I'm more like you than I thought. I'm adaptable—and hardy."

I reach for her hand, squeezing gently. "Don't forget brave."

Our attention is drawn as Kennard mounts his horse. Katherine, Josef, and Davion gather around him, shaking hands and patting his leg. Ayleth runs to him with an item gripped in her tiny palm. He accepts it, glancing at the item in his palm before slipping it into a hidden pocket under his leathers.

Favion Alphonse climbs upon another horse, Henry secured to his chest and looking about as he smiles at his grandfather.

"Should we say goodbye?" Laila stands, eager to bid farewell to the baby she came to know so well when she was still in Devlishire. The nephew who remains a stranger to me.

"Of course. I'll be right along."

Laila's gait is light as she nearly skips to the earl's horse and tugs at the baby's toe. She smiles up at the earl, and they exchange words before Laila moves on to Kennard.

My body resists as I propel myself to the riders. I offer what I hope is a kind look to the earl. I can't have him leave here as my enemy—or disliking me. "I thank you for protecting the prince, my lord. When all of this is behind us, I shall ensure you are well-rewarded for your loyalty."

He meets my look with a steady assessment, his mouth tight and a glint in his eye. I can't decipher if it's a look of pleasure or contempt that I would make such an offer. "It's an honor to protect my grandson—as well as the crown, My Queen." He nods, the moment passing. Again, he is just a noble in a dirty surcoat, pleased to have a purpose.

I smile as he turns his horse, and, with a quick tap, rides away.

Kennard issues a clicking sound, and his horse follows. He holds my gaze as he passes, and the burning that spreads in my chest prevents me from saying anything. I can only nod and hope that he understands everything I can't say.

Kennard offers a single nod in response. As they're enveloped by the shadows of Fairlee, he looks over his shoulder one last time—at camp, at his friends, at his queen.

I want to call him back, to tell him there has to be another way, that we'll find it together. But that isn't the case. If King Kyste can offer the same safety to Henry as he has to my brother all these years, don't I owe it to Henry to give him that chance? My family certainly owes it to Melaine to protect her son.

As much as I want Kennard at my side, I feel confident he's Henry's best chance. To be near me is too great a danger. This is a truth, proven time and again by those I've loved.

When I can't bear to watch the empty space the horses rode into any longer, I walk to the creek. Rushing water, fresh and new, bubbles as it cascades over boulders, long ago sealed into the earth. I step onto a fallen tree, making my way across the water where I stand, staring downstream. The rush of water provides a respite from camp sounds, from the reminders of war, and the odds that are constantly against us. The freedom of the flowing, unencumbered water is hypnotic, and soon my thoughts evaporate—only the water under my feet and the sun on my face exist. For one moment, I'm free from all that's led me here, and all that lies ahead.

Isobel rolls to my side like the wind. "He'll be back."

"Are you so sure?"

"You could send him away a thousand times, and he'll always return. He's something to prove to you. Until he does, he won't give up."

A small spark of hope exists in me that Kennard will take this opportunity to find I'awn, to find happiness. But the greater part of me will always hope he'll return to fight for me—beside me. My eyes will always find the dark that hides between the trees or on the distant horizons, looking for him to emerge.

"What's our plan?"

"Find Mereck de Grey. Tell him to retrieve the riches of Allondale. Once I conquer Claxton Landyn, I'm going after Phoebe. If I'm to declare war on Travión, we'll need a bigger army. Send word to Legion E. We'll need every man and woman who can ride with us. And then ready the horses. We ride at dawn."

I knew you'd be on your way. I'll see you soon, mortal.

The Beginning: The Propagation of Origin Lore in Simplistic Societies by Master Entwistle Lidgeon, First Unification Council.

WITH ALL PRE-UNIFICATION SOCIETIES—AS WELL AS WITH THOSE still existing outside the enlightened sphere of the Unified Kingdoms—one will find that the entirety of literature relating to creation centers upon the existence of a single entity. That single entity then gives rise to all other life, though the method varies greatly among the societies.   Let us first examine the Elyphesian society's myths, which have passed into extinction with the emergence of the Church of the Heavens and the Earth.

According to Elyphesian belief, Omnilus was the first breath in the universe. He existed in darkness for five thousand years before growing tired of the persistence of it. Acting on impulse and spurred by creative genius, he placed a single, pulsing bit of light in the firmament.

The light was magic, and Omnilus grew enamored of its beauty from its initial spark in the heavens. He soon placed another, and then another, marveling at the way each new star twinkled against the darkness with the promise of more magnificence. Each year, Omnilus hung a new star until the vast darkness sparkled reaching far to the ends of the night sky. And the light made Omnilus happy.

When the sky was nearly filled, Omnilus crafted a single larger star. This one eclipsed all the others. Although it was exquisite and cast warmth upon the nearby stars, it shone so brightly that the moon was startled and hid behind the earth.

Omnilus saw how the sunlight was cast unencumbered across the barren earth, so he raised the land high in places and pushed it farther down in others so shadows were cast upon the surface and the difference in color and texture sparked his interest.

He then created blue and set it in motion until it washed across most of the surface—undulating in a rhythmic dance, taunting and luring the immovable earth to join it.

Seeing the blue's majesty, Omnilus created green to cover another portion of the lands, while others he left bare and in shades of brown and red to reflect the beauty of the sun back into the atmosphere.

Across the green lands, Omnilus spattered flowering blossoms in majestic hues. From the heavens, he watched, amazed as the light and colors danced across the earth in vibrant colors and movements.

But Omnilus realized that, for all the magnificence he had created, he was alone and without anyone to share it with. And so, he created six entities to share the heavens and earth with. He gave them each the ability to adopt a physical form with which they could wander upon the earth and partake of its perfection. He also created Elyphesus—so named for it was a utopia for gods and all things constructed with god-like perfection within the beauty and magnificence of the earth.

Omnilus created Rūvolo, and then Liræmor, Kūbialus, Nemii, then Whenorríga. Finally, he created Nithenia, and he favored her for a while. The others were initially in awe of his creations, but they soon became jealous of each other and filled with greed, each trying to claim dominion over parts of Omnilus's creation.

And then the gods began to craft life of their own to walk amongst them and keep them company in their own likeness. Then they experimented with animals to sustain the appetite of mankind and for man to hold dominion over. The gods selected humans they favored and granted them station over the others, calling them kings.

After thousands of years, the goddess Albati was created from the essence of all the gods and from that which was most favored and feared on earth.

But the gods' thirst for dominion over man—and each other— grew unquenchable. They created ever larger and more dangerous creatures, which the kings hunted, feasting upon their flesh. And the monarchs employed servants, forcing them to hunt increasingly dangerous animals on their behalf.

Omnilus watched with growing sadness as all he created grew

ugly with death and greed. And he saw that it was no longer good, nor was it within his control. When the gods created dragons, Omnilus realized the beast would soon claim all he had created if he didn't bring it all to an end. But, as Omnilus prepared to draw the air from the world and bring an end to all things living, Nithenia intervened, begging for mankind to be spared. It wasn't the mortals who were to blame, she argued, but the gods themselves who inspired their devotion and acts of domination over others.

Omnilus relented and spared the living things. But he was saddened by what had become of his creation. He cast a curse upon the gods, preventing them from ever creating new life, and he cast the dragon from the earth before Omnilus himself abandoned his creation, retreating to the heavens to create anew.

But the gods were left behind, and their compulsion to claim the earth and mankind was unchallenged. They crowned kings and inspired wars. They favored humans, and they lay with them, managing to create life in that way. Their children, the godlings, walked as manifestations of the gods on earth.

And with their children, the gods continued to inspire war and then turned against each other...

THE GODDESS ALBATI, FROM *ROMANTICISM, BETRAYAL,*
AND THE MYTH OF THE FEMININE IDEAL BY MASTER IGNAVIOUS
TORSKEY, THIRD UNIFICATION COUNCIL.

AS PREVIOUSLY MENTIONED, IN THE MYTHS OF PRE-UNIFICATION societies, Whenorríga, goddess of the night winds and the swift-footed, was first-born amongst the goddesses. Though, at first impression, she was the embodiment of the feminine ideal—passionate and loving as well as benevolent—she was also prone to great rage.

During one tremendous fit of rage *(reference: Volume 4, Article 28, Page 437)*, Whenorríga called upon the night winds, driving them into a tempest as she pushed them farther into the heavens than ever before, unleashing them upon the land.

Great winds swept across the earth, churning dust into the sky, blowing the petals from flowers and leaves from the trees. Animals fled to the thick, protective cover of the forests in terror. Mankind soon followed, aware that the gods were angry at each other. Men, women, and children wept as they huddled against the storm, praying their deaths be swift to spare them the torment of being caught in a battle between the gods.

Autumn gave way to winter. Still, Whenorríga's fury remained unabated, so she increased the power of her winds. They swept from the earth into the heavens, pushing the moon until it passed in front of the sun. At that moment, the moon and the sun caught their first sight of each other, and each recognized the glory and perfection of the other. Their attraction caused a surge in light and the wind, carrying a mix of both the heat of the sun and the cool breeze of the moon swept down from the skies, sweeping through people who clung together, declaring their love for each other as they feared the end. The winds swept over them, infiltrating their being, carrying the essence of their emotions with it. When the wind—and Whenorríga's fury—finally ebbed, the particles that had swept throughout the world were deposited on the Candor Islands.

As the moon and sun began to part, they reached their essence toward each other, struggling to remain together. The last rays of their conjoined light shone upon the Candor Islands, infusing the remnants of love, yearning, and loss into a new life. Water from the Great North Sea—a gift of apology from the god Liræmor—nourished the particles as they fused and grew together.

One day, Mandiah Pellah, the son of a fisherman, was scouting the northern shore for mollusks that had washed ashore during the exceptionally high tide the previous night.

In a narrow ravine, Mandiah noticed a large gray lump and investigated. There, lying among the detritus of the high tide, was a small woman covered by a shiny membrane. Although she had the appearance of a grown woman, she was only half the size. The lady was lying on her right side underneath the membrane, her abdomen and chest lifting and subsiding with breaths.

Gulls screamed overhead and dove, grabbing at Mandiah's hair and exposed skin as he neared the woman. He attempted to swat the birds away, but their attacks grew bolder.

Mandiah stood over the sleeping half-woman, so mesmerized by her that he nearly missed the low rumble of an angry animal. On the sheer face of a low cliff directly over Mandiah, loomed a wolf unlike any he'd seen. It was the height of a human, its coat red and orange with deep amber highlights. The fur of the animal glistened in the light of the sun, giving the appearance of fire.

Another growl erupted and the animal pulled back its upper lip, baring a full set of sharp, pointed teeth of the most brilliant white. Mandiah held up his palm to show the animal he was no threat. With his other hand, he reached to pull the driftwood that littered the beach near him. As the wolf looked on, Mandia pushed the logs deep into the sand around the sleeping figure, then layered large leaves over them. When the structure was stabilized and the girl in the safety of the shade, he backed away. Mandiah returned to the tree line and observed from the shadows as the wolf lay back down, watching over the girl.

Deep in the forest, Mandiah pulled the thin cord from the

mouth of his mollusk bag. He fashioned a snare, leaving it in the brush, then he ventured to a different region of the beach where he wouldn't interrupt the wolf—or the girl.

After hours of digging and foraging, Mandiah returned to his snare to find a small rabbit. He cleaned the animal and returned to the ledge where the wolf loomed over him, watching with distrust. Mandiah averted his eyes and laid the rabbit at the cliff's base, then walked to the woods without looking back and followed the tree line back to the village.

He returned the following day with a fresh fish for the wolf. The rabbit was gone, but the girl still lay on the shore, nestled between the dunes, the cliff, and the Great North Sea.

The wolf watched Mandiah as he dragged more driftwood from the beach and arranged it to better conceal the girl should anyone happen by—though he had no doubt the gulls and the wolf would do their part to protect her. The gulls continuously dove at Mandiah, nipping at his ears and the back of his neck each time he neared the girl, but it wasn't with the same fervor they had done so the day before.

Each day, Mandiah returned to feed the wolf and see how the girl had grown. One day when he returned, he found the girl fully grown and sitting atop a dune. She was looking out over the ocean as Mandiah approached, the wolf lying next to her as she stroked its flaming fur. The girl's hair, a mixture of amber and fire, glistened in the rays of the sun.

Mandiah approached with caution, reluctant to scare this new life he helped preserve. But as he spoke, the girl only watched him, her amber eyes following him with interest. The girl's brows constricted, and she cocked her head to one side, her mouth mimicking the movement of his own. A sound then erupted from her throat, harsh and unpleasant. She tried again, the result smoother this time. Soon, the girl was repeating the words that Mandiah spoke.

"I am Mandiah," he said while gesturing to himself.

"I am Mandiah." The girl repeated the words and the motions.

The wolf nuzzled the girl, a whisper seeming to slip from his snout to her ear. She looked from the wolf to Mandiah. A smile spread across her face, and, in that instant, Mandiah belonged to her.

She held a hand to her breastbone. "I am Albati."

"Have you a home?"

The wolf nuzzled her again with his silent guidance, and Albati shook her head.

A storm loomed on the horizon, and the sun drifted low in the distance. As dark fell across the land, Mandiah led the girl into his village. He pushed the fishing nets and poles from the gear house and laid out blankets for Albati. He placed a jar of salted fish and a few dried apricots on a stool and ushered Albati inside with a warning to remain quiet until the morning. The wolf refused to join her, returning to stand watch in the shadow of the forest.

Albati became a fixture in the village, and soon people could no longer recall a time when she wasn't at Mandiah's side. And as young people are likely to do, Mandiah and Albati fell in love. But as Mandiah leaned toward Albati in the moonlight, his heart intent on finally kissing the lips of his beloved, the wolf leapt from the shadows. Mandiah was knocked to the ground, and a great wind blew in, lifting Albati into the night sky and sweeping her away as Mandiah called her name into the vast night.

Albati was transported to Elyphesus, where she was welcomed by her brethren. Rūvolo approached the young goddess first. The warrior god, his muscled chest bare and bronze, his long dark hair highlighted with orange, red, and gold, was fierce. The god whispered, "Welcome, sister," in her ear. At that moment, she recognized him as her wolf companion.

Albati felt the connection to her brother and sister gods, felt their very essence in her own being. But as awed as she was by the magnificence of the gods and Elyphesus, she yearned for Mandiah.

Each day and each night, Albati tried to return to the village and her love, but each time, the gods interfered.

"You may take lovers, but not him," she was told. For the gods knew that true love for a mortal would draw Albati's allegiance from the gods. They also knew that a war was coming, and they each risked loss if Albati turned against them. And so, they threatened not only Mandiah, but also all mankind. "If you return to him, a plague will be unleashed upon the earth and love will never exist again. If either the sun or the moon sees you with the mortal, all living things will be damned."

Albati retreated to a private garden in Elyphesus, mourning for her love. Whenorríga and Nithenia sent men to her—great warriors as well as artists and poets—but Albati would take no other lover and host no guests in her garden. She lingered alone and aching until she realized there was a way for her to see Mandiah without being spied. Four times per year, when the moon and sun passed each other, they only saw each other. On those days, Albati slipped from the gates of Elyphesus and returned to the forest to meet Mandiah. And she loved him and bore him a child, a godling daughter they named Mysápi, for she was love. And then Albati retreated forever to Elyphesus so as to protect her daughter from the awareness of the other gods.

And as the gods feared, Albati held an affinity for the mortals that her daughter knew and loved, so when men turned against the gods, Albati supported them. Nemii discouraged her allegiance to the mortals, whispering in her ear that if Albati sided with him, he'd ensure Mandiah was secured amongst the gods when his natural life ended. Albati wanted nothing more than to see Mandiah again in the Elyphesian afterlife. But Nemii tricked Albati, for Mandiah was slain by Nemii's blade. Mandiah's body was left for the birds to pick apart, and his soul for the rats to carry into the darkened tunnels of Targatheimr where he would be tortured for eternity. And then Nemii lured Mysápi into the tunnels with the other godlings, and Rūvolo caused the earth to shake, trapping the godlings in the underworld for evermore.

And so Albati, the goddess of love, ill-fated lovers, and alliances, conceived of the night winds and the fertile seeds of the earth, swore to her brother and sister gods that she would rejoin them in Elyphesus where they would wait until the prophecy was fulfilled, and they could return to the lands to destroy the disbelievers and those who entombed their offspring. And she would turn her back on the ill-fated lovers who had turned their backs on her and would await the vengeance that simmered deep in her heart.

THE NITHENIAN ELEMENT: ORIGINS OF THE GODDESS —FROM THE FALLACY OF ARCHAIC BELIEF SYSTEMS IN THE PRE-UNIFICATION KINGDOMS: A STUDY IN ANCIENT MYTHS

A note from the Grandmaster of Religious Studies, First Unification Council – It is of note that the following account of the Elyphesian entity identified as Nithenia has been presented in the manner it was intended upon its conception: that of a fictional story intended to inspire bravery and achievement among ancient civilizations. The presentation of this tale in fictional format is by no means intended to condone the worship of, or insinuate the existence of, any entities besides the God of the Heavens and the God of the Earth. Following the myth, you shall find Master Rosew's extensive essay that exposes the inaccuracies and blasphemous implications of this tale.

THE YOUNGEST OF THE SIX ORIGINAL ELYPHESIANS WAS named Nithenia, for she was brave and champion of the victorious. But though she was beloved by her brothers and sisters, they also envied her, for she was favored by Omnilus. The Great Creator instilled in Nithenia all that was good and just in his own spirit, trusting that one day his daughter would lead the others and return the earth to the utopia he intended it to be. With his daughter in the heavens, and beloved by her siblings, Omnilus retreated to the great beyond, certain he'd done all he could to preserve the beauty of the lands he'd created and the life that sprang from it.

But the gods knew Omnilus preferred Nithenia, and that she was intended to rise above them and serve in the place of the Great Creator. And so, when Nithenia was a girl, her brothers and sisters cast her from the heavens. She was to walk the earth, live among men, and come into her powers on her own. They hoped the young girl would suffer among the harsh life of peasants and that she would retreat from her obligation, leaving Elyphesus—and the earth—to their whims.

Nithenia was young and afraid. For seven weeks, she cried to be permitted to live in the heavens with her brothers and sisters. But her cries went unanswered. Even the godlings turned their backs, warned by the Elyphesians that Nithenia must make her own way. They warned that the young goddess would grow to be bitter and callous to all the gods and their offspring if she didn't do this alone.

For seventy years, she wandered the earth, taking the appearance of a small boy, a young man, a woman, and even a dog. She embraced every iteration of human and animal she thought would lead her to lessons or teach her what it means to be a god in the world of humans. And though she learned what life was like for humans, she could not reconcile that knowledge with her position as a god among humans.

One day, hungry and tired from having swum across the Great North Sea from the Candor Islands, and finding herself in the ancient Kingdom of Albrách, Nithenia came across Strovmore.

The elderly man was walking along a deeply rutted path on the outskirts of the village, his back hunched with age, exhaustion, and the heat of the day. Each step was tenuous and labored, the swollen joints of his left hand clutching the contorted end of an aged walking stick that bowed dangerously with each step. In his other hand, he clutched the handles of a cloth sack, which dragged on the ground behind him. The old man pulled the bag along, paying no mind as it bounced off the heels of his cracked leather sandals. Wooden twigs stuck from the top of the bag, poking him in the back of his calf with each step. His legs, bare under the thigh-length tunic, were purple and red from the constant assault.

As Nithenia followed the old man, she felt compassion for him. Though his task seemed difficult, he continued along, determined to reach his goal.

"Please, sir. Can I lighten your load for even a short while?" Nithenia, in the form of a young girl, stared up as the old man assessed her. His pale blue eyes, red-rimmed with age, were kind but also seemed to hold more wisdom than Nithenia had seen in another human.

"Only if I can repay your kindness," the old man said.

Together they walked the short distance to the outskirts of the city—Nithenia having assumed his heavy sack, which she dragged behind her only so as not to betray her strength in front of the old man. Strovmor explained that he had been in the fields where the farmers worked hard to clear the yearly growth of danailor. At her look of confusion, he told her about the narrow trees that grow as straight, rigid reeds and then blossom into thorned tangles of impassable shrubs if left untended. Each year since the Venbrúids first invaded, the people of Albrách have had to pull Danailor roots from the ground each spring before the crops can be sown.

Every day, Strovmor walked to the fields and bought the thickest and straightest of the reeds to craft arrows. He would then sell his arrows in the city, earning enough money to feed his family and his neighbors for the year.

When they reached Strovmor's narrow, two-story house, Nithenia thanked the old man for keeping her company.

"And where do you think you're off to?" The raspy, winded voice beckoned Nithnia to turn. Strovmor stood in the doorway of his home, his wife beside him, gesturing for her to join them. "Did I not say I intended to repay your kindness?"

The elderly couple stood aside as Nithenia approached. In all the time she'd walked the lands, she'd never been welcomed by anyone.

Unaccustomed to kindness, Nithenia was certain she misinterpreted the couple's intent, certainly they only meant to share some small bit of food. "I'm happy to wait on the stoop. If you can offer some bone broth or perhaps a piece of bread, I'd be appreciative."

Strovmor's wife wrung her hands as she looked from her husband to the dirty girl in front of her. The old man's voice was gruff. "Nonsense, you'll come into the house and eat a decent meal at the table. We don't have much, but you'll have what we do."

Nithenia marveled as Strovmor and his large family—his children and grandchildren—gathered for the meal. They had an easy manner with each other, conversing with a comfort she found herself being drawn into. After the meal, Strovmor's wife divided sweet bread among the children, including her as the adults looked on with smiles.

After the meal, the children and grandchildren retreated to benches in front of the house to enjoy the cool evening. Strovmor remained by the fire, pulling one of the Danailor sticks from his bag and a knife from his pocket. As Nithnia watched, the old man shaved the outer layer of the wood away.

He worked intently, telling the girl about the wood, how sturdy it was in comparison to others. "It's strong enough to hold an arrow and pliable enough to be shaped. But most importantly, it has just the right amount of motion that when the arrow is shot, it will move ever so slightly, increasing the distance the shot can travel."

Nithnia found herself quickly enfolded into the daily activities of Strovmor's family. They were kind, treating her as one of their own, and even provided her with a mattress beside the other grandchildren.

Each evening, Strovmor told the grandchildren bedtime stories as his sons whittled arrows and the ladies sewed. The stories about animals were Nithenia's favorite, particularly the tale about porcupines. Strovmor's voice was smooth and reflected the emotion of each element of the story, causing Nithenia to listen with rapt attention. "The poor porcupine was a sweet, kind, and curious soul. Sadly, he was cursed with quills that both protected him from all who meant to hurt him—but also hurt his friends. How could he ever protect himself and be loved? And so that is why he wanders the forest alone, coming out only at night when he can't hurt others."

Nithenia had been with the Strovmor's for several weeks when she awoke one night to warnings on the wind. They weren't intended for her, but Nithenia recognized the whisperings of her brothers and sisters. Something was coming from the Great North Sea that lapped at the eastern edge of Albrách. Whenorríga and Liræmor had conspired to allow the threat to ride in on the night winds and the tide.

The Venbrúids raided the city with brutal efficiency. Strovmor and his wife urged the children to run as they could not. They were to flee in all directions. The adults gave each of the children a diamond—their earnings from the sale of Danailor root—to flee with. "It will afford you a home and food wherever you end up if we can't join you."

Nithenia had never before experienced a threat to her life and was curious as she watched the villagers run through the streets. Her curiosity turned to horror and fury as she watched the Venbrúids slaughter the people, then struck down Strovmor as he stood on his step, yelling at the children to run.

Knowing she wasn't yet skilled enough to face an army of grown marauders, Nithenia fled with the old man's grandchildren into the Argralands. In the thick darkness of the forest, Nithenia became separated from the other children. For hours, she wandered alone and afraid among the thick trees. The young goddess worried the Venbrúid would find her—or worse, that they would find Strovmor's grandchildren and she would be unable to save them.

Determined to find the children, Nithenia ducked under low branches, crawling into a clearing. As she stood, she saw the prickly creatures who gathered around her.

Nearby, the other children screamed. As the sun lightened the sky, Nithenia saw that porcupines had begun to surround them as well. The encroaching animals—though trying to protect them—frightened the children. Their cries drew the Venbrúids nearer, and Nithenia knew the children would be killed or taken into servitude.

Nithenia looked at the porcupines surrounding her, willing one to come close—and it did. With one rod of Danailor, Nithenia fashioned an arrow and used porcupine quills as fletching. She used the diamond in her pocket as the tip and stood, the arrow in her grip as she sighted in the approaching Venbrúids. For a moment, Nithenia thought of praying to her brothers and sisters to guide her arrow, but decided against it, praying only to herself and the goddess she was to become.

As the men walked through the narrow path, Nithenia unleashed the arrow, throwing it with all her might and taking them all with a single shot.

With this one act, Nithenia earned her place amongst the gods. Her weapon of choice was a bow with her arrows sculpted from Danailor, her fletching from porcupine quills, and the arrow tips from diamonds.

ABOUT THE AUTHOR

JODI IS A YA & ROMANCE WRITER, BLACK belt, and registered nurse. She lives with her husband, three sons and an evolving herd of undisciplined animals in Colorado. She has a well-earned fear of bears, but tolerates the Teddy and Gummy variety. She has been obsessed with books, both reading and writing them, for most of her life and prefers the written word to having actual conversations. The most current projected completion date of her To Be Read book collection is May 17, 2176.

ACKNOWLEDGEMENTS

AFTER SPENDING SO MANY YEARS ON THE HIGH Crown Chronicles, I'm thrilled that it has been published and now has a sequel. So many people have helped take The High Crown Chronicles and Queen of the Ruins from the earliest versions to what it is now.

As always, I owe a huge thank you to my family for their ongoing support and the fact that they continue to believe in me. I also owe a special thank you to Logan (aka Fade), who wrote and recorded an amazing theme song for the High Crown Chronicles series (dark and angry as instructed!).

I'm forever grateful for the support, love & shenanigans of The Sinners Club.

Thank you to Robin, Amy, and Elaine for having read the earliest, and ugliest versions of this series (please tell me you've deleted all copies!).

To Kate Angelella, Kate Foster & Rebecca Carpenter who all (at some point) gave me excellent early feedback. And for being amazing, inspirational, and highly creative forces of nature in their own rights.

A deep thank you to Tessa Elwood for choosing me for Author Mentor Match and mentoring me through a significant phase in the development of The High Crown Chronicles. You truly helped me break through a huge wall and there were so many amazing new possibilities on the other side).

Thank you to my Sifu, Troy Miller for all the years of teaching me to fight and how to wield a weapon (I couldn't have described it all-or even imagined it-without having been on the receiving end of some decent blows!).

To James L. Weaver who always offers the best insight and never says no to a beta read (or hasn't said no yet!).

To S.C Alban who gave me a lot to think about and spurred some great questions. And who has challenged me in my creativity...and the creative use of a few words that weren't right for this book but will be used elsewhere!

Thank you to Cynthia Shepp and Chris Kridler for tightening the words and putting the commas in the right places and making this book infinitely better.

To Marya Heidel, who always creates the most stunningly beautiful covers, I am in awe of your artistry and appreciate you more than you know. Thanks for keeping it, dark, ominous, and badass—just the way I like it.

Thanks to Melanie Newton for telling me (over and over) not to panic unless she does...and she still has not (that I know of!).

I have so much love for everyone at CTP for giving me the chance. I'd especially like to thank everyone who first read The High Crown Chronicles and said "yes".

Thank you to the best writing groups ever: The Forge and The Insane. Writing can be a long lonely path and it's amazing to be surrounded by creative, supportive, encouraging, and energetic people.

And finally, thank you to everyone who's ever picked up one of my books, read them, and to those who maybe haven't bought one, but always ask how my writing is going.